THE
TENTH
BLACK BOOK
OF
HORROR

Selected by Charles Black

READ ORDER

131	91	22	66
81 (10)	170	52	5
	182	138	35
	193 (12)	205 (14)	151
			102

Mortbury Press

Published by Mortbury Press

First Edition

2013

This anthology copyright © Mortbury Press

All stories copyright © of their respective authors

Cover art copyright © Paul Mudie

ISBN 978-1-910030-00-4

Mortbury Press
Shiloh
Nant-Glas
Llandrindod Wells
Powys
LD1 6PD

mortburypress@yahoo.com
http://mortburypress.webs.com/

Contents

Dedicated to Sir Charles Lloyd Birkin
1907-1985

*****

Acknowledgements

Stiff © by Angela Blake 2013
The Easter Bunny © by Tom Johnstone 2013
The Last Testament of Jacob Tyler © by David Surface 2013
The War Effort © by Carl P. Thompson 2013
The Pre-Raphaelite Painting © by David A. Sutton 2013
Christmas in the Rain © by Chris Lawton 2013
Deeper Than Dark Water © by Gary Power 2013
Marshwall © by Paul Finch 2013
Exploding Raphaelesque Heads © by Ian Hunter 2013
The Best Christmas Ever © by John Llewellyn Probert 2013
The Pygmalion Conjuration © by Mike Chinn 2013
The Boy © by David Williamson 2013
The Last Wagon in the Train © by Andrea Janes 2013
Dad Dancing © by Kate Farrell 2013
Guinea Pig Girl © by Thana Niveau 2013

Cover artwork © by Paul Mudie 2013

*****

STIFF

Angela Blake

It's hard to say when Amanda Worthington first went insane.
She was just days past her eighth birthday when the nuns found
her on the convent steps, playing in a most inappropriate
fashion with the tomcat they kept to control the rat population
in the nunnery yard.

The nuns had been alarmed by the cat's surprised meowing,
and a couple of them had peered out the door to be confronted
by the hellish sight of the animal splayed out on its back with a
mousy-haired little girl touching it in a place that could only be
described as sinful. A plaque around the girl's neck
proclaimed: THIS CHILD IS DEVIL'S. Sister Mary screamed
and ran to get Mother Superior, while Sister Martha passed out
and had to be carried inside by two of the younger sisters. It
was left to Sister Florence and Sister Magdalene to ascertain
that there was no sign of an attending adult in the vicinity, and
to whisk the girl away into the bowels of the nunnery to decide
what to do next.

After much debate and a half-hearted attempt to find the
girl's parents without involving the police, the nuns decided to
keep the child. The good Lord had obviously sent them the girl
to test their faith through the task of saving her immortal soul
from eternal damnation. And test their faith the good Lord did,
as Amanda's obsession with genitalia in general, and male
genitalia in particular, grew day by day. Had the nuns paused
to consider what trauma could have induced such aberrant
tendencies in a child, they might have sought professional
help, but, aware that they'd been forced to break the law in
order to carry out God's work, and convinced that they were
fighting the Devil himself, they chose instead to administer
their own brand of discipline. But corporal punishment only
seemed to induce an unhealthy excitement in the girl, and the
one time Amanda had been locked on her own in the chapel to

5

pray for forgiveness, Sister Martha had found her rubbing herself up against the life-size wooden carving of Saint Francis. It took Sister Florence and Sister Magdalene twenty minutes to bring Sister Martha out of her dead faint.

By the time Amanda was twelve, the nuns had been forced to sack all male staff who helped out at the nunnery. Even the seventy-year-old gardener had to go when it was discovered that Amanda had cornered him in the cabbage patch and attempted to give him a blowjob. Whenever a grocery delivery boy, a repairman or a visiting priest was expected at the nunnery, Amanda would be locked up securely, and often gagged so that her cries would not alarm outsiders of the male sex.

But Amanda's life at the nunnery was not all doom and gloom. Sister Theresa was a kindly woman and a firm believer that every creature on God's earth was a creature of God. In this, Sister Theresa differed from the other nuns, whose war with the Devil over Amanda's soul was beginning to take its toll on their mental health. Rather than punish Amanda's nymphomania, Sister Theresa tried to distract her with other interests: she taught Amanda to type on the old PC in the office, and, on finding that the girl's talents stretched to more than pleasuring the nunnery cat, she also taught her to carve wood. Amanda's patient practice in carving figurines of the Virgin Mary paid off in due course, when she was able to make herself a splendid set of wooden dildos decorated with the faces of her favourite male saints.

Things might have carried on in this relatively peaceful manner, disturbed only by the odd period of bondage and incarceration occasioned by the grocery deliveries to the nunnery, had it not been for Bishop Ramsey and the beetroot soup.

Amanda had just turned sixteen. A couple of days earlier Sister Theresa had baked her a small cake and decorated it with candles, which Amanda had blown out in the presence of a couple of the younger sisters. But today she was tied securely to a heavy chair in Mother Superior's locked office, her mouth taped firmly shut, while the nuns ran around in a panic, preparing for a visit from the local bishop.

Bishop Ramsey had spent all morning inspecting the chapel and the nunnery grounds, where the nuns grew vegetables and fruit for their famous preserves, which they jarred themselves and sold for a little extra income. After his tour, the bishop surprised the nuns by deciding to stay for lunch. Luckily, Sister Mary was cooking that day, so the meal was both plentiful and tasty.

"You'd better go and see to Amanda," Sister Theresa whispered to Sister Florence once dessert and coffee had been served. "Take her some soup and a piece of bread for now, and she can have something more substantial in the kitchen once the Bishop has gone."

"Yes, Sister." The younger nun hurried off to the kitchen, then headed for Mother Superior's office, carrying a food tray. She unlocked the door and went in.

"Oh dear," she commented on seeing the trussed-up girl. "I'm just going to put the tray down, then I'll lock the door and untie you. You won't do anything stupid, will you?" Amanda shook her head. "Okay then." Sister Florence untied the girl and went to pass her the bowl of soup. Unfortunately, her foot caught on the edge of Mother Superior's favourite cream-coloured rug, and the bowl went flying, sending thick purple-red soup all over the offending textile.

"Oh my God!" Sister Florence cried, clapping her hand over her mouth as she realised her blasphemy. "Mother Superior's rug," she moaned. "I'll be back in a minute. Please, stay here!" Amanda nodded enthusiastically, and the nun ran off in search of a cloth, locking the door, but leaving Amanda untied. It wasn't long before Amanda had picked the lock, and was heading for the dining room, where she figured the action to be. She hadn't been near a man in longer than she cared to remember, and, if there was one in the nunnery, she'd have him – no matter who he was or what the consequences.

7

Stiff

The bishop had finished his coffee and was just rising from the table, when the teenage girl burst into the dining room.

"What the de ...?" cried Mother Superior, then realised what she'd almost said and turned bright red. "I'm sorry, Bishop ... Amanda, stay where you are!" But it was too late. Amanda had already ripped off her top and bra and was running at the bishop, a frenzied look in her eyes. The nuns recovered from their shock and ran to intercept the girl, but it was too late. The topless sixteen-year-old flew at the dumbfounded bishop and, with one deft movement, her hand was under his cassock. The bishop screamed, the nuns screamed and Amanda screamed – in delight, as months of sexual frustration melted away in a warm climax. Then the sisters had her firmly by the arms, and dragged her to the broom cupboard where she would stay locked while her fate was decided.

Later that night, the verdict came in: eternal damnation or not, the offender couldn't stay. Next day, Sister Theresa reluctantly escorted Amanda to a women's shelter, run by her sister Grace Kelly. Mr and Mrs Kelly must have been having a laugh when they named their elder daughter, for, even as a baby, Grace was intolerably harsh on the eye, and on each of the remaining four senses. But her heart was as big as Theresa's and, if anybody would put up with Amanda, Theresa knew that it would be Grace.

The nunnery was in disgrace. It took all of Mother Superior's persuasive powers, an unprecedented quantity of strawberry preserve and a sworn oath that Amanda would be removed immediately to stop the bishop from implementing the strictest disciplinary measures against the convent. Amanda was simultaneously thrilled, apprehensive and a little tearful to be leaving what had been her home for eight years and, despite everything that had gone on in that time, a couple of the nuns shed a tear too as they waved her and Sister Theresa goodbye.

"Please," implored Sister Theresa as she handed Amanda the two hundred pounds that Mother Superior had seen fit to send her off with, "try to be good. Grace will take care of you

and she'll help you get a job. But you must try to be good."
Amanda hugged the nun and followed Grace to a small room,
which was to be her new home until she was able to fend for
herself.

"We don't allow men here," Grace explained. "Many of the
women have had bad experiences. So we don't bring men back
to the house." Amanda didn't respond so Grace decided to
delve further on the topic of the uglier sex. "Theresa tells me
that you … like men." Amanda grinned. "Well, I can't stop
you seeing them, but as someone older and perhaps a little
wiser, I'll just say that … I hope you use protection." Amanda
looked confused. "Christ," said Grace. "Those bloody nuns
…" She sighed in exasperation; she would have to take
Amanda to a pharmacy as soon as possible.

Even though Amanda had been banned from using the nuns'
computer – after Mother Superior switched it on to check her
emails and was confronted by a naked woman being penetrated
in all orifices by several unusually well-endowed men – she
had nevertheless managed to become pretty good at typing and
surfing the net. So it was no surprise that, after a simple typing
test, she was taken on by a local temping agency. Within a
couple of weeks she was offered a job at a post-production
house, taking in and logging the video tapes and film reels that
were brought in for transfer. At first she worked front of house,
greeting clients and interacting with the general public, but her
outrageous clothes and lewd behaviour soon saw her
transferred to a storeroom in the back, where she stacked
shelves and had sex with any male member of staff who
ventured onto her turf. The boss tolerated her behaviour as he
made use of her himself several times a week, and Amanda
loved her job, but the office was small – there were only four
male members of staff, including the boss, and they had work
to do. The attention that Amanda got just wasn't enough.

At night she trawled the bars, looking for sex. Some of the
men gave her money after she had sex with them, but soon

stopped when they realised that she'd give it away for free. And it was in one of her habitual nocturnal haunts that Randy Mandy – as she quickly became known – met the aptly named John Thomas. One night with John changed Mandy's life.

Mandy had been flirting with two men at the bar, and had accidentally backed right into John Thomas, who was waiting to be served.

"Oh, I'm sorry." She turned around to find a tall, well-built man standing at the bar beside her. "Or maybe I'm not," she added in sultry tones. "Hi, I'm Mandy."

"I'm John," the stranger said after a moment's pause, toying nervously with his wedding ring. Mandy noticed.

"You're married?"

"Yeah," replied John, relieved that Mandy had been the first to broach the subject.

"That's okay," she said. "I don't mind." John felt a bit awkward, but as the pretty little thing before him continued to chat away, smiling at him and leaning forward in such a way that her generous bosom almost popped out of her skimpy attire, his inhibitions soon melted away and he noticed a strong and uncontrollable stirring in his nether regions. Mandy noticed it too, and her own urges got the better of her. She reached down and cupped her hand around John's manhood; even through the denim she could immediately tell that it was huge. John took a sharp intake of breath and placed his hand over Mandy's, intending to remove it, make his excuses and hurry home, but changed his mind at the last minute.

"Can we go back to your place?" he asked.

"Sure." Mandy had left the shelter three years earlier and rented a studio flat in a modest part of town. "It's not far."

Nothing she'd ever experienced had prepared Mandy for John's manhood. The sight of it would have made the porn stars she'd surreptitiously admired while pretending to work on Mother Superior's computer green with envy. It had been a struggle, but Mandy had accommodated it fully, and the pleasure for both her and John was almost unbearable.

"You must be a witch," John told her after the fifth time that night, "coz you've put a spell on me." When he left, after two more rounds, Mandy felt satisfied for the first time she could remember. And John would have been enough for her, if she could have had him all to herself. But she couldn't. Despite assurances that he would leave his wife, he scampered home every time and his promises came to nothing. So their romps were restricted to whenever John could make time to see her and to see to her. And Randy Mandy was not happy when she wasn't getting any. She continued to see other men, but found that she was so stretched by her frenzied sessions with John, that no one else could fill her sufficiently. Even double penetration couldn't satisfy her lusts. She contemplated confronting John's wife and revealing his infidelity, but she knew deep down that if she were the one to break up the marriage, John would never forgive her. So she decided she would have to use some other means to separate them and have John, or rather John's tackle, all to herself. Whenever and wherever she wanted it. Which was pretty much anywhere and all the time.

There was only one thing for it. John's wife would have to be removed from the equation by some other means. An accident would have to be arranged. Mandy took to spending her spare time watching Lucy Thomas's comings and goings. She observed her rival zipping around in her red sports Jag, and soon found that John wasn't the only one getting some extracurricular action. Still, that was irrelevant now, as Mandy's mind was already focused on a firm plan of action.

One day Mandy trailed Lucy to the local garage, and watched her leave her car for a routine check-up. Mandy knew the mechanic who was working on the vehicle, and paid a visit to the garage just as he'd finished working on the car. In no time at all, she and the lusty garage attendant were bouncing up and down on the back seat. Afterwards he fell asleep – as Mandy knew he would – and she took the opportunity to sabotage the Jag. The 'accident' worked almost as planned. The brakes failed and the car sped off the road, hurtling to a devastating collision. There was just one flaw. A fatal one. It hadn't been Lucy who had come to collect the car – it had been John.

In a brief moment during her despair, Mandy recalled how she had always called Lucy a lucky bitch! Her lover might be dead, but Mandy had to see him one last time. Fortunately, her wide circle of male acquaintances included a laconic young man who worked at the undertakers. She had often visited him at the funeral parlour and romped with him amongst the velvet-lined coffins. Mandy still had the key to the funeral parlour that he had given her when they were doing their thing. But this was the first time that she'd had sex with someone in a coffin. And okay, John might be cold, his face hideously mutilated. And yes, dead. But his penis was rigid with rigor mortis, and Mandy needed it inside her so badly. When her climax subsided, it dawned on Mandy: one last time was not enough. She continued to sneak into the funeral parlour every night, but she wanted more – she wanted John back for good.

Mandy had paid little heed to the prattle she'd been subjected to in the convent, but as her mind raced during the days before John's funeral, she found herself returning again and again to the nuns and what they'd tried to teach her. They'd always been telling her about the Day of Judgement, when all the dead would rise from their graves. And that sinners like her would inevitably cause the end of the world, and bring the Day of Judgement forward. Mandy didn't need to bring the Day of Judgement forward, and she didn't need to raise all the dead from their graves. Only one.

Mandy threw herself into intense research, and ended up in a small occult bookstore in a dingy part of town. The elderly proprietor looked like an extra from a 1960s Hammer film. After an hour with Mandy in the back room, the old timer admitted that he owned the last remaining copy of the *Dark*

Grimoire. It contained a powerful spell for raising the dead. The spell was as long as it was complex, for, rather than the usual practice of summoning the spirit of a deceased person for the purpose of conversing with it, the resurrection spell in the *Dark Grimoire* summoned the soul back into the body, commanded the body to rise, and bound the resurrected individual – body and spirit – inextricably to the summoner.

The man allowed Mandy to copy out the spell, creating a kind of mini-grimoire of her own, and made sure that she accurately drew the seals of the entities that she would call upon to help her, and the protective signs and symbols she would need to shield herself from her diabolical aides. Replication of the spell in her own hand took Mandy all day and all night, allowing for short breaks during which she expressed her gratitude to her mentor. When Mandy left the following morning, the man wished her luck and gave her a complimentary copy of a book about Crowley's Sex Magick.

"Come back any time, missy!" he said.

Mandy had to work fast. She had until the next full moon – the night of the day following John's funeral – to gather and prepare her materials. The spell she had copied not only comprised the core necromantic ritual, but also listed all the magickal tools she would need to obtain or make, and how to purify them in preparation for the ceremony. She tracked down parchment, herbs, oils, candles, human bones, a bull's penis, a black hen and a cornucopia of bizarre materials. She also learned the lines of the spell by heart, fasted and – a feat truly extraordinary – abstained from sexual activity. The tension in Mandy caused by the latter generated an unprecedented amount of energy – all of which would aid her in the ritual to be performed.

By the time of John's funeral, Mandy was as prepared as she could be, with a day to spare. She decided to attend the Christian ceremony, before conducting her own. She followed the mourners at a distance, and positioned herself behind a large oak tree, just out of sight of the funeral party. The priest's inane ramblings didn't reach her here. *Thank heavens for small mercies*, she thought. Her wry smile faded when she caught sight of Lucy Thomas – dressed in an expensive black suit and dabbing a black silk handkerchief theatrically to one eye. On either side of her stood her lawyer and her landscape gardener, both of whom she'd been 'seeing' before and during her marriage to John. Tears of anger and regret welled up in Mandy's eyes. How she hated that bitch, how she hated herself and how she hated God who'd twisted all her plans for a happy life with John into this obscene nightmare.

A cloud passed over the sun, and Mandy shivered in the sudden chill. She stood silently as John's coffin was lowered into the ground. The priest uttered a few more platitudes, the mourners threw some clods of earth onto the casket and then everyone drifted away. As she watched John's widow turn her back on his grave and walk away, a realisation dawned on Mandy: the bitch was gone, and would not be coming back. John belonged to Mandy now. She waited until the gravediggers had finished their work, then lay face down on the soft soil of John's grave.

Mandy had done incredibly well to abstain from any sort of sexual activity for what seemed like an eternity (several days), in her desperate bid to do everything right ahead of the ritual, but now the thought of John's manly body just feet below her own started to drive her crazy. She fought with her unwanted desire, but a vision of her lover's magnificent member – thrusting proudly through the earth towards her – swelled in her imagination, and she was overcome. She writhed to a climax against the compacted earth of John's grave, and fell asleep moaning her dead lover's name, waking up shivering once the sun had set. At closing time, a couple of cemetery guards spotted her on their rounds, dragged her off John's grave and marched her to the exit gate, sending her on her way in no uncertain terms.

"I'll be back for you tonight," she promised John, "and we'll be together forever – just you and me." But as she made her way home, she couldn't shake the feeling that she might have made a grave error.

Mandy slept for the rest of the day. Her alarm clock woke her an hour after dusk and ninety minutes after the cemetery closed. She packed all her props, including the hen in a basket and a set of heavy-duty chain-cutters, into her second-hand VW Beetle, and headed for the cemetery. She had sedated the hen with some drugged seed, and the bird dozed quietly in its wicker prison. Mandy knew the risks involved in what she was doing and feared that, despite all her preparation, she might still not be ready for what was to come. If all went well, she would be back by morning with John. If it didn't, neither of them would be coming back.

The lamps on the street leading to the cemetery were dim and spaced far apart, but the full moon provided ample light for Mandy's purposes – too much light, perhaps, should there happen to be a passer-by. But the street was deserted, and Mandy was able to cut the chain on the cemetery gate with an ease that surprised her. Little by little, she carried all her equipment to the side of John's grave and laid it out carefully, starting with her silk-wrapped magickal tools and ending with the captive hen. Fortunately, the grass was kept short, and Mandy was able to scratch through it, and draw two vast chalk circles around herself and the grave – one circle within the other. In the space between the circles Mandy scratched out the symbols of the planets, the names and seals of the angels and deities whose aid she would call upon, and protective signs that would control the spirits and stop them from harming her, copying them all carefully from her notes. Next she inscribed a pentagram within the inner circle, its points touching the circumference. When she had finished, she reinforced the two vast circles and the pentagram with salt that she had purified in preparation for the ritual.

By the time Mandy had prepared her circle, it was almost

15

midnight. She peered into the wicker box and made sure that the hen was still sedated. She stripped naked and donned a fine cloak of black and red. She lit a fire of myrtle, cedar, willow and cypress wood in a large chafing dish. Using the dish as a censer, she poured on a few drops of wine, some mastic and aromatic gum, then added a mixture she had prepared of aloe wood, saffron, henbane, mandrake, hemlock and opium. The heady fumes rose into the night sky. At exactly midnight, Mandy took a deep breath and began the resurrection rite.

"I invoke, conjure and command you, gods and goddesses, angels and demons inscribed in this Circle."

One by one she called upon the entities that would help her bring back her lover from the other side and give him to her – body and soul.

She called upon Hecate, the goddess of life and death. She summoned Lilith, queen of the succubi, and Lilith's lover Samael – Malach HaMavet, the angel of death. She called forth Isis, who brought her brother-husband back from the land of the dead. Mandy beckoned Frastiel, who can bring you anyone you want – whether dead or alive. She cried out to Israfel, the burning one, angel of resurrection. She invoked the evil angel Iabiel, who can separate a husband form his wife. She summoned Asmodeus, the demon of lust, and Anael, the angel of human love. Finally, Mandy conjured the Unnameable, lord of primeval chaos, that can disrupt the laws of nature and God because it is older than both.

A wind stirred, and shadows started to form beyond the circle. Mandy gently lifted the hen out of its basket and held it in one hand; with the other she picked up her dagger.

"For you whom I summon do I spill this blood, that you might aid me this night!" Mandy called to the entities that were starting to materialise around her, and with a single deft stroke she painlessly slit the hen's throat; the drugged bird didn't even stir. She let some of the blood spill into the chafing dish, where it spat and sizzled. Then she stepped swiftly to John's grave and let the remaining blood drain onto her beloved's burial place. "For you, John Thomas, do I spill this blood. A life for a life! A life for a life! A life for a life!"

The shadows around Mandy thickened and began to take on a more tangible form. Mandy placed the dead hen on John's grave, along with the bull's member, and held the dagger to her own hand.

"For you whom I summon do I spill this blood, that you might aid me in my work!" She made a small cut and let a few drops fall from her hand into the chafing dish. Moving to John's grave, she let her blood drip onto the earth. "For you, John Thomas, do I spill this blood. A love for a love! A love for a love! A love for a love!" Mandy stood in the centre of the circle, at the foot of John's grave, and concentrated her energy on visualising him coming back to her.

Somewhere in the distance she heard the baying of hounds, and with it came Hecate the Crone, queen of the dead and of the changeable moon. The shadows thickened, and the combined stench of sulphur and putrefaction assailed Mandy's nostrils, so strong that even the heady scent of the incense did little to combat it. One by one the lords of death and masters of the Underworld started to take on form around her. Samael brought with him a legion of his fallen angels, which whirled around Mandy, crowding around her salt circle, but never crossing it. A shriek split the air, and dark queen Lilith appeared, her succubi slithering and crawling about her feet. Isis stood behind Mandy, Asmodeus at her left shoulder and beside him Iabiel. Anael glowed golden-white on Mandy's right. Frastiel materialised and stood nearby – hooded, no face, eyes burning like cold stars. Four-winged Israfel came in a tower of fire that reached from the earth to the stars.

The Unnameable appeared last. It was hideous like the primeval void, like chaos, like the death of all hope. Its malevolence was stronger than that of the others. It stood opposite Mandy, on the other side of John's grave, just beyond the circle. Mandy's eyes widened in terror, but she did not falter. She dropped her gaze to her beloved's grave and raised her arms, bidding the deities and demons around her to lend her their might. So determined was Mandy to succeed in her ritual or to die, that she bent the immortals to her will. Slowly her body filled with energy – like an electric current – from the angels, gods and demons who, having performed the arduous task of materialisation in our world, now channelled their strength to the one who'd allowed them to walk the earth once more. Mandy shouted above the wind that had intensified and now howled around her.

"By the power of Lilith, maid of desolation, who rules the midnight realm – John Thomas, I command your spirit to leave the mountains of darkness!

By the power of Frastiel, who can bring back the departed – John Thomas, I command your spirit to return to its rightful abode!

By the power of Isis who reclaimed her lord Osiris from the land of shadows – John Thomas, I command your spirit to come back to its earthly body!"

The fire in the chafing dish dimmed, then burned brightly once more. Flames danced wildly in the wind.

"The earth shall give back that which has been entrusted to it!

And the grave shall give back that which it has received!

And the abyss shall give back that which it owes!"

Mandy never lifted her eyes from John's grave, but there was no sign of movement.

"By the power of three-faced Hecate, who commands the cycle of life, death and rebirth – John Thomas, I command you, rise!

By the power of Samael, who can give back that which he has taken away – John Thomas, I command you, rise!

By the power of Israfel, whose voice quickens the lifeless – John Thomas, I command you, rise!"

Lightning struck above the cemetery, and hail started to pelt the ground around Mandy. A violent gust of wind ripped off her cloak, and she stood naked to the night and elements that raged around the grave. The salt that she'd used to strengthen her circle was blown clear off the ground, and the demons surged forward, looking for a way to enter Mandy and corrupt her with their filth. But the chalk circle and the powerful symbols within it impeded their entrance and held them firm to do Mandy's bidding.

"By the power of Iabiel, I tear aside your previous bonds and make you mine!

By the power of Asmodeus, lord of the flesh, I bind your body to mine!

By the power of Isis and Osiris, I bind your mind to mine!

By the power of Anael, I bind your sex to mine!

By the power of Samael and Lilith, I bind your soul to mine!

By the power of those that have gathered at my command, I bind you to me!

By the power of the Unnameable that crouches at the Threshold, I bind you and command you to rise!"

The entities encroached as close as they could upon Mandy and the grave. The air was thick with writhing darkness and the stench of hell. But nothing stirred in John's grave. Despite the strength that the angels and gods gave her, the unprecedented amount of energy required by the resurrection spell was starting to drain Mandy's life force. She started to feel faint, but forced herself to carry on.

"John Thomas, your eyes will seek only me! Your body will seek only me! Your mind will seek only me! Your sex will seek only me! Your soul will seek only me!

John Thomas, I bind you and command you to rise! I bind you and command you to rise! I bind you and command you to rise!"

The demons and deities lent their power, compelled by the commanding voice of the desperate mortal before them. But still nothing stirred in John's grave.

Tears streamed down Mandy's face. Her world darkened further and she knew that her life force was being been sucked from her – perhaps the abominations that she had summoned were taking it back. She knew that she couldn't hold out much longer, and still no movement from the grave before her. Her soul had almost been sucked dry. It had shrunk within her to a few mere grains of light. She mustered what life she had left within her and screamed the penultimate words of the ritual over the howling wind.

"For mine is the love and mine is the will! And love is the law! Love under will!" Mandy swooned, teetering on the verge of unconsciousness. Exhausted and hoarse from shouting, with her last gasp she managed to scream into the storm.

"Such are the words. So mote it be! Such are the words. So mote it be! Such are the words. So mote it be!"

A profound darkness descended over Mandy and she fell to the ground at the foot of the grave. When she regained consciousness, the entities had disappeared, the flame had gone out and the candles had been extinguished. Clouds had crept across the moon, and the cemetery was in total darkness. Mandy raised herself painfully to her knees and turned on her flashlight. Tears stained her face as she looked at John's intact grave. She crawled over to the tattered remnants of her clothes, which had been blown onto a nearby bush, and dressed herself as best she could. She gathered up those items that she could see and dragged herself back in the direction of the unlocked cemetery gate. She didn't feel the ground tremble. She didn't notice the fist that punched through the earth or the fingers that grasped at the night air. She didn't see the figure pull itself from its own grave, or smell the musty cloth as it tore at the garments in which it had been buried.

As Mandy crawled into bed, Lucy Thomas was woken by the sound of breaking glass and something heavy lumbering up the stairs. She dialled 999 from the phone next to her bed, and risked a peek out into the hallway. The sight that greeted her sent her screaming back to the bedroom, locking the door behind her. As she looked around for anything that would make a potential weapon, the doorknob turned, then rattled;

then the door splintered and came flying off its hinges. Lucy screamed again as the mud-covered hulk lurched towards her, a huge erection protruding from its tattered trousers – an erection that could only belong to one man.

"John?" Recognition and incredulity dawned in her ice blue eyes. "Oh my God!" Reeling in horror, fear and astonishment, Lucy Thomas backed her way right through the open window, landing full on the iron railings beneath and dying instantly. By the time the police arrived, the intruder was gone, leaving nothing but muddy smears on the staircase.

Mandy had cried herself into a deep, exhausted sleep. She didn't hear the sound of breaking glass or the footsteps on the stairs or the laboured breath leaving and entering lungs that had so recently been still.

The first thing that she became aware of was penetration by a member so large that it could only be that of John Thomas. As the powerful thrusts roused her and brought her back to the world of the living with a shuddering climax that she'd feared she'd never experience again, Mandy opened her eyes and gazed at the mud-streaked face of her lover. The glazed look in John's eyes convinced her that – despite the initial delay and confusion resultant from her failure to follow the ritual to the letter by masturbating on his grave – the sexual binding element of the spell had worked. For John was oblivious to the world around him. All he could see was Mandy. He now had no memory of his previous existence, his wife or anything else. He had no desire for anything other than Mandy, and she welcomed him with open legs.

Now if Mandy could just find a spell to halt the decomposition of dead flesh, she and John Thomas would live happily ever after.

THE EASTER BUNNY

Tom Johnstone

"Alright, Simon … Yes, of course I'll bring her to you by Sunday morning … Alright, Saturday night then. Yes, I know it's a very special day for you. It's special for me too …"

This last parting shot she muttered to herself, because Simon had hung up. Barry Thomas sighed. Marie was still letting that bastard control her even now.

"He says he'll bring her back on Friday," she said, rubbing her forehead.

"Morning or afternoon?"

"Morning."

"Well, that's something anyway."

"Yes. But he's adamant that he wants her to spend the whole of Easter Sunday with him. Says he wants to take her to church, show her the true meaning of Easter. As if *I* wouldn't!"

"It's like Christmas all over again." Barry opened a beer.

"Bit early for that, isn't it?" Marie frowned.

"You're starting to sound like *him!*"

"Point taken," she conceded, allowing herself a careworn smile. "Apparently my local C of E's not good enough. She's got to go to *his* church."

"You can say no, you know. I mean, I know Cassie's not … mine and everything, but, well …"

"Go on," she said in that unnerving way of hers, the direct, unblinking (*and beautiful*, he added to himself) blue stare that said, *say what you're going to say even if it makes me slap you in the face.*

"I just don't think it's healthy, a young girl like her spending all that time in that happy-clappy church of his … But you know my views on that subject!"

He shot her an appeasing grin. She returned it after a painfully long pause. Religion was something she and Barry had agreed to disagree on, though she was in two minds about her faith, unlike Simon. She wasn't in two minds about splitting up with Simon, and Simon wasn't in two minds about much of anything, least of all religion.

"Simon and I agreed that he would get access at weekends and some nights too, and that means Sundays."

"But surely that doesn't mean he gets her on high days and holidays as well?"

"Look, Baz, like you said, she's not actually yours, so it's kind of none of your business, alright?"

That threw him. All right, Cassie was just his stepdaughter, but he still cared about the kid, even though she'd been giving him the cold shoulder lately, something he put down to approaching puberty.

Seeing he looked hurt, Marie reached towards him, stroking his shoulder.

"Look, sorry for snapping, love. You shouldn't take me so seriously when I fly off the handle like that. I know you've been there for her as much as anyone, I mean you've been more of a dad to her than he ever was in a lot of ways. It's just … Well, I still feel guilty for being so rotten to him, you know …"

"*You've* been rotten to *him*? He's the one that knocked you about, Marie, not the other way round!"

"After he found out we were seeing each other."

"And that makes it alright, does it? I'm sorry, babe, but any man that raises his hand to a woman—"

"Alright, alright, but that's in the past, Baz. He's trying to make up for it now. I know the religion thing's a bit weird, but it's his way of showing Cassie he cares, that he can be a good role model."

"But why's he so into it? He never used to be, did he?"

"No, not really," she admitted, looking thoughtful. "But I think it's helping him move on, and that's got to be a good thing, hasn't it?"

"I suppose so. D'you think he *has* moved on though?"

Marie considered the question for a moment.

"I'm not sure."

"*I* don't think he's over you, babe," murmured Barry, his voice softening and deepening, his body snuggling up to her on the sofa. "Can't really blame him either …"

They smiled at each other, and Barry reached around and stroked the soft curve of her belly. He loved this part of her, but the way its curve seemed more pronounced, even swollen, reminded him of something else that was on his mind.

"So when *are* you going to tell him then?"

"Tell him what?" she purred, her voice languorously drowsy from his caresses.

Gently he tapped the rounded flesh he'd been touching, to remind her of the cells dividing inexorably inside her.

"Oh, yes," she sighed. "I don't have to tell him yet, do I?"

"I suppose not. You'll be showing soon, so he'll know anyway."

"So? What d'you think he's going to do, turn purple and explode?"

"Hopefully."

In the event, the big set-to didn't happen. Marie's pregnancy was beginning to show, but she didn't have an obvious bump yet, and she had got into the habit (perhaps not consciously) of wearing baggy clothes whenever she met her ex-husband for 'hand over'. Simon had noticed though, Barry felt sure, by the way he cocked an eyebrow and bit at that irritating little wisp of beard under his bottom lip with his two front teeth. Then he opened his mouth to say something but seemed to change his mind. He ushered his daughter in hastily, without acting as though he was delivering her into the jaws of hell, the way he usually did; then he said he had 'just remembered something' he needed to do after dropping Cassie off. Barry wasn't sure how Simon knew, if he did. It was possible that Cassie had tipped her father off. It wouldn't surprise him if Simon had put her up to spying on them, the way the girl had been acting lately, all the 'you're not my dad' stuff whenever he tried to assert some kind of domestic authority. They hadn't officially announced their news to her either yet, but Barry suspected she knew something was afoot, even if she wasn't certain what.

But Barry and Marie momentarily forgot all their worries over when to come clean about her pregnancy to her ex-husband and daughter, when they noticed what Cassie was carrying. It was small and thin, emaciated even, with dark fur, and long floppy ears, nestling like a baby in the crook of the child's arm, its whiskers twitching fitfully.

"What's that, honey?" asked Marie.

Cassie returned her mother's unblinking blue gaze. In that respect, thought Barry, the resemblance was uncanny. However, in other respects, he noted sourly, she looked more like her sallow-faced, lank-haired father. Perhaps the last few days away had seen a growth spurt that now seemed to emphasise this. Barry couldn't help thinking the onset of puberty was going to make her shoot up like a pencil rather than blossom into a miniature version of her curvaceous mother.

"It's a rabbit."

"I can see that, love. But what's it doing here?"

"He's a present from Dad: an Easter present."

Cassie smiled.

"Right." Marie sighed. "That's very kind of him, but where's it going to live?"

"Here. He says he hasn't got space for him at his."

"Oh."

"He's a rescued animal," said Cassie, her voice assuming an exaggerated air of adult authority. "And he's very well behaved. Look!"

And she gently placed the scrawny-looking animal on the hall carpet, where it made a dash for the kitchen.

"Must be hungry," said Barry, who fancied he could hear the half-starved creature's ribs rattling in its fur like spoons in a sack.

"Oh, I don't want it getting in there. Your dad should have

asked me before he did this."

"I'll get it," Barry offered, and gave chase, as Cassie argued in the hall that she was old enough to care for an animal. He caught up with the rabbit as it made for the compost bucket. Admittedly it needed emptying, but he didn't like the idea of the animal just diving in. He didn't like the way its big saucer eye gawped at him from the side of its head either. As he bent down to pick it up, saying, "Come on, Flopsy", the possible evolutionary reason why rabbits have their eyes in that odd lateral position suddenly struck him: To make it harder for predators to creep up on them. He was expecting it to run away then, but instead it did something quite different: Its jaws yawned open, and it sunk its two buckteeth into the flesh of one of the hands he was holding out to pick it up.

His cry of pain summoned Marie and Cassie.

"Well behaved?" he spluttered, wrapping a tea towel around the wound. "Damn thing tore a dirty great chunk out of my hand!"

"I told you he's a rescued animal!" Cassie retorted. "He can lash out a bit if you're too rough with him. And his name's not Flopsy, it's Eli."

"Really," replied Marie with weary sarcasm.

"Yeah, really. Me and Dad named him. Dad says—"

"Dad says a lot of things. But Dad obviously didn't feed him. Come to that, did he give *you* any breakfast? You look famished."

"No, there wasn't anything in. No time either, what with you wanting me back at the crack of dawn."

"That's enough," snapped Marie. "Now, rescued or not, that rabbit's going to have to look for another home."

"Mum!" Cassie whined, then stumped up the stairs. A door slammed.

Marie sat down at the kitchen table, head in her hands. Barry had been washing and dressing his wounded hand while the row had been escalating, trying to stay out of it. He was still feeling slightly woozy, shaken by the bite from the rabbit, but he tried to make himself strong for Marie: he could see she was upset, on the verge of tears. Tentatively, he laid a hand on her shoulder.

"Babe," he murmured.

"She's drifting away from me, Baz. I know she is."

"You know that's not true." He tried to put some conviction into his voice, but it was a struggle.

"You know it is. He's done it deliberately, to get at me, like with those flashy presents at Christmas."

"Oh, I don't think it's that," he said, trying to lighten the mood a little. "Probably just thinks it's his Christian duty to rescue distressed bunnies and use them to show us all the true meaning of Easter ..."

He could see his attempt at levity was working a little, drawing the strained corners of her mouth up in the beginnings of a smile.

"Tell you what," he continued. "You ring up Saint Francis of Assisi and have it out with him, and I'll go and find Flopsy, er ... Eli, and bag myself a rabbit for Easter Sunday dinner, eh?"

"Baz!" she mock-scolded him in a whisper, glancing towards the stairs in fear of Cass over-hearing.

"Only joking," he laughed. "Mind you, I've always wanted one of those lucky rabbit's feet—"

"Stop it!" She was laughing as she said this.

"Sorry. But seriously though, if you want to send him back to the rabbit sanctuary or wherever he came from, we'll have to find him first. He's done a runner – nowhere to be seen. Maybe I'll go and get Cassie's help. I'd rather *she* winkled him out of his hiding place than I did. She seems to be able to pick him up without being eaten alive. So are you going to ring him then?"

"Oh. Yes. I'll tell him, next time he wants me to adopt a pet he'd better ask me first."

"Especially one that hasn't been housetrained," agreed Barry, rubbing his bandaged hand ruefully.

"More housetrained than Simon is," she added, but despite

her defiant and irreverent tone, he could see that she was dreading making the call, avoiding moving towards the phone.

"Ookaay. Well, I'll go and fetch the rabbit whisperer," he said, heading towards the stairs.

"D'you mind?" she asked, screwing her face up in a way that said *sorry-you've-drawn-the-short-straw*.

"No, that's fine," he replied, with a studied neutrality that suggested otherwise.

As he stepped gingerly towards the stairs, she called after him:

"Baz …?"

"Uhuh," he replied.

"Thanks."

We all have our crosses to bear, he thought as padded up the stairs.

Marie was sitting opposite her sullen-faced daughter at the kitchen table. "Honey, I was thinking, maybe we should keep the rabbit after all."

"Yes!" The thirteen-year-old victoriously punched the air on hearing this climb down.

"On one condition," her mother qualified the concession. "The rabbit's got to have some kind of pen. He can't just roam around the place like he owns it."

Cassie's expression was guarded and quizzical.

"That can be your project for today," Marie smiled brightly, in that way that's guaranteed to infuriate a teenager. "Building a little home for Eli. You'll help her, won't you, Barry?"

"Sure, if we can find him," grumbled Barry, turning around from the teapot he was warming and the hot cross buns he was buttering.

"Oh, has he still not turned up?"

"No, mum," lamented Cassie. "I hope he hasn't got out onto the road and got run over."

Some hope, thought Barry sourly. Despite the kid's apparent way with rabbits, all they'd found were droppings dotted around the house. They probably contained traces of his digested flesh. Maybe that was why they smelled so bad. But he didn't mind helping her construct some kind of rabbit hutch. The woodwork lessons he'd been giving her were one of the few success stories of his fractious relationship with his stepdaughter, and they were certainly going a damn sight better than his own carpentry and joinery business. Come to think of it, maybe he *really* could do with a lucky rabbit's foot to help him through this recession!

But when he and Cassie had reported back to the kitchen from their failed rabbit hunt, Barry had noticed the drained, defeated look on Marie's face. Just a phone conversation with Simon still had the power to leave her cowed, even after she'd somehow found the strength to boot him out. It made Barry's blood boil. It wasn't as if he had some great aura of charisma, with his spindly frame and reedy voice. When she'd phoned him, he had apparently pontificated at great length about how traumatised the animal was, and how important it was for Cassie to learn compassion for God's creatures.

"I'm sure it hasn't got out," Barry said. "I think I heard it scuffling and scratching around somewhere, in one of the cupboards or something, just couldn't find it before it snuck off somewhere else. Probably got into the wall cavities or something – it's a skinny little thing, so it might be able to get into all sorts of nooks and crannies!"

"Oh, don't say that," sighed Marie. "It might be chewing up all my clothes!"

"Not to mention the wiring!"

"Eli's a he, not an it," protested Cassie.

"Well, you and I had better go and build *him* a hutch for when he finally turns up."

But he didn't.

The rest of Good Friday went by without them finding Eli, though occasionally Barry's proximity to a wall would appear to arouse a renewed bout of scuffling or scratching behind it.

Perhaps the creature could scent the congealed blood on his wounded hand.

Perhaps, being the Easter bunny, he would reappear on Sunday.

That night, his arm thrown over Marie's prone form, Barry awoke to the sensation of something gnawing on his toes. The moonlight caught the large unblinking eye, glinting on the side of Eli's head.

His legs sprung back in repulsion, and he leaped out of bed: No more Mr Nice Guy.

He heard the bony little rabbit scuttling off into the darkness, down the stairs it sounded like. Marie was stirring, half asleep, wondering drowsily what was happening, as Barry bounded down the staircase in pursuit of the rabbit. It was only when he felt his foot catch on fur-covered ribs, that he realised Eli was halfway down the stairs.

But by that time, the floor was rushing to meet his head.

*

He awoke shivering and wondering if the pain in his head was simply due to the impact of the fall. It seemed sharper, not as localised as he thought a knock on the head might be. Maybe it was worse than a simple bump, maybe a fracture. In which case …

But he definitely wasn't in a hospital, though he wasn't at home either.

It wasn't lit like a hospital for a start. Torches were throwing out jagged yellow flares of light that hurt his eyes and fitfully revealed scales of leaf mould on the ground and ghosts of tree trunks around. The people were ghostly too. They could have been doctors in their white garments, but the white things they were wearing were robes, not coats. Barry had that sick, nervous, disorientated feeling you sometimes get in hospitals.

But there the resemblance to a hospital decisively ended.

They were outside for a start. The nausea could be concussion, but there was something else about the pain in his head, or rather pains. He was wearing something on it. He felt the pressure of numerous razor-sharp metallic teeth digging into his scalp from the object he was wearing. Indeed, apart from his boxer shorts, it was all he was wearing.

Still shivering, he tried to rise, but the effort was too much, and he retched up the previous afternoon's half-digested hot cross buns. A white-robed figure approached him and took an arm to help him to his feet. He recognised the man's reedy voice:

"Sorry Marie couldn't make it. She had a fall. Like you. But unlike you she was pregnant." Simon exhaled, a pantomime of regret. "Sorry about your baby, Barry. Marie will be alright, in the end. And when she recovers she'll realise it was all for the best. We'll be a proper family again, like we were before!"

Barry let out a sob, which was almost another retch, and thought he was going to fall back down again and never get up. But Simon was there to help him up, more forcefully this time and with help of the strong hands of other robed assistants.

"Of course, you know well that I don't believe in murdering the unborn, but some things aren't meant to be. So it was kind of the hand of God that pushed her. I know you don't believe in all that, Barry Thomas. *Doubting* Thomas."

Simon and the others had now encircled Barry's trembling form, and were herding him towards a clearing lit by torches whose flames rose and fell in the breeze, revealing what he at first took for two trees in the dim, fluctuating light.

"Our Church was dying," Simon went on, "haemorrhaging souls, people leaving in droves. What we needed was a sign, something that would let Him know the time was right for Him to begin His reign on Earth. Then I thought of you, your name: Barry, like Barabbas, the one the Christ killers chose to spare instead of Him!"

Simon's eyes were shining now.

Now they were properly inside the clearing, Barry saw that

the twin objects were too straight for trees, too regular and symmetrical in their lines and right angles. And there two groaning, barely conscious figures attached to the identical wooden structures.

In fact, he realised there were three wooden crosses, two already vertically upright and occupied, with their bases firmly embedded in the ground, the other one lying horizontal and awaiting a tenant.

"Who are they?" gasped Barry.

Simon shrugged. "Just a couple of thieves."

"They're people!"

"We took them into our Church when they had nothing, and how did they thank us? They robbed us."

Barry saw where this was going now, where the symbolism was pointing.

"But I'm not—" he began.

"No, you're right. You're not." Simon's reedy voice was beginning to rise to a pitch of cold hysteria. "But don't you see the beauty of it? Your name. Barry. Short for *Barabbas*. The one who *should* have been crucified that day! And by making it happen as it should have done, Christ will know that mankind is ready for Him to return once again."

Barry began to struggle, feebly at first in his weakened state, but then more vigorously as they dragged him inexorably towards the central cross, but it wasn't enough to resist the cultists' weight of numbers.

"Of course, you might be Him after all," gasped Simon, breathless from helping to wrestle Barry onto the horizontal cross and tie his thrashing limbs to the wooden beams. "After all, you are a carpenter: In which case you'll rise again on the third day, so, you see, either way we win! Oh, I know it's all just symbolism and metaphor, like you people are always saying: The Bible shouldn't be taken literally and so on. *But metaphors can be very powerful things, Barry ...*"

Through his terror, he realised he'd never heard Simon talk so much. A bit weird certainly, but a man of few words. With an insight that he knew couldn't save him, it suddenly struck him that he'd never seen Simon in his element before.

"People like you are always picking holes in the Bible, saying, *how could God have built the world in six days?* We all know it's a figure of speech: Days are longer for Him, aren't they? Maybe for Him one day's like several billion years. And that crown on your head isn't really made of thorns: Had to make do with razor wire. Symbolic, see? And what about doubting Thomas? He wouldn't believe Christ had come back from the dead unless he could stick his fingers through the holes in the Lord's hands. Now of course all the research points to the nails going through the wrists rather than the hands, because the little bits of flesh and muscle on your palms wouldn't be enough to hold your weight up there."

Just then, between the silent and implacable figures that surrounded his prone form, Barry could make out another slighter figure emerging from the darkness of the woods into the clearing. Her movements were so uncharacteristically graceful and stately that at first he didn't recognise his gawky stepdaughter.

"Cassie," he pleaded. "Baby, it's me! It's your—"

"You're not my dad," she replied. Then she hissed: "And you killed Eli!"

And he remembered the sensation of brittle bones snapping as he'd tripped over the rabbit. Then her father handed her something, a number of things: A large lump hammer and three very long nails. Simon's acolytes gathered round eagerly, preparing to hoist the crucifix into an upright position.

"I think *you* should be allowed to do this, Cassie," smiled Simon, placing a paternal arm around his daughter's shoulders as he led her to her stepfather's taut, sweat-bright body. "Short for Cassandra, the prophet no one would listen to. It's seems only fair that you should be the one to smite the false prophet Barabbas! I always knew those woodwork lessons of yours would come in handy. She built these crosses herself you know, my little Cassie, out of reclaimed floorboards. Now

33

remember what I told you, darling, aim for the wrists not the palms of the hands …"

THE LAST TESTAMENT OF JACOB TYLER

David Surface

My name is Jacob Tyler. Let there be no mistake or controversy about my identity – Jacob Tyler is my true legal name, no other false name or names that I have provided my current employers for reasons which will soon be made clear in the story I am about to relate.

My personal effects, such as they are – a pocket watch and my Tryon rifle – I bequeath to whatever man discovers my remains and gives them a Christian burial. These items – in particular, my rifle – I would have preferred to leave to a son. But in this, as in much else, I have been disappointed – cursed, some would say. So to the man who takes this rifle from my hands, may it serve you better than it has served me.

Any property holdings that were once mine – namely twenty-five acres in lower Dutchess County, New York – have long since been liquidated and passed from my hand. And it is in that place where I lost my name and every other good thing that holds a man in the circle of human society that my story must begin.

All my life I have earned my living at the barrel of a rifle. It is true that no sportsman will ever earn his living by settling in one place – not until beavers and turkeys grow from the ground like corn.

Until the age of thirty I did right well for myself as a hunter of wild game, providing food for the tables of wealthy men from Manhattan to Albany, and later as a trapper for Mr Astor's company. When the fur trade dwindled and the price of game did also, I hired out my rifle for other enterprises, such as protecting properties in dispute or returning escaped slaves to their owners. I know some men, good hunters, who refuse such work, but I have never seen the point of such scruples. Say what you will, as long as there are slaves, there will be those who escape and those who hunt them down. It seems to me that such work is best done by professionals – I am, as I have said, a hunter and trapper by trade, and those skills have served me well.

Still, by the autumn of 1845, I was unable to find work – none that suited me. A man too long out of work will grasp at the first thing that looks like salvation – as will a man who has spent too much time alone.

My wife's maiden name was Kathleen van Cortland. Like all women, the advantages she promised seemed at first to outweigh the disadvantages. Her sharp tongue that I took at first for wit and her quick temper that I mistook for passion soon made their true selves known to me.

The property I have mentioned came to me through marriage. It had been in my wife's family – as she was fond of saying – for the better part of a hundred years. It was in its day a decent piece of land yielding a good crop of wheat as well as milk and apples. But in the absence of any male heir, it had lain fallow for many seasons.

I had been married but a fortnight when a man approached me in the tavern where I spent my evenings and began to make offers to purchase the twenty-five acres. When I told my wife of this she became much incensed and made it known that no amount of money could bring her to part with her birthright. I asked her what good was a birthright that cannot put food on the table. She then made bold to say that it was not the land, but I who was to blame. "This land will give back what a good man puts into it," she said, and went on to revile me for my drunken and wasteful ways. Not wishing to hear more, I left her at her raging and went to the tavern where I drank many glasses of brandy to still the angry voices in my head.

You might well ask why I did not exercise my right as lawful head of the household and sell the property without my wife's consent. Indeed, I could have done so. However, I would then be free of the property but not of my wife – and the misery she had caused me before would be nothing compared to what she would inflict upon me afterward.

The Last Testament of Jacob Tyler

It was about this time that my wife fell victim to consumption and soon took to her bed. Doctors came and went and she spent her days and nights in the most dreadful fits of coughing until I thought she would choke. The only thing that gave her any relief was a tonic that the doctor had prescribed for her of which she took four doses every day. This alone seemed to provide her with some repose.

As my wife's illness increased, so did my hours at the tavern where my debts likewise grew. The man who had wanted to buy the twenty-five acres continued to press me with his offers, which, in my circumstances, I was more and more loathe to refuse.

It was when I was preparing my wife's nightly dose of medicine that the idea came upon me. Taking the bottle to the kitchen, I poured a third of the tonic into the basin and replaced it with spring water. If the taste was any different, my wife did not seem to notice, but I could hear her wracking cough grow worse throughout the night.

The next day I poured out a little more of the medicine and replaced it with spring water. Indeed, my wife's fits grew worse and worse till I could scarcely bear to hear them.

I congratulated myself for my own cleverness – there would be no poison left behind, nor any sign of wrongdoing whatsoever, only the illness that God Himself had seen fit to visit upon her. In this manner I told myself that no action of mine would bring about her end – I was merely allowing nature to take its course.

One night as I was preparing my wife's nightly dose, her hand suddenly flew out and clutched my wrist with an iron-like grip. Her sunken eyes remained shut and her breathing was shallow and weak, but her grip was as unbreakable as a vice. I could feel the strength of her intent, though whether it was entreaty or accusation, I could not be sure.

After a few long moments had passed, I felt her grip release, and I fled the house for the tavern where I spent several hours waiting for that which I felt would not be long in coming.

I waited until midnight had passed before I returned home. There was such a pall of silence within the house that I fully expected to find my wife's lifeless body in the bed where I had left her. When I entered the darkened bedroom I could hear what surely were her last laboured gasps of breath – so far apart they came that at first it seemed she was no longer breathing at all.

Hearing her struggle so, and knowing that the end I had worked for was near, a feeling of victory rose within me – fed, no doubt, by the brandy I had consumed – along with a feeling of – dare I say it – sympathy, almost a tenderness. I turned and fumbled to light the candle that sputtered and sent wild shadows swelling across the walls. *Are you ready to die?* Those were the words that had formed themselves in my brain and were now on my lips, ready to be spoken, when I turned and saw my wife sitting bolt upright in bed, her lips curled back from her teeth and her eyes wide open with a look of malevolent fury that was not human. I cried out in terror and dropped the candle to the floor where it instantly went out, plunging the room into blackness. I now felt ten times the terror as before and scrambled desperately to strike a light – but not before I heard my wife speak out in the darkness in a terrible voice I could scarce recognise as her own. *"Are you ready to die?"*

Hearing these words I had meant to speak myself coming from my wife's lips, and in such a terrible, inhuman manner, I might have fainted away in terror, but I could not, so overwhelming was my desire to strike a light – if I was going to die, I wanted to see the agent of my death.

Somehow my trembling hands managed to light the candle. When I did, I was amazed to see my wife once again lying in bed on her back, her eyes still wide open but with no light left in them. One touch at her throat confirmed it – she was dead.

It was the work of less than a week to sell my wife's property for a greater sum of money than I had ever seen. I have often heard it said that the more money a man has in his possession, the quicker he loses it. Once my debts were paid it did not take long for me to incur more, and life once again became difficult. Moreover, rumours had begun to circulate that my wife's death may not have been entirely due to her illness; indeed, word reached me that certain members of her family who were no doubt behind these rumours were planning to bring the matter before the law.

It was for those reasons that I made plans to leave Dutchess County. I had read in the newspapers of a property dispute in the Kansas territories where a man who was handy with a rifle could earn decent pay. But my resources had dwindled to such an extent that a journey of that distance was beyond my means. Imagine, then, my great pleasure when I learned that Governor Seward was seeking armed men to help put down an uprising among tenant farmers in Delaware County. Delaware County – scarce two days journey! It was – so I thought then – a gift from the Almighty. So it was on a cold October morning that I cleaned my rifle, put my remaining money into my boot, and set out with a group of twelve other men for the village of Andes.

On the second morning of our journey we were joined by twenty men of Sullivan County looking to cast their lot with us. It was then we were required by Sheriff Henricks who rode with us to sign a document swearing allegiance to the Governor of New York and agreeing to the terms of payment we had been promised. It was thus that 'Jacob Tyler' became 'Jonathan Brown' and I rode the rest of that day with a feeling of lightness and well-being in my breast, as if, by the stroke of a pen, the past and all its ills had been erased.

By mid-day we were already deep into the Catskill Mountains, as dark and difficult a range as I have seen in this part of the country. We followed the meandering Esopus and before sunset we came upon the first homes of the residents of Andes, pleasant-looking white clapboard houses set back off the road. The men, women, and children who witnessed our approach did not come forth to greet us but watched from their porches and windows with caution and, it appeared to me, some degree of suspicion as we rode past.

"You can hardly blame them," said Jonas Petersen, a young man of Sullivan County who rode with us. "It's not *them* we've come to protect."

Petersen was one of those young men whose education was greater than any practical use he had for it. Thus anyone in his company was subject to the excess of fact and opinion that could not remain inside his head. It was from him that I learned the nature of the conflict we had been called in to resolve.

"Even the rich must pay their debts," Petersen said as we passed along the road through the village. "The men who own this land but do not work it owe great debts to men who are even wealthier than they. In that sense, they are just as trapped as these poor families you see staring at us from their meagre homes. The men who own this land can pay their debts by exacting the money they need from these poor men and women. But for these people, there is no one lower to turn to. That is why they have taken up rebellion."

I asked Petersen if he was prepared to use violence against those for whom he felt so much sympathy. He looked at me with some alarm and said – as though he was explaining something to a child – that Governor Seward had brought us here to prevent violence, not to be the cause of it. When I saw that he actually believed this, I nearly laughed, but seeing the look on his young face, I decided to say nothing more and we rode the rest of the way in silence.

If young Petersen had weak and ill-formed notions about our purpose, there were none in Sheriff Henricks' mind. The rebels we were about to face were desperate men, he warned, and would not scruple to use violence to achieve their goal. When I asked where this army of rebels might be found, he said without pause, "All around you." I cast my eye about the room at the local men nursing their tankards of ale and at the tavern keeper counting his coins.

"They do not appear to be as fearsome a foe as I have been told," I said.

"And what have you been told?" he asked, fixing me with a cold glare.

"Merely that a few farmers have taken up arms against their landlords and wealthier neighbours."

"And what have you heard of the Indians?"

I confessed that during the ride from Dutchess County I had heard some of the men speak of 'the Indians' although I knew of no tribes in New York that still made war against white men.

"They are not true Indians," Henricks said with much disgust in his voice. "They are cowards who put on savage dress and mask themselves with the hides and bones of dead animals to hide their identity. They meet in secret and roam the roads at night to frighten the landlords and their own neighbours who are in sympathy with the forces of law and order."

"I would like to see these Indians," I boasted. The brandy had made my blood run hot. Besides, I wanted Henricks to see that I was not afraid of the childish tricks of a few poor farmers.

"You will see them," Henricks said, still unsmiling. "Tonight."

So it was on the evening of our arrival that Sheriff Henricks ordered us to assemble with our horses and firearms in the field behind Hunting Tavern. After muffling our horses' hooves with burlap and rope, we proceeded down the road that led into the woods north of town, taking care to go slowly so as not to raise any alarm.

Our goal was an abandoned barn about a mile from town where an informer had told Henricks the Indians would meet. Before setting off, Henricks cautioned us to be wary of ambush. Looking about as we rode, I was reminded of why I had never liked hunting in the mountains because of how the land rises up on every side and lets no light pass through the trees – in that darkness, there could be a hundred of the enemy crawling near and you would never see them until their hand was at your throat.

After we had ridden for a half an hour, a light came into view, a small white flame hovering motionless in the darkness. Drawing closer, we could see it was a solitary candle burning in the window of the barn we sought, a black, dilapidated structure that squatted alone in a clearing. Henricks raised his hand and signalled two dozen men to spread out in a wide circle to prevent those of us who were going in from becoming surrounded. The rest of us then dismounted and proceeded to make our way on foot through the trees toward the barn and that solitary candle. I thought it odd that these rebels had placed a candle in the window of what was supposed to be a secret meeting place. It did not bode well.

Henricks himself approached the barn door, rifle in hand. After waiting for us to gather around, he gave the door a mighty kick. It swung open and Henricks leapt inside with a shout. The rest of us rushed in behind him, quickly deploying along one wall so as not to shoot our fellows in battle.

Within a moment it became clear – we had been deceived. The barn was empty. There was only that one candle burning and, for some reason, a lingering smell of tar. Henricks walked over to the candle that had been set on the rotting windowsill and touched it with curious fingers. It was at that moment that one of our party cried out in a voice that was terrible to hear. Looking about for the source of his alarm, I thought at first that we must be under attack but saw nothing moving in the shadows around us. I then looked at the man who had cried out and saw his gaze fixed on a point high above our heads.

There above us in the rafters of the old barn was a man, or what had been a man. His limbs had been bound and stretched so far apart that he looked like a bird stripped and splayed for gutting. And now we could all see where the smell of tar had come from. If you have seen drawings in the newspapers of men who have been tarred and feathered – those comic figures of fun like creatures from children's books – then you have not seen the bulging, blinded eyes, the skin burnt black by the molten pitch, the places where the skin itself has been torn away by the victim's struggles.

It was at that moment when we heard cries of alarm and gunshots from outside. We swiftly ran out – glad to quit that barn and its horrible tenant – and saw two men running toward us, their faces white with alarm. They related how they had been standing watch when a face suddenly appeared between the trees, a face one man described as *like a scarecrow* and the other described as *a withered corpse*. Both men claimed to have discharged their firearms in the direction of that terrible face which remained motionless, looking at them, then melted back into the darkness.

As these two men were relating this story, there arose all around us a terrifying clamour like the howling and braying from the throats of a thousand unseen animals. I saw more than one of the younger men looking wildly about, naked fear in their eyes. Henricks shouted at us to stand fast. We followed his command until that terrible noise died down and finally ceased altogether. Afterward came a silence that seemed even more threatening than the awful din that had preceded it.

Before departing, Henricks ordered the barn burned to the ground, so we rode the first half-mile back to town with that conflagration at our backs, obliging us to watch our own shadows writhing ahead of us on the ground. Whether Henricks ordered that poor man be cut down or left him hanging there to burn, I do not know to this day.

After we had stabled our horses and returned to our quarters for the night, I asked Petersen if he was still in sympathy with the rebels, now that he had seen their handiwork. The young fellow seemed shaken but still undaunted in his opinions, stating that the rebels were decent men driven to indecent acts by awful circumstances. It occurred to me that one might say the same of any man, and I thought to engage young Petersen on this point, but he had already taken to his cot and turned his face to the wall.

The following morning, I noticed that our tavern keeper was not to be found in his usual place. I later learned that he was the informer who had led us to that barn – and the same unfortunate wretch we had found hanging in the rafters.

Henricks was not daunted by the loss of a single informer. In a village where every soul knew someone or something worth telling, new informers were all around.

After breakfast, Henricks ordered ten men including myself to accompany him to the village stables. Upon arriving we found no one but a young buy of twelve or thirteen who looked upon us with great suspicion and, it seemed to me, fear.

"Where is your master?" Henricks inquired.

The boy said nothing but continued to stare at us with the wide eyes of a frightened animal.

"Speak, boy," Henricks raised his voice. "Where is your master?"

"Gone," the boy finally stammered.

"Gone where?" Henricks demanded.

"To Bovina – to shoe a horse."

"So," Henricks said, "the horses in Bovina have no one else to shoe them?"

To this the boy made no reply. I was sure that Henricks was about to lay hands on the lad – then he spoke more quietly. "Come. There is something I want to show you."

Henricks led the boy – who came with some hesitation – out of the stable and into the sunlight where he stood squinting at the other members of our militia standing by with their rifles in their arms.

"Do you see it?" Henricks asked. The boy looked around, even down at the dirt at his feet, a look of confusion on his young face.

"You do not see?" Henricks said. "Then you must look closer." At that he grabbed the boy by the hair and plunged his head into the trough, holding it deep underwater. The boy thrashed and kicked but Henricks' grip was iron. Finally, he pulled the boy free from the water, still holding him by the hair.

"Do you see it yet?" Henricks asked. The boy was gasping and choking and could not answer. "Then look again." He plunged the boy's head back underwater and held it there while the boy flailed and kicked. When he pulled the boy out again, the lad's face was blood red and water poured from his nose and mouth.

"Where is their meeting place?" Henricks shouted into the boy's ear. "Where do the devils meet tonight?" Without waiting for an answer, Henricks shoved the boy's head underwater again and held it there longer than before. The boy's thrashing grew weaker and weaker and when Henricks pulled him up again he seemed already half-drowned.

"You want to breathe?" Henricks said. "Tell me where they are meeting tonight. Then you can breathe." I saw the boy's lips moving but could hear nothing. Henricks put his ear close to the boy's mouth and closed his eyes, nodding slowly. Then he rose up and spoke in a gentle sounding voice, "Now you can breathe." He then patted the boy on the shoulder, put his pistol to the back of the boy's head and shot. A black hole opened in the boy's forehead with a great spray of blood, a look of surprise on his young face – then he slumped forward into the trough, sloshing water that Henricks took care to step away from.

I confess that I was startled by Henricks' action. In my time I had seen men do terrible things with some goal or result in mind, but what Henricks had just done seemed unnecessary, wasteful, even more so when I asked if the boy had told him where the rebels would meet and he said, "No." Then he added, "Now we don't need to look for them – they will come looking for us."

If I was startled by what Henricks had done, young Petersen was completely undone by it. I found him alone in the inn, a half-empty bottle of brandy in his hand. He sat staring into the cold hearth with his back to me so I could not see his face. I called his name three times before he finally spoke in a hollow, ragged-sounding voice.

"He will die for this."

I cautioned Petersen that he could be shot for such speech, and that he was no match for Henricks when sober, let alone drunk as he was now.

"It's not *me* he needs to fear," Petersen said in a voice so low I could barely hear it. Suddenly he turned and fixed me with a red-eyed stare and spoke in a hollow-sounding voice, "Are you ready to die?"

The shock of hearing my wife's last words to me from Petersen's lips was like a cold hand at my throat. I had to close my eyes for a moment and shake my head – it was a strange and cruel coincidence, nothing more.

"Death will come when it comes," I finally said. "It matters little if I am ready or not."

"How can you know that?" he asked, a look of great earnestness and intensity on his face. "How can you know what Death wants?" He took a long draught from the bottle, emptying it, then turned back to stare into the cold hearth. "Every man with a gun thinks he can make death his slave. But death will not be any man's slave. Not his. Not yours."

After this drunken speech Petersen's eyes closed and he laid his head on the table where I left him to sleep until nightfall.

That night Henricks ordered us to assemble once more behind the inn at moonrise. This time there was no muffling of our horses' hooves, no orders to move quietly. We rode for a half hour north of town to a quarry where flint had once been taken from the ground, now a deep bowl in the forest floor. Henricks ordered several men to descend into the quarry where they struck tents and built a campfire that they lit and left blazing. Then Henricks ordered us to climb high into the trees around the quarry's edge and be ready with our rifles. We smeared our rifles with mud to avoid reflecting the firelight – some of the men darkened their faces too. Then we waited.

The moon had almost climbed to its highest place in the sky when I heard them coming – first, nothing more than the distant snap of a twig, then closer. Then I saw them moving through the trees below. Dark shadows, the moon illuminating a grotesque painted mask, a set of antlers, then more and more of them until it seemed the whole forest floor was alive. They poured down the sides of the quarry and I thought of a herd of deer I had once trapped in a dead-end gulch and shot, one by one as they'd struggled to leap the steep walls and climb over each other as they fell. The figures below moved closer to the empty tents and the campfire, their grotesque faces illuminated in its reddish glow.

Then Henricks gave the order and the trees all around exploded with volley after volley of rifle fire. Figures below fell to the earth and were trampled by more figures running to escape the hail of bullets from above. I shot one man in a red and yellow robe with a painted scarecrow face who was waving a scythe and shouting, then another with a pair of bull's horns on his hooded head who fell to the ground screaming and writhing like a snake until I silenced him. Altogether I shot fifteen men.

When Henricks shouted the order to cease fire, the forest was full of the haze and stink of gun smoke, and the quarry below was carpeted with bodies, some of them still moving. We climbed down from the trees and walked among them, shooting the ones who were still alive.

Before we left, Henricks ordered two men to douse the bodies with coal oil and set them afire. From the cries that rose from that smouldering mass, I knew we had left some alive, despite our best efforts. So I stood and fired my rifle in the direction of those cries until either the bullets or the fire had silenced them.

When we had done with this work, Henricks led thirty men, including myself, north along the Kings Road where he believed some of the rebels had fled. He left behind a contingent of twenty men to make sure that the fire did its work. Petersen was among those left behind at the quarry. His face, when I last saw it, was ghost-white in the firelight. I didn't know if he had fired any shots tonight, and, seeing the haunted look on his face, I determined never to ask him.

We rode along in silence halfway to Delhi, not encountering a soul along the way. Finally, Henricks gave the order to turn and go back. As we rode, I became aware of the darkness ahead growing thicker and heavier, the way the sky feels just before a storm. I cursed the mountains around us that blocked out the moon, and the trees that crowded close and let no light through. When I saw a dark figure coming toward us, moving in a halting and unnatural way like a scarecrow being pulled along on strings, I raised my rifle, and all the men around me did the same.

Then we saw – it was Petersen, but a horrid, changed version of the man we knew. His head had been laid open with a great wound from which the blood flowed, soaking his white shirt red. Worst of all, he was burnt – black, scorched marks covered his hands and face, and the smell of burnt cloth and flesh hung heavy upon him. As we ran to meet him, he stumbled to his knees and by the time we reached him he was lying full on his back in the middle of the road, staring up at the moon and the trees with a look on his face that was terrible to see.

"Where are the others?" Henricks demanded.

"Dead," Petersen answered in a choked whisper.

"Dead?" Henricks said. "How? Not *all* dead …"

"All dead," Petersen rasped out. "They came … they came out of the fire. Still burning. With their masks and pitchforks. And their scythes. Still burning. They are coming."

"Who?" Henricks demanded, although by now he knew the answer as surely as we all did.

"The men," Petersen said, "The men we killed tonight."

"They are *dead*," Henricks spoke loudly and deliberately like someone trying to wake a child from a bad dream.

"They are dead," Petersen said, "And they are coming."

With that, a sudden rushing sound rose up from the dark road ahead of us, like a great wind moving through the trees. And with it a smell of smoke, tar, and burnt things.

When I looked back down, Petersen had ceased breathing. Suddenly, there came a hideous torrent of noise out of the darkness ahead of us like the one we had heard before, like cries from the throats of a thousand unseen animals. At that, several of our men broke ranks and took off running through the trees. Henricks shouted at the deserters who did not stop, and took a shot at one, although he missed. He then ordered us to retreat to a barn that stood just off the road where we bolted the doors, positioned ourselves at the windows and made ready to face what was coming.

There is nothing like hot-blooded action to push back fear, so it was by making these familiar preparations for battle that the doubts and terrors of just a few moments ago began to seem small and distant. I now believed, as Henricks surely did, that another rebel force had discovered their slain brethren, taken vengeance on Petersen and his fellows and were now on their way to engage us. Petersen had been drunk, destroyed by his own fear and weak will, and his words were the ravings of someone who could not face the truth. I checked my rifle, wiped the sights clean with my thumb and fixed my gaze on the road, waiting for a target.

As I stared into the darkness, I saw a flickering glow through the trees that grew brighter and closer. *Torches*, I thought – then I saw. The figures that approached by the hundreds were not carrying torches. It was they themselves who were burning. God help me, they were all burning.

In a second they were on us in a great howling rush of wind. Doors and walls burst inward in a shower of sparks and the nightmare figures stepped through, laying about with their scythes and pitchforks, butchering men like pigs at a slaughter. All around me, men screamed and fired their guns uselessly. I saw Henricks firing his Colt again and again at one of the burning devils who lifted him by the throat with one hand and forced a pitchfork through his chest, pinning him to the wall while the poor man kicked and squealed in a thin, shrill voice that was horrible to hear.

A tall robed figure appeared before me, burning antlers rising from its head, its face the skull of a great stag painted red and black with the skin dried and cracked like leather. It was on me in one stride, grasped the back of my neck in a grip like iron and pushed me to the floor, pressing my face down into the dust. I could feel its great head lean closer, hot breath and heat from the smouldering skin licking at the back of my neck. Then it spoke into my ear through the burning cloth and leather in a voice that I knew.

It was my wife's own voice.

"Are you ready to die?"

It was then that I screamed as I had not screamed since I was a child. I screamed like a sick man emptying himself of the poison that burns his insides. Something left me then. I don't know what, but something went out of me, and with it, the feel of that hand – of *her* hand on my neck. I did not feel it release me – one moment it was there; the next moment, it was gone.

At first I believed I had been dreaming – then I woke at dawn and saw the terrible slaughter all around me, the scorched and blackened bodies of men where they had fallen. I rose and walked away from that burning ruin, away from those black mountains, away from Delaware County. I went as far as my money would carry me and put as many miles as I could between myself and that cursed place. I finally reached the Nebraska territories where a land company hired me to watch over a large property and keep all unwanted persons from entering. And so I come to the end of my story.

And yet, it is not really over – not yet. Every day I sit here with my old Tryon rifle across my knees, looking out over this strange, unbroken horizon, and wait for them to come. Let them. Let them come. I am ready now. Still, when I dream of dark glades and vales, and hills pressing close on every side, I am relieved to wake and find this flat and empty landscape that stretches all around me. Because if there is something coming for me, as it surely must, I want to see it when it comes.

THE WAR EFFORT

Carl P. Thompson

"What will you be doing, Horace?"

Through his partially open door, Horace Renwick looked up at the man who stood on his doorstep. His suit was smart, but Horace didn't think much of the man's parking skills. The way he'd left his car slung across the pavement in front of Horace's small, neat garden was both untidy and inconsiderate, causing an obstruction for any pedestrians passing by.

"What do you mean?" replied Horace, trying unsuccessfully to ignore the car.

"For the war, Horace. For the war."

Horace twitched, his broken spectacles lifting on his pink nose.

"How do you know my name?"

The man lifted his arm barely an inch from the side of his body, a spasm more than a gesture, under which he carried a thin brown book, which he tapped with a long, pale finger. "You're on the list."

Horace squinted, and nodded towards the next house on the left.

"You shouldn't call at number sixty-two. She's an old lady on her own."

"She's not on the list, Horace. You are."

Horace looked at the man's highly polished shoes, and at his sharply pressed suit

"Could I have a look? At the list, I mean."

"We're wasting time, Horace. You are my last call. I won't be going to see the old lady at number sixty-two, or anyone at number sixty-six, whether old or not; nor will I be knocking on the door of number sixty-eight. They are not on the list, Horace; you are. So could I get an answer?"

Horace peered over the man's shoulder at the car again.

"I'm sorry, what was the question again?"

The man leaned forward, blocking his view.

"What will be your contribution? To the war effort?"

Horace looked at the man with wide-open eyes.

"The war?"

"Why, yes, Horace, the war! Defending our island against the mighty Hun!"

Horace blinked. It was bright outside, but he had not expected it to be so cold.

"I don't understand; I really don't. I don't mean to be rude, but I must close the door, there's a draft coming in, and I can't afford to lose any more heat."

The man took a step forward.

"Would you like me to come in, Horace? I do wish to resolve this today. You wouldn't want me to call again tomorrow, I'm sure you have more pressing business than standing and talking to me, Horace."

"Not really. I need to clean the pantry, and I have a ship in the bottle, which I want to finish making. Who is that, sat in your car?"

"That is a friend of mine, Horace. I told her to wait in the car, as I knew we wouldn't be long."

The man took another step closer.

"I can make suggestions."

"What do you mean?"

"If you cannot decide. I can offer suggestions for your contribution. You can pick one; I'll get a signature, and then leave. If you'll allow me to do so."

Horace looked at his wrist; he'd left his watch upon the kitchen table, next to his cold toast.

"What sort of suggestions?"

The man cocked his head, grinned, then took the brown book from beneath his arm and a short bookmaker's pencil from a pocket inside his overcoat.

He licked the lead tip, and held it above an open page.

"Okay, okay. How about a postal order? Say, a guinea?"

"A guinea?"

"As an average, a mean, that would be the general contribution, yes. A guinea."

Horace twisted his neck inside his shirt collar.

"No, I'm afraid not. I have no savings. What I have is what I have, and no more."

"Shame, Horace. We could have finished there and then. Never mind."

The man put the pencil to his temple. His face twisting into a grotesque expression as he thought.

"Ah, ha! I have the answer. A parcel. A few simple items will suffice. Nothing fresh, mind you. A can of spam, or corned beef. A quarter of tea, and perhaps some sugar. Shoe polish is always a bonus, if you have any. Cigarettes would be a most generous and welcome addition."

Horace looked again at the man's shoes, then at his stained fingers. He stepped back an inch further inside the narrow hallway.

"I'm sorry, I have barely enough for myself. If I could spare such things, then I would. But I am not in such an enviable position."

The man moved his polished foot to the edge of the step, the toe of his shoe protruding over the wooden doorframe.

"You are to some, indeed many, Horace. Those that fight for King and Country, they would gladly swap places right now."

Horace shook his head. "I understand, but this is a difficult time for all of us."

"Think of your father, Horace."

Horace stared at the man. "My f-f-father?"

"Yes, Horace. That is one of the reasons why you are on the list. We knew you would understand."

Horace leaned against the door, putting considerable force behind it.

"I th-th-think, y-you better l-leave now," he stuttered.

"If I do, I will only need to call tomorrow, Horace. Should we not end this now?"

"Pl-please, do not c-call tomorrow. I cannot h-h-help you."

"Silver? Gold? Unwanted precious metals, Horace, are the most generous of gifts."

"No, n-no, I can't, sorry."

"Old medicines? Tools?"

"Please move your foot," begged Horace, leaning hard against the door.

"Clothes? Spectacles? Come on now, Horace, we've all got to do our bit! Besides, I get the weekend off if we resolve this today, and I promise you, that, I would be grateful for."

"Who is it, Horace?" a female voice called from inside the house just as Horace began to speak.

"Bill!" Hardwick yelled through the narrow gap. "Bill Hardwick, miss, from the War Office!"

"Let the man in, Horace!" the woman called warmly from the rear of the hall. "I'm sure he means you no harm."

"I certainly do not!" Hardwick laughed, shouldering the door open and sending Horace crashing into a coat stand.

"I do apologise," said Hardwick, holding out a conciliatory hand, not meant for Horace, who was bent picking up his spectacles, but for the tall, well-appointed woman who stood a couple of feet away. "Bill Hardwick, at your service."

"I heard you the first time, and the second, Mr Hardwick," the woman said with a smile, waving Hardwick's hand away. "Now what can we help you with?"

Horace opened his mouth to speak once more, but the woman gave him a withering glance.

"I have explained to Horace, Mrs …?"

"Mrs Elliot. From number sixty-two."

Hardwick looked at Horace, whose gaze was fixed on the wooden floor, then back at Mrs Elliot.

"I'm here for the war effort. A collection for our brave troops, the young boys taken from the bosoms of their mothers to fight the filthy Hun. To raise their spirits, and boost their morale." He leant in a little closer. "To let them know that they are not alone, that all of us, and I mean all of us, are one hundred percent behind them."

Mrs Elliot scowled at Horace. "Why on earth would you not allow this gentleman entry, Horace? Furthermore, why would you not offer him your hospitality?" She turned to Hardwick, the scowl now a smile, her surprisingly white two front teeth smeared red.

"I don't have anything to give," Horace grunted, like a naughty schoolboy. "Besides, he has a woman outside."

"She won't mind waiting," blurted Hardwick. "This is my last call, and then we're away. Just a little jaunt, nothing much."

"Well that settles it then," said Mrs Elliot. "Why don't you take Mr Hardwick into your living room, Horace? I will pop next door and see what I have. I am sure we can rustle up something for our boys."

Hardwick grinned at Horace. "Many, many thanks, Mrs Elliot," he exclaimed, as she headed towards the kitchen. "This way is it, Horace?" he added, nodding towards the door to his left.

Horace didn't answer. His gaze followed Mrs Elliot as she entered the kitchen and then closed the door behind her.

"Horace?" Hardwick barked, and Horace turned his head in an instant.

"What?"

"The living room. I presume it's through here."

Horace looked back towards the kitchen. He heard his back door slam shut, and jumped where he stood.

"Yes, yes, it is."

Horace led Hardwick into the room.

"Very nice," Hardwick lied. "Very cosy indeed, Horace." The room was sparsely decorated, with old brown wallpaper, and a wooden floor with a threadbare rug barely concealing the scuffed planks. Two old chairs faced each other in the centre of the room, like nearly dead geriatrics without anything else left to say, wearing matching, holed green cardigans. Hardwick sat in one of the chairs, and its springs groaned a broken last breath.

Horace sat in the chair opposite, though on the edge, as if ready to leap.

"Good to have friends like that, eh, Horace?" Hardwick asked.

"I suppose so."

"That's what this is about you know, Horace. The freedom we have in this country to leave our doors open. The trust we have for the people on our doorstep, those who we share our lives with. The knowledge that they are like us, Horace, you and me. Like your father." Hardwick pointed at a blurred black and white photograph on the mantel above the hollow fireplace and its meagre cold ashes.

"That him?"

Horace looked at the photograph, as if he was seeing it for the first time.

"Yes."

Hardwick stood tall, and lifted it from the mantelpiece.

"The infant, Horace. I presume that is you?"

Horace nodded.

"I imagine he was proud as Punch seeing this, Horace. His newborn, in his arms. Proud as Punch."

"He never saw it." Horace stood and held his hand out. Hardwick took another look and then handed it to Horace. "He left the next day, before it was developed, so my mother told me."

"I'm sorry Horace, really."

Hardwick put a firm hand upon Horace's shoulder. "This picture is something to be treasured, Horace. A real treasure."

Horace carefully placed the picture back on the mantelpiece.

"Now, could you find out where Mrs Elliot is, Horace? I don't mean to be rude, but time is pressing."

Horace nodded. "Your weekend off, I know." He turned towards the door. "I'll go and find out what's keeping her."

"Much obliged, Horace, much obliged" Hardwick yelled, rubbing his hands together as Horace stepped out of the room. Hardwick sat back down, crossed his legs, and took a cigarette case from his inside pocket. As he lit up, he looked around the room, and allowed himself a quiet chuckle and a shake of the head.

As he exhaled smoke upwards, Hardwick heard the sounds of the back door closing, and voices in low conversation. He heard Mrs Elliot's calm, authoritative tones, but it wasn't Horace she was speaking to, Hardwick was sure of that. He heard another female voice, this one throaty and raw, and perhaps another female, older and less comprehensible. He also heard a male voice, a low distinctive tenor, rattling through the house, even though it was not raised in anger.

The voices stopped, but now he heard footsteps approaching the room. Hardwick stubbed his cigarette out in between his spittle-moistened fingers, and stood and faced the door.

Mrs Elliot entered the room, ushering in two elderly and rather hunched characters. "This is him! Mr Hardwick," she said, smiling. They simultaneously looked up towards him, their movements suggesting that it took a great deal of energy and effort, as though they would rather keep their eyes on the floor given the choice.

"Mr Hardwick, this is Elsie Humble, from number sixty eight, and Mr Wilkinson, from number sixty six."

"Pleased to make your acquaintance," Hardwick offered, clicking his heels, and bowing slightly, before straightening. "How may I help you folks?"

"They are interested in the war effort too, Mr Hardwick."

"Good to hear it. It doesn't surprise me one bit to see people like yourselves eager to help out. People who've already been through it once, dare I say it? It warms my heart, it really does."

Mrs Elliot, who had left the room momentarily, returned with a pair of wooden stools.

"Come now, Elsie, rest those bones. You too, Seymour."

The two neighbours took their seats, both facing Hardwick, who took his seat once they had slowly taken theirs.

"Now folks," said Hardwick earnestly. "I don't want to keep

you, I'm sure you've got better things to do than listen to me. But one minute of your time will make all the difference."

Elsie and Mr Wilkinson nodded slowly in unison, while Mrs Elliot simply listened, sat forward in the chair opposite Hardwick, her hands clasped together upon her skirt.

"Our boys are fighting for our freedom. We need to support them. We need to feed and clothe them. We need to show this axis of evil that we are the second front, right behind our brave boys, prepared to do, and to give whatever we have. Prayers mean a lot, they do, but your donation, no matter how small, means more."

Mrs Elliot smiled. "Have you given yourself, Mr Hardwick?"

"What do you mean?"

"Exactly what I said, have you given yourself?"

Hardwick looked around the room. "Of course," he answered, becoming indignant. "Of course I have, though not perhaps what you could measure in pounds and ounces, or shillings and pence, Mrs Elliot, but I have given my time!" Hardwick jabbed a finger against the arm of the chair. "Time is what I have given, that most precious commodity, one that this dreadful war has robbed so many of!"

"You have not given time, Mr Hardwick," said Mrs Elliot, shaking her head. "Not in the same way that Elsie's grandson has, barely seventeen and buried at sea; or Horace's father, a proud man whose last days lay in the horror of Ypres; or Seymour's beautiful wife Jean, taken from us only last year by the Luftwaffe."

Hardwick shuffled uncomfortably in the uncomfortable chair. "You are right, Mrs Elliot. I apologise most humbly, I did not mean any offence, certainly not to the memory of your dearly beloved. What I meant to say, was yes, I have given service. Not at the front, though I wish I could, I promise you. This, this is the next best thing I could do."

Elsie Humble laughed. "You don't know the half of it!"

"Quiet, Elsie!" hushed Mr Wilkinson.

59

"I will not!" she snapped, then turned to face Hardwick. "You come here, asking young Horace for help, asking for corned beef, or tobacco, or some such things that he ain't got! You tried livin' on our rations? You wondered whether we can even feed ourselves, our families, our little ones? You ever thought about that, Mr Hardwick?"

Hardwick raised his palms like two white flags.

"I think perhaps you misunderstand me, Elsie. If I may explain? I simply asked Horace to look into his heart, and to find his conscience. Perhaps cut down for a day, or skip a meal, just one, so that our lads don't end up weak from hunger. That's all."

"Pah! Cut down on what. You can't cut down from nowt! Not unless you start taking from others, and we don't do that. Not round here."

Mrs Elliot leaned forward.

"What Elsie is saying, Mr Hardwick, what we are asking, is that you give as we give. You sacrifice what we sacrifice. For the war."

Hardwick shifted forward on his seat, moving his face closer to Mrs Elliot's. "Fine. You lot ain't got much, so I know it's not gonna cost me. I will match what you give. I ain't got a problem with that at all; in fact I like the idea greatly."

Mrs Elliot sat back in her chair, and smiled.

"So what is it you people do then, Mrs Elliot? I presume you're enjoying retired life. Same for you, Mr Wilkinson? Elsie? Taking it easy, as you very much deserve to do?"

"No," Mrs Elliot replied. "No, we're all still very much active. I am a notary, in a part-time capacity, and I am also heavily involved in the Women's Institute, amongst other things. Elsie here, has her own store in the town: a haberdashery. Seymour still undertakes certain duties for the funeral business his great-grandfather established in the last century."

Hardwick heard someone, presumably Horace, drop something heavy in the hall. Something that crash-landed with a metallic *badum!* and echoed through the house.

"Good for you lot," said Hardwick, arching his neck towards the door. He heard that same someone groan as he picked up whatever he had dropped, and then drop it again, or perhaps something else, something equally as heavy, equally as metallic.

"What, er, what does Horace do?" Hardwick added, surprised that no one so much as blinked at the sound.

"Horace?" Mrs Elliot replied, getting up from her chair and heading to the door. "Horace is a butcher. Our butcher."

She left, closing the door behind her. Hardwick smiled at Elsie and Mr Wilkinson. "An undertaker, then, Seymour," he said. "Fascinating work, I imagine." Elsie Humble scowled. "Terribly tragic too, I suppose," Hardwick added, though her scowl did not disappear. "And you, Elsie, a haberdashery. Lovely. You must enjoy that."

"It's the people I enjoy, Mr Hardwick. The people. The company. Their lives and their stories. I consider my customers my friends."

"I'm sure you do."

"I certainly do. Occasionally I may even bring them along to meet Horace, and Seymour, and Elizabeth."

"The evenings must fly by."

"You'd be surprised, Mr Hardwick," Mr Wilkinson replied. "You'd be surprised."

The door swung open, and in stepped Mrs Elliot, holding in her outstretched hands a brown paper parcel.

"For the war effort, Mr Hardwick."

She opened the parcel, revealing a large, pale and bloodied liver, and held it beneath his nose. "Now, the agreement was that you match it."

Hardwick laughed a little tremulously. "What is this? Bloody pigs liver? I'm afraid I can't accept fresh produce. Take it away, missus. Take it away."

"Fresh produce is all we've got, Mr Hardwick," replied Mrs Elliot. "We don't have any jars of potted shrimp, no corned

61

beef or ham. Only what we can harvest. Fresher than anything you might have tasted recently."

"You should show some gratitude, young man," added Elsie Humble, gesturing towards Hardwick with a finger that resembled a gnarled chess piece. "Horace worked hard to get that."

Hardwick stood up. "Thanks, but no thanks. I think you lot are wasting my time. I'll see myself out, ta."

Mrs Elliot stepped in front of him, blocking his exit, her hands still outstretched, blood dripping through her fingers onto the wooden floor.

"You don't think our boys would appreciate liver, Mr Hardwick? It has a lovely metallic taste, don't you think?"

"It needs to be fresh, lad, otherwise it just isn't the same," added Mr Wilkinson, who rose hand in hand with Elsie Humble. "The Jerries eat it raw, so I've heard. We can't have our lads malnourished now, can we?"

"You 'ave to be kiddin', you lot! You're bloody demented!" Hardwick sidestepped Mrs Elliot and headed for the door.

"Tell Horace I won't be calling again. He can keep his bloody rations" Hardwick spat, half-turning before opening the door.

"Tell him yourself," Mrs Elliot replied, as Hardwick opened the door.

"What the Christ?"

Horace was standing in the doorway. He had removed his cardigan, and replaced it with a filthy bloodstained butcher's apron. In one hand hung a massive cleaver, in the other, another piece of meat, this one larger and bloodier.

"I've told them lot, I don't want your bloody pigs' liver, Horace. We can't use it."

"This isn't liver, Hardwick," said Horace, quietly. "And it certainly is not from a bloody pig."

"Get out of my way, Horace!" Hardwick pushed past Horace, but not in the direction of the front door. Instead, he took two steps towards the kitchen, and then stopped at the threshold.

The room was bathed in a red glow. Horace stood behind Hardwick, accompanied by his houseguests.

"What's this Horace?" Hardwick asked, without turning.

"What the bloody hell is this?" he repeated.

He held on to the doorframe as his eyes scanned the room. The kitchen's worn floral wallpaper, torn in places revealing the brickwork beneath, had been splattered a vivid crimson, its black and white floor tiles were slick with fresh, thick blood. The light fitting above had a curved scarlet smear, and the large white sink appeared two thirds full, of deep, dark, viscose, blood.

"This is unsanitary, Horace, to work this way! I should report you, the lot of y ..." Hardwick stopped mid word. Upon the broad, heavy, blade-scarred oak table lay the remnants of Horace's butchery. A ribcage, as one would expect, from a calf, one would assume. Endless intestines, marbled pink and grey, trailing upon the floor at one end, kept because waste is a crime in these times, one would agree. And the inverted head of the butchered animal, bobbing in its scooped brain juice in a white porcelain bowl in the centre of the table, missing its lower jaw and eyes, but still recognisable, most definitely identifiable, as human.

"Jesus Christ!" croaked Hardwick; and though he wanted to turn away, he couldn't. His gaze inexorably drawn to a visual feast of grisly delights in that abattoir of horror. Skinned cats hung on steel wire from the window sash, dripping rot into the bubbling sink. A further two human heads sat upon the windowsill, grinning, with scalps and lips and eyes removed; three disembodied torsos were suspended from the washing rail, swinging slowly, in various stages of decomposition. Yet the most terrifying vision within this horror show was the pressed dress hanging over the back door. The last time Hardwick had seen that dress it contained the shapely body of Mrs Eleanor Pearce, the young wife of his sappy, diminishing boss Reginald Pearce; she had been sitting in the car not fifteen minutes ago, her white thighs visible below the short hemline, save for the flesh hidden beneath Hardwick's hand.

Hardwick put his hand to his mouth, shaking his head.

"This ain't right," he mumbled between his fingers.

"Sorry, what was that?" Mrs Elliot replied.

He continued shaking his head, but now his whole body shook, and he stood convulsing in the doorway.

"We should thank you," added Elsie Humble, tapping Hardwick on the shoulder. "We ain't seen any fresh meat round 'ere for ages!"

Hardwick took his hand from his mouth, his throat filling with vomit.

"She should keep us going for a while, eh, Seymour?"

"Yes, Elsie. Decent bit of rump she 'ad, I reckon."

"Ooh, Seymour, you are a devil."

Hardwick belched a guttural roar and spun round, ready to run.

Above him, catching the sunlight from the stained-glass hall window, and descending down like the glittering wings of an angel, was Horace's cleaver.

It struck Hardwick cleanly, in the centre of his skull. The moment it hit, Hardwick felt a pain he had never felt before, as clean and as accurate as lightning, rippling in waves through his body, starting at his forehead and ending in the extremities of his fingers and toes. His body did not fall, not just yet.

A second after the blow, his hearing popped, the only sound remaining a fierce ringing. In the following second, he saw lights exploding in the air around him, as though he were in the midst of a thousand flashbulbs.

He inhaled an acrid, sulphurous smell and he closed his eyes, but despite this, the dazzling lights persisted; and he felt his blood running down his face. In his final second, amidst the final flashbulb before he ceased to be, he saw the sepia picture of Horace and his father. Then he was gone, and his body slumped to the floor at Horace's feet.

Horace, Mrs Elliot, Mr Wilkinson and Elsie Humble

huddled over the body, now no more than a corpse.

"I didn't trust him to keep his end of the bargain, Horace," said Mrs Elliot, putting a hand on Horace's arm. "Besides, what sacrifices did he ever make?"

"Remember how your dad died, son," added Seymour Wilkinson. "With those shells whistling past him, sending him deaf and blind. He had a terrible death. Not like this 'un."

Horace nodded, putting his bloodied hand on Mrs Elliot's.

Seymour bent down, and grabbed Hardwick's thigh.

"Big bugger isn't he!"

Mrs Elliot smiled at Horace.

"He'll see us through t'end, he will! Till Hitler gets what's comin'!"

Elsie Humble laughed. "Eee, Seymour, stop, you'll put me in an early grave."

"Don't tempt me!" he replied, and the sunlit hall was filled with their cheery laughter.

THE PRE-RAPHAELITE PICTURE

An adventure with Roman Blackwood

David A. Sutton

Last month my work took me back to Moseley again. I was anxious about it, though that little village in the Birmingham suburbs was pleasant enough to assuage my fears. More upmarket these days than in former years when an excess of residential lettings deprived the shops and restaurants of the kind of income expected from an upwardly mobile clientele, Moseley – as I arrived – was humming.

Generally speaking everything still appeared unchanged. The shops were as ever a cosmopolitan mix; a charming little Greek delicatessen and Indian restaurants; an art shop and boutiques; banks and wine merchants and newsagents. Gone was the W. H. Smith, located in an old half-timbered building. New were two express supermarkets, but estate agents were still superimposed on their ancient facades. A Saturday farmers' market came once a month, surrounding the minuscule village green where once a foul public lavatory stood. Gone too, it seemed, were the winos who drank cheap cider, oblivious to the roar of traffic as it passed them along the high street.

I had an appointment with an old friend, Clive Foster, who I hadn't seen in years. Not official business, though what came later makes me wish I had been hired in my usual capacity – psychic debunker (or 'ghostbuster' as my PA always quipped).

It was about seven-thirty in the evening and I'd just left the Prince of Wales pub and was standing on tiptoe reading the menu on the window of *Ponte Di Legno*, a restaurant at which I had earlier booked a table. The street it stood on, Woodbridge Road, had become over the years a little Mecca of restaurants, with Italian, Thai and Middle Eastern establishments clustered near the main road.

"Skulking about, as usual, Roman?" The whisper was close, almost in my ear.

I turned and there stood Clive, still bent double to my ear level. I uttered what I hoped sounded like a jubilant shout and we slapped our right hands together and embraced. As we drew apart my old friend cuffed me gently around my head.

"Roman, you haven't grown any taller I see," he jested. He knew I could take any amount of ribbing from him about my being a midget.

Ignoring his remark I said, sallying forth a little jibe back at him, "I'm impressed, Clive, that you managed to get here on time, if at all!"

"Ah, my usual skill and perseverance with the A to Z." He pushed open the door to the restaurant and we strode – well in my case waddled – in as if we owned the place.

Despite the dim lighting inside, I could see that Clive's appearance had changed quite a bit in the eight or nine years that had elapsed since I'd last met up with him. He had become heavier and paler, and more stooped in the intervening years. We had been friends through university, even though Clive had been a challenging individual to be friends with. He was disliked by many of our peers because he was a womaniser par excellence. His influence over the fairer sex was, to someone like me, uncanny; women fell under his spell, attracted by some charm he possessed. Yet he was downright callous in his affairs. Clive just experimented with them, dumped them, and then went on to his next conquest. Most of the other young men in our group begrudged him his success but they also secretly admired it too.

He had few close friends, apart from me. I knew this used to concern him. He badly wanted to be one of the boys, but could not stop himself and went out of his way to conquer the girlfriends of more than one of his acquaintances.

We sat on a brown leather sofa while we waited to be called to our table, and I thought a little more about the Clive I had known.

Unlike me, Clive had really been the alpha male. He was an accomplished horseman, a wild and undefeated drinker, an inveterate – and often winning – gambler. As I said, he had been horribly handsome, with a head of long, dark wavy hair, one that many a lady hoped to run their fingers through. The combination of his impressive physique, disarming smile and cheerful disposition made him irresistible.

Our friendship had been abiding despite his foibles and the huge difference in our characters. Being a somewhat lacklustre individual myself, I admired Clive's flamboyance, and he in turn enjoyed what he called my 'seriousness and dependability'. I had in some ways regretted losing touch with him, though our paths were never in any logical sense parallel. We veered off on our own byways as old university chums must do, but I was understandably pleased to meet up with him again.

While we waited, Clive ordered two glasses of Islay single malt, with what I recalled as his usual breeziness, and he smiled at me in the knowledge that I hadn't demurred from his selection of aperitif and therefore I must still be the old Roman he had known. Yet I found I had difficulty responding to him in the same way, because now, in the diffuse light from several spotlights, I saw the full extent of the changes in his appearance. Clive's once muscular body had blossomed to the point where his paunch imitated pregnancy. Shadows were slung like soiled canvass under his eyes and his skin was a pallor I would have associated with a corpse. His dark hair, somewhat bedraggled, was highlighted with streamers of grey.

What remained was his smile. It had about it a sense of childlike innocence and enthusiasm, and it made you feel important and convinced of his genuine liking for you.

He smiled again as my puzzled eyes took in the rest of him.

"Let's see," he said, almost shouting over the restaurant chatter. "My guess is that you're married by now, of course. You have two-point-whatever it is offspring and you are very unspectacularly happy. Am I right?"

Having no children and one divorce successfully completed, I laughed. "You must be losing your marbles, as you are unspectacularly wrong!" By the look of him I knew there were more important things to discuss than my recent history, so I spoke again before he could. "And how about you?"

My question took him by surprise. I could tell he would rather have had more time before he opened up. He coughed, embarrassed. "Me? I'm well. That's to say ..." His eyes twitched. "... all things considered ... ah!"

The waiter had brought the whisky and we both paused to savour the aroma and taste of peat.

"To the drowning of sorrows." He tipped his glass up and the liquid vanished down his throat.

"Sorrows?" I asked.

"We all have them, don't we?" He fell silent, opened the menu and stared at it with a glazed look. Then his familiar smile returned and he glanced over at me.

"Are you in some sort of bother, Clive?" I asked.

Embarrassment swept across his face and he hastily looked down at the menu. "I'm all right. How about the seafood linguine?" he changed the subject.

"It's been too long a time since I was last here, so—"

"Tell me, Roman," he interrupted, his voice starting to break up a little, "Are you still the same? Dull and dreamy?"

Had I not worked out that he was in some kind of difficulty, his comment might have irritated me. No one likes to be called dull, however true, but I had moved on since the old days. I guess he knew it. Clive smiled wistfully.

"Don't take offence," he said. "I am in a bit of a pickle. In fact, I'm in one hell of a mess. But if I tell you everything you'd think I was straightjacket material." He glanced around, obviously very agitated, as if seeking help from the other diners. "There is a woman, you see. She dangles me like a marionette. I'm at a loss as to what I can do."

"Clive," I said. "Can't you be more explicit?" His face was a sad mask indeed. I began to feel sorry for him. He had been such a happy-go-lucky student once. Something terrible had taken its toll on him.

"Yes," he replied, lowering his gaze to stare at the dregs of amber liquid in his glass, rotating it between twitching fingers. "Explicit, yes, by all means, let's be explicit. I see you find me changed, don't you?"

I nodded.

"I look like a wreck?" He tried to be flippant.

"Somewhat," I said noncommittally.

"Let me tell you that what you see on the surface is merely a shadowy reflection of the shambles in here." He tapped his head. "And yet ... I'm full of pride in a way. A man redeemed perhaps." The satisfied smile of a man older and wiser, and somewhat rueful about it appeared on his face.

He was starting to make very little sense, but I let him continue without interruption.

"I was a rascal. But life is just a single chance, so I went for the one thing I was accomplished at, with women."

At that moment, the waiter arrived to take our order and show us to our table.

"Sex became a drug," he continued after the waiter left. "But one without satisfaction, yet I supped low the last few years. The more sluts I bedded, the worse I became. Hopeless, eternal repetition. Women became a sedative, whose efficacy diminished over time. Night after night I spent in the throes of monotonous bonking. But now I've found what I never realised I'd been searching for: the perfect female. After all those one-night stands, and the prostitutes ..."

He reached into an inside pocket and brought out a photograph. He looked at it as if this was the first time he had seen it and his expression changed into something like awe – and not a little trepidation.

"This is her."

He slid the picture across the linen tablecloth. I took it and almost laughed. It was not the expected photograph of a stunning blonde, but a picture depicting a nineteenth century

70

painting of a rather wistful looking woman. I was put in mind immediately of the Pre-Raphaelites ...

"She's perfection," he stated.

I tried to study the snapshot with seriousness. The woman in the picture was very beautiful and imposing. She was a classical Pre-Raphaelite beauty. Standing tall, slender; she had a very pale, sad face, and long, red hair. Above her, an apple tree seemed to hem her into the frame of the picture and she was reaching up one delicate hand to grasp one of the ripe, red fruits. Matching the apple's colour was her lips and her flimsy dress was also crimson; the folds clung to her body, especially her thighs, so that you could see the contours of the flesh beneath. Her eyes were an intense black melancholy burning into those of the painting's viewer. I was put in mind of the female form in Burne-Jones's *The Beguiling of Merlin* and wondered if this artist had been a student of that great romantic painter.

"Amy Grignon," Clive said in a whisper that was barely audible over the babble of the other diners. "She died on April the fourth, eighteen-ninety-three."

I tapped the photo against the knuckles of my left hand, uneasiness creeping upon me.

"I love her, Roman. Since the moment my eyes met hers I've not had a single lecherous interlude. She has ... solved my problems, shall we say, in that respect."

The way he spoke, it was hard to believe he was talking about someone who had been dead for something like one hundred and twenty years. Whatever was wrong with Clive, it was no joking matter. He noticed my anxiety and chuckled.

"I can almost feel your brain throbbing," he said. "You think I've tipped over the edge, don't you?"

I said nothing at this point and tried to affect a neutral demeanour.

"I'm not mad," he declared. "I know she has been dead a while." He paused and stared at me intensely. "But time, what is it, really?" he added.

71

Looking at the photo again, at the strange smile that was set on the voluptuous lips of Amy Grignon, I noticed there was something about her that was unsettling. That wistful smile and those deep-set, dark eyes smouldered with a melancholic passion that was reflected in Clive's expression. For a moment I thought, she seemed capable of almost anything, even in death. Clive reached across the table and took the picture back, snatching it from between my fingers.

"A goddess marooned among modern day masses. She died a virgin. Nobody was good enough for her and when her father made the mistake of forcing marriage upon her she committed suicide on her wedding night." He raised his eyes and they were moist with tears. "She was in love with the painter who did this – Cecil Crawley – painted after her death."

Clive was under the spell of a self-inflicted delusion. I needed to persuade him to see a doctor. He read my thoughts.

Resting his elbows on the table, he looked at me, blinking away wetness in his eyes. "Roman, tell me, have you ever loved? I mean the real passion?"

"I think so," I said hesitantly. My ex … well I *had* been in love I suppose.

"If you merely think so, you most certainly have not." He paused, gathering his thoughts. "I've become a better historian than I ever proved at uni. I came to own this painting and it did not take more than a few glances at it to lose my soul. I also came across some of her clothes and belongings and I read her diaries and her love letters and read them over and over again. Would you believe it, every word thrilled me. She broke the lovelessness that has surrounded me all my life. Is that really so odd? I fell in love with her. And then she started to come to me during the night, in dreams. God!" He paused to smear a tear from his eyes. "I know this must sound insane … Anyway, as I was saying, I fell in love with her. Not with her portrait, mind you. No, with her personality, as I pieced it together from all the little relics surrounding me, and my research. She is a strong willed, passionate female, yet gentle, tender. Despite the century, she came to me, in my dreams. Dreams that I wanted to prolong because of the passion they brought.

"Can you picture the misery of waking the morning after? I so needed those dreams. The pain and despair of a world without her was unendurable." He paused again, looking at me sternly and raising his right hand as though to stop me from interrupting him, which I did not intend to do, despite being troubled by his wild and rambling talk.

"I know what you want to say," he said. "Get a grip! Well, the pure fact is that she, Amy Grignon, is precisely the woman for me and that I began to realise – without a shadow of doubt – that I would have been precisely the man for her. We were made for each other, only, we were many years apart. But the dreams began to fade, become less frequent and less intense. What to do?"

He gave me an odd look.

"What could I do? There was nothing. Nothing. I might have gone to her grave and committed suicide on her coffin like some Victorian fop. And yes, the thought crossed my mind more than once, but ..." Here he straightened himself and a sudden twinkle brightened his eyes. "I just could not believe that her radiant presence in my dreams, her potent sexuality was only the result of my feverish imagination. There was more to it. I sensed her presence, close to me, very close, despite the passing of time." He laughed, so suddenly and unexpectedly I jumped, for it was raucous, like the screech of a night owl.

There was the crash of cutlery on plates at the next table. Clive nodded an apology towards the other diners and continued in a husky whisper.

"My conviction was that she was reaching out to me across the desolation that separates the living from the dead. Somehow she had escaped the nothingness that is death. I started to scorn our human notion of death. My Amy was still with us."

"For Heaven's sake, Clive!" I exclaimed, finally managing

at last to get a word in edgeways, "You know what this sounds like?"

"Psychosis," he answered softly, lapsing into a thoughtful silence He lowered his head, a tremor passed through his head and hands.

I refrained from saying anything more and the starters arrived and interrupted me in any case.

Slowly he raised his head, after demolishing his food. Now his eyes were brimming with tears but when he spoke again, he was apologetic.

"Roman, I've said too much. I've worried you unnecessarily. And I couldn't expect you to want to help me after all these years."

"Of course I want to help. But she's dead and gone, Clive. Nothing's going to bring her back, even as a disembodied voice at a séance."

He appeared not to hear me. His attention wandered across to the other patrons; the clink of cutlery and hubbub of voices coming in waves.

When his focus returned to me, he said, "I could not give her up without having tried everything. So I started to search every dark, obscure niche of human experience. Mystics, black magicians, writers of supernatural fiction, ancient scribes. I managed to achieve one thing, a love potion. It was like reproducing her perfume. A single droplet on my pillow *ensures* her presence during the night. Suggestion perhaps, but it works and I depend on those dreams like an addict depends on his drugs."

"Suggestion definitely," I replied. "Reinforcement. I could almost believe you'd been up to no good with the dark side of magic." I squirmed uncomfortably.

"Well … sort of." His head dropped forward so I could not meet his eyes.

"Jesus! I don't believe this. I mean, for heaven's sake. I can understand that this vision of Amy has taken hold of you but there are limits. Black magic, indeed! It's pathetic." I should have been more professional, sympathetic, I suppose, but the disdain in my voice just came out.

He sagged back into his chair, defeated, staring at the table, looking so lost and forlorn and so utterly washed up that I swallowed my anger. "Clive, you've got to work your way out of this."

Without looking up, he nodded.

"I know. I'm driving myself nuts with this whole business. But it can't be helped. Life without her is total agony ... Will you help me?" he added.

"On one condition."

"Being?"

"That you come to see a friend of mine as soon as I've explored your situation."

"A shrink, no doubt."

"An analyst, yes, but a very good friend, Philip Ashe."

"Okay, it's a deal. Come to my house with me." He grinned.

"All right, I'll come, but not until next week. I've some business to take care of first."

"Fine. Come whenever you want, day or night, as long as it's *before* the tenth of the month. That's the decisive night. It will be either then or ..." He cut himself off and gazed out of the window into the busy street outside the restaurant.

"You really will come, won't you?" he asked, softly.

"Hey, I said so, didn't I?"

"Yeah, of course. It's just that I desperately need someone I can trust by my side. The thing is that I not only love her, I dread her, too. She has a frightening quality sometimes. A way of observing me, of stealing up on me."

"All this in your dreams, of course?"

"Yes, my dreams. Only, they are unlike any dreams I ever had before." He looked at his watch. "Gosh, look at the time. I must be going."

"But we haven't even had our main course yet."

"It doesn't matter. I must go. Here. This is on me." He threw some banknotes on the table. "No, I insist. Don't forget, now.

Be at the house before midnight on the tenth whatever you do." He gave me his business card showing his address and jumped up, shook my hand and dashed off.

I was left shaken. I did not doubt that he had become unhinged by his fascination for that woman – painting rather – but there was also much structure in his madness. I wondered whether I should not have made a greater effort to get him to see an analyst immediately.

The waiter brought me my pasta, grumbling about Clive's sudden departure and the waste of a perfectly good dish. I began on my meal with reluctance, not feeling much like eating. I tried to make light of the matter as I ate. Necromancy indeed.

*

It was good to step out into the damp, cool night. The rain had stopped and the overcast sky had broken to allow a luminous moon to drift among the grey-streaked clouds. It was almost full, in a day or two it would be.

No matter what poor old Clive believed, I was certain that the dead were just that – dead, harmless, objects of grief or relief, distaste at worst, but nothing more. These thoughts absorbed me as I drove to Clive's mansion in the country. Clive had never been short of money. I was also conscious of the fact that my other work had taken me longer than I expected. It was the tenth of the month and close to Clive's so-called deadline. But it was a deadline in his imagination, not in reality, so I was not too concerned.

After twenty miles or so, I saw someone hitchhiking. I don't usually stop but this time I thought it might not be a bad idea, get my mind off things. I pulled up. The hitchhiker was dressed in dark cloak with the hood up. It turned out to be a woman, quite young and pretty with light blue eyes. She did not say much, only smiled and gave one-syllable answers to my questions. Still, I was glad to have the company.

When I asked her where she was going, she shrugged her shoulders. "I'm going to Horden House."

"That's nice," I said, surprised. It was Clive's place. Quite a coincidence. "Funnily enough—"

"You also," she said simply and then clammed up.

A bit disappointed by her unsociability I concentrated on the country road, which was just as well, because it wound a treacherous way through the Worcestershire countryside. I almost forgot about her presence until an intensely cold draft beside me made me glance her way. I shouted. The hood was pushed back revealing a dark-eyed redhead, with a lunatic grin on her face. I struck out instinctively at her with my left arm and … she vanished. The next moment my car dipped from the road into thick undergrowth, groaning, shattering the headlamps, banging and bouncing down a slope until it came to a standstill against a tree. My seat belt had kept me from serious injury, but I was shaking with fright. I sat huddled in my seat, my face in my hands. I don't know how long I remained like that but eventually I calmed down a little. The engine itself had stopped running, but the windscreen wipers were still on. I looked round. Nobody there. I switched off the ignition and the wipers came to a standstill. A squall of raindrops from the tree pattered on the roof. Steam escaped sizzling from the crumpled bonnet. I got out and saw that both front tyres were flat. Looking at my watch, I saw that the glass was broken and it had stopped at eight p.m. I'd never reach the house in time for Clive's deadline unless I could raise the AA on my mobile, but – sod's law – there was no signal. In any case, there would be no replacement car suitable, for with any car I had to have adaptations to the pedals for my short legs. I estimated that it was at least another five miles to Horden House. That meant a four-hour walk with my short stride.

Thinking about the car had taken my mind off the reason for the accident. Yet, as I groped my way back to the road, a shadow stole over my thoughts. Even though the appearance of that woman was only a hallucination, it didn't diminish the effect it had had on me.

Along the lane, the trees stood dripping noisily in the dark. Gusts of wind came and went, shaking the boughs and bringing down avalanches of water. I found that I dreaded the reappearance of my female phantom. She did not come, of course.

*

When I arrived at Horden House, there were lights on in a few of the rooms. It was a big place, fronted by a curving gravel drive, the front door a huge wooden block with Romanesque style pillars on each side.

I was about to tug on the bell pull when I noticed that the door was open, so I pushed it further saying, "Clive, it's me. Roman."

I went into the living and dining rooms and the kitchen, but he was not there. Then I ascended the stairs, calling again.

In what I assumed to be Clive's bedroom was the picture, nearly taking up the whole wall opposite the bed. I hadn't realised how large a work it was, the photo Clive had shown me gave a very false impression. It definitely had the look of a Pre-Raph. Dreamy woman standing with a sad look in her eyes. Voluptuous lips, wavy red tresses. And the black eyes, though they were doomy, they penetrated into mine as though piercing into my very thoughts.

Though the painting was mesmerising, I was more interested in finding out where Clive had got to. There were other rooms in the house I hadn't entered, and there was also the garden ... maybe outhouses and a greenhouse. Which thought made me look out of the window. I cupped my hands over my face to get a clearer view in the murk, and there was someone moving about in the grounds. And it had to be Clive. I released the catch on the window, shoved it open and called down, "Clive!" But he'd disappeared into the shrubbery.

After I'd dashed downstairs and across the lawn, I got a

surprise. At the back of the extensive shrubbery there was a low walled area in which stood several tombs, highlighted by the brightness of the moon. I had stumbled upon a family cemetery. The nearest chest tomb had on its upper surface, a motif that was very badly worn, but I think it was of doves. Below that I could just about read the name incised there and of course it was Amy Grignon. The moonlight sparkled on glints in the age-worn stone. Horden House, I now realised, had once been the home of the Grignons ...

I moved closer to look at the other chiselled details and as I did so Clive rose up from behind the grave as if he were the resurrected dead. It gave me an initial jolt that set my heart racing. He was not alone. Clive was embracing a female wearing the dress that I remembered from the painting. She had her back to me and her loose russet hair swayed across her shoulders. When the couple turned, Amy's face was haggard and deathly pale, but adorned with an ecstatic yet monstrous grin.

"Clive ...?" Although he did not seem to hear me, there was something about that dream-like tableau that filled me with terror. Perhaps he was performing his dance macabre with a mannequin. Clive sat the woman on the tomb, where she remained, motionless, convincing me that she really was lifeless. I shuddered. He looked down at the woman with a sickly smile. Then, under my horrified gaze, she began to stand, her movement wooden, like a puppet. Then she sat again.

The expression on Clive's face showed its fear. "What is it, my love? Why do you look at me like this? What's wrong?" Then his scream. It still rings in my ears occasionally, an echo from the past. An outrageous, renting howl, followed by noises of mental disintegration and then sudden, total silence as Clive retreated from the tombstone.

"Clive!" I yelled, moving around the grave to reach him and on my way I stretched my arms, reaching up to the dressmaker's dummy's shoulders, intending to stop this charade. My stomach turned as my fingers felt the emptiness under the thin fabric of her dress and I sprang back with a shout. When she fell backwards a white, gleaming skull parted from the rest of her body and went skittering across the ground, shedding its elaborate wig. It would have been laughable had it been a scene from a Hammer second feature I'd been watching, but as it was, there was something about that grinning, clattering skull and the wig giving it a mere semblance of life, that went under my skin. Went under and shuddered there like goose bumps on the inside.

Explanations? I can't think of any that *fully* satisfy all the events. Perhaps I only imagined the haggard face superimposed on the skull and the movement of the skeletal corpse. Perhaps Clive was only playing with the carcass like some men play with sex dolls, but the fact remains that I was unable to help him that day. Oh, I was happy enough rationalising Clive's 'resurrected woman', but not too happy to see my old friend committed and with some considerable time to serve in the mental hospital.

And I still can't fully account for the apparent phantom in my car. But I think it's having seen that photo, and then the painting, of course. It's amazing, isn't it, what flair some artists have, what skill to influence one's imagination?

CHRISTMAS IN THE RAIN

Chris Lawton

Abbie sheltered from the piercing winter rain in the darkness behind Edinburgh's shining facade. Just off Princes Street, in an alley between two department stores, she cried quietly. Hidden in the shadows, her tears muffled by the winter storm, no one among the thousands of revellers would ever have known she was there. It was Christmas Eve, and Edinburgh was blind to the suffering being played out on its streets.

She ached all over, the wounds from her last beating still yet to subside, and the hunger pangs of days without a proper meal were beginning to wear her down. Wiping her eyes left big panda smears behind, old crusted make-up finally being washed off by her sadness. It had been four days since she had turned sixteen. Four days since she had been beaten for the last time and thrown out of her home. Her mother had gotten rid of her as soon as she could; she was sixteen now, time to fend for herself. Her mother had taken joy in telling her this whilst she dragged her out of bed. Abbie laughed dryly at the thought of it, wiping away tears that refused to stop coming.

Shivering, she huddled herself tighter in her sleeping bag before taking a big swig from her cheap whisky. Rotten stuff, it made her cough and splutter every time she drank it. Her cheeks stung from the cold and the salt as she remembered being dragged from her bed to find her bag packed and ready. She begged and pleaded with her mother, desperate for her to have a change of heart. She hated being there, but needed a chance to find her feet and a place of her own. She would do anything, anything at all if only she would let her stay a few more weeks. Her efforts earned her only a savage beating. Mother's new sugar daddy watched and laughed before eventually joining in. He kicked her in the stomach so hard she crumpled into a ball and vomited into her mouth. She swallowed it to avoid another kick. Pulling her hair, he

81

dragged her up towards him before spitting in her face. He dropped her back down and walked out. "You have ten minutes," Mother had said. "Get dressed and get out, or you'll get worse."

For two years she had kept a Stanley knife hidden under her mattress, but was always too afraid to use it. She had dressed in jeans and an old black hoodie, and put the knife in her pocket. It might come in handy she had thought at the time. She quickly put on some make-up to hide the marks left by Mother, then checked through the bag. Mother had left her thirty pounds, and had put a sleeping bag and some clothes in her backpack. No doubt she would tell the social she had stolen the money and the sleeping bag, if they ever came around. Abbie hated the social workers. They had never been on her side, only ever doing as little as they could to seem to be doing their jobs. They always listened to Mother's lies: that she was acting up in school because she was a vicious little monster. Quite unlike her God-fearing mother, who was always in church and helping out in the community. Abbie never feared God, never honestly believed in Him, but she did fear that Bible-thumping bitch she called Mother.

How was a kid supposed to thrive in school when she was beaten with a belt every night and forced to pray by a hypocritical, hateful guardian? Her father had died when she was very young, and Mother somehow seemed to blame her. She wished it had been the other way around. Maybe then she wouldn't be sitting here in the dark, with just a bottle of whisky for company. Finally feeling overcome by her hunger, Abbie decided to rake through the large bin behind her. She was in luck. There were some unopened M & S sandwiches, which had only just gone out of date. She didn't like prawns, but it would do. She didn't like the smell of piss either, but this alley had kept her drier than she would have been otherwise. She stuffed the extra packets into the bottom of her bag, which was now pretty empty as she had most of her clothes on in layers. She sat in the dark for another half an hour drinking herself into a stupor. After a while the tears stopped. Even through all the layers of clothing, Abbie was freezing. She had heard of homeless people lining their clothes with newspapers for extra warmth, so she decided to raid the bins again.

She found a small stack of unsold tabloids tied up with string and took them out into the light to cut them free. Out of interest, she unfolded the top one to see what was going on in the world. Her blood turned to ice. 'Third Body Found in Three Days – Edinburgh Cannibal' was the headline. Terrified, she read the article then went on to each paper's version of events. According to the *Daily Record*, dismembered remains of three bodies had been discovered in Edinburgh, all female and all young. The *Daily Mail* had announced that three prostitutes were missing, and a torso had been found with the same 'tramp stamp' as one Isabel O'Lafferty, whom it referred to as a well-known local working girl. The Sun had run the headline 'Cannibal!' The reporter stated that, according to his unnamed Police source, the body parts that had been found so far all showed evidence of the flesh being chewed from the bones. The teeth marks were definitely human, and forensics teams were working to identify whether they were male or female. Abbie had never felt so alone.

Where was Sarah? Abbie was supposed to have met her here hours ago. She dug her phone from her pocket, a cheap pay-as-you-go Sarah had given her two days before. The battery was dead. Abbie was worried. Both for herself and her friend. The fear and the alcohol combined and made her head swim. Think. Think. Where might she be? Abbie leaned against the wall, tears of a different sort now blurring her eyes. Sarah was level-headed and reliable. She wouldn't knowingly let her down. Suddenly, Abbie remembered Sarah mentioning meeting her boyfriend on Cockburn Street before coming to see her. That must be it, she thought, she's been held up. Probably on some pub on the Royal Mile. She packed her sleeping bag away, put on her backpack, grabbed her whisky and headed out on to Rose Street.

On Rose Street, the throng of revellers smoking outside the pubs made her feel safe, though she was wary of everyone. Never allowing herself to come within easy reach of those around her, she wound her way through the crowd. One woman tried to grab her bottle out of her hand, drunkenly slurring that children shouldn't drink, but slipped on the icy ground and hit the floor. While those around her picked her up, Abbie slipped out of sight. She hid the bottle up her sleeve, not needing that kind of attention right now. Crossing on to Princes Street she found it bustling with drunks singing in an impromptu street party. She quickly passed them by and crossed the road on to Waverley Bridge. The wind was picking up, and the rain was turning to sleet, so she took another big swig from her bottle. It was strange, she noticed, that there was almost no one else around here. She quickened her pace, checking all around her as she moved towards the bottom of Cockburn Street.

When she reached the bottom, she could hear screams, shouts, and windows smashing as a massive fight broke out up ahead. She stopped in her tracks, and thought better of heading up the main path. Best to stick to the shadows, she thought; if the police caught her, she was likely to be taken back to Mother, and another beating. It had happened before. She walked down Market Street towards the little alley that ran all the way to the top of the hill. The noise the crowd was making was getting ridiculous. It must have been one hell of a fight. Distant sirens could be heard approaching. As she climbed the first few steps in the alley, Abbie began to get worried. If Sarah was here, she would be half way up, probably half-naked with her boyfriend in the dark of the alley. She had caught them there before accidentally more than once. There was no sign of anyone around. When Abbie arrived at their usual meeting place, she found it empty.

The noise of the fight was still going strong, so she decided to stay here hiding in the shadows till it had blown over. Sitting with her back to the wall, she drank more of the drain cleaner she called whisky. Its septic burn warmed her a little at least. About an hour passed, the fight had died down long before, but Abbie had stayed waiting to see if Sarah would arrive. She didn't. This wasn't a good place to sleep, so Abbie tried to get up. Disoriented, she staggered forward into the wall in front of her. She almost dropped her whisky, but managed to save it at the last minute. Slowly, she straightened up and realised how quiet it had become. Where is everyone? she thought.

*

She must have fallen asleep, and awoken past the closing time of the nearby pubs. Picking up her bag, Abbie tried to get her head straight enough to find somewhere safe to sleep. As she began walking out of her shelter towards the steps of the alley, she heard movement to her rear.

"Alright, hen?" slurred a voice.

Looming directly behind her, stood a huge silhouette. Before she could move he grabbed her and threw her back in the direction she had come. She managed to turn just in time to hit the wall with her bag, sparing her from injury. The base of her bottle shattered against the wall. He started unzipping his trousers and unbuckling his belt as he walked towards her. Blood raced in her ears, drowning out all sound.

For a moment, the light fell upon the man's face. It was clear to Abbie that he was completely out of his mind. His pupils were huge black pits; his forehead soaked with sweat. He was frantically chewing and gurning, the corners of his mouth covered with white flecks, and his lips twisted into a vicious grin as he moved closer. He was erect and oblivious to the fact that his trousers had fallen around his knees. She was terrified, but she was determined not to go down without a fight. Not again.

She lunged at him as he staggered towards her, driving the neck of the bottle into his face.

His flesh tore all around his cheek, a splinter bursting his right eye. It took a moment for the realisation to hit him. He screamed in pain, stumbling backwards towards the steps. She rushed him, hitting him as hard as she possibly could, fury replacing fear. He fell, his body tumbling down the steps. Finally, he crashed onto his back, upside down at the bottom, with his trousers round his ankles. Abbie grabbed her bag and started down towards him.

She reached his body and knelt down to check if he was breathing. Fuck, she thought, I killed him. Tears in her eyes, she knelt there for a minute, trying to work out what to do. She needed to get out of Edinburgh, and quickly. But she had no money. But he might ... She rummaged through his front pockets and found his wallet. She opened it to check for money and found a stack of notes, his credit cards, and pictures of his children. Two little girls. She felt sick.

Suddenly, he coughed a shower of blood and tried to sit up. She panicked again, standing and trying to back away from him. He reached out towards her, so she kicked his hand away and sprinted, wallet in hand, back into Market Street. There was no one around, so she ran as fast as she could into Princes Street Gardens.

*

Down in the darkness of the gardens she noticed the party still continued on Princes Street. She figured it must be a few hours yet before the clubs kicked out. She could hear music and joy coming from the street above, which only made her feel more alone. Opening the wallet to take out the money, she noticed a small pouch stuffed underneath the notes. It contained a handful of tiny black pills. She looked at them in the half-light. Not knowing what they were, but feeling like she had nothing left to lose, Abbie poured some onto her hand and then swallowed them. They might get me high, she thought. Or kill me. Either way was fine by her. She found a tree hidden away from view from the street and sat down under it, soaked through by the icy rain.

She sat there for what seemed like hours, worrying about the man in the alley. Sure, she had defended herself and he had deserved it, but she really struggled with the thought of the man's children. How would they cope if she had killed him? How would they cope if she hadn't? She knew she had caused him terrible damage, enough to frighten a child. She remembered her own father, and how terrible it had been for her when he died. She cried until she couldn't cry any more. Inside her, she felt a change growing. She was becoming warmer in spite of the bitter freeze that had overcome Edinburgh. She felt a kind of joy rising in her, and the man started to slip from her mind. She began to forget her thoughts of her own father, of Mother, of herself.

The world around her began to fade away, a divine white light replacing it. She could hear music, such beautiful, sweet music that she felt compelled to dance. Tears welled in her eyes once more, but this time they were tears of unbridled joy. A joy so pure she felt she had never felt anything like it before. As she danced around and around, beautiful, bright colours began to form and flow, encircling her. She felt herself start to float in the air, rising up and up into the pure, radiant white glow from above. It felt like the greatest moment of her life, nothing else mattered, only the white light. She reached up to touch it.

Abbie plummeted into darkness. She felt like she was falling forever, the swirling colours became depictions of her life. The beautiful music turned sour before becoming the screeching voice of Mother, howling foul abuse at her daughter. She saw her whole life, every beating, every burn. She felt the pain of every wound and torment afresh. She could see the two little girls crying their eyes out at the funeral of their father. It felt like all the hands of hell were dragging her further down into her suffering. She screamed her lungs hoarse, but no one came to help. "You are all alone," the voices laughed, "you belong to us." She felt the world tumble and spin around her, gathering momentum until total darkness took over.

*

She came round, soaking wet in an alleyway, lying face down in a pile of vomit. She had pissed herself; at least it smelled that way. Her mind was a complete haze, the walls swimming when she dragged herself to her feet. For a moment she couldn't remember who or what she was. She had no idea what she had just been through. And then she heard the laugh. The laugh Mother used when she was around men, an overbearing, hideous, high-pitched wail. Suddenly everything came back to her, along with an anger she had never experienced before. Her rage was all-consuming. Her vision snapped back into focus, and she ran to the end of the alleyway.

Mother was walking towards her, hanging drunkenly off the arm of a man. A different man than the one who had spat in her face. This man looked almost nice. He certainly didn't look drunk; he was very smartly dressed too. Nothing like the kind of bullyboy she would normally chase down. He must be rich. Whoever he is, she thought, he'll see her for what she is in a minute. Abbie realised where she was, they must be heading for the train station. She checked that there was no one else around then skulked back into the darkness and set her trap.

When the couple had just passed her, Abbie rushed forward, throwing the man off balance and causing Mother to tumble to the floor. Abbie landed on top of her, clawing at her face. "Remember me, you twisted old bitch?" she screamed, raining blows down upon her.

"Who the fuck are you?" Mother cried, striking back with an intensity Abbie didn't expect. It threw her off balance leaving the pair struggling on the floor. Mother grabbed Abbie's hair, and smashed her head into the pavement leaving her reeling. The concrete split her eyebrow, blurring her vision with blood, but she managed to hit Mother again and make her let go of her hair.

Separated, the pair stood up and threw themselves at one another again. Mother got the upper hand once more, shoving Abbie backwards, slamming her head into a wall. She started lashing out, punching her daughter again and again, both screaming at one another. Abbie suddenly remembered the Stanley knife, and reached into her pocket. Before she knew what she was doing, Abbie had sliced a deep gouge into Mother's throat. The arterial spray painted them both deep red. Horror spread across Mother's face as she looked into the eyes of her killer before collapsing backwards in a heap.

Something was wrong.

She crouched down and looked deep into the dead eyes of her victim. It wasn't Mother. Abbie's skin crawled. How could this be? She knew it was Mother, she had heard her laughing. She knew what the evil old cow looked like, what she walked like, how she behaved. But this broken, empty shell in front of her now – that was not Mother. Desperate to convince herself that she was wrong, that this *was* Mother, Abbie grabbed the woman's handbag out of a puddle and rifled through it. Inside she found a purse. Looking inside, the bottom fell out of her world. Her name was Ashley Anne Farley. She had a beautiful baby boy.

What have I done? she thought, recoiling from her kill and her guilt. Mother's laughter erupted into the night, its sound reverberating through Abbie's very soul. Terrified of what she had done, and of being caught, she looked desperately around her. Where was the man, she thought. He was here a minute ago. What if he has run off to get help? Shaking, drenched in rain, sweat and blood, Abbie picked herself up. Looking around once more for the man, she saw the alleyway was empty, and turned to run into the shadows. In that moment she was tripped and fell. Her world shattered into darkness on the concrete.

*

Black shapes danced before her, slowly congealing in muddied forms before dissipating into twilight. Her head ached, worse than she had ever remembered. As the light began to re-enter her world, she began to recognise forms around her. A poster, a bed, a teddy bear. The world was still grey, but she felt she knew these shades around her. Her head swooning, Abbie reached up to where she knew it would be, and flicked the switch. The light burned her eyes, she clenched them shut again. Eventually, she slowly reopened them.

Her room was exactly as she remembered it. Confused, she started to climb out of bed. She was clean, wearing her favourite pyjamas. She had no idea how she had gotten here, or where she had been. She strained to think what had come before. She got flashes of alleys, of parks. Of people. Suddenly she thought she would cry out, waves of emotion overtaking her. She remembered a face, a woman. A dead woman. She remembered blood, blood she had caused. She remembered a fight.

Quickly, Abbie crossed the room to her mirror. Nothing, not even a scratch. She checked herself from head to foot. Surely, she thought, there must be something. Some mark to let her know where she had been, what she had done. Smiling, she burst into tears in front of herself, feeling absurd and wanting to laugh at her own reflection. It had been some nightmare, she thought, but that was all. The smell of freshly grilled bacon wafted into the room from downstairs. Breakfast time, she thought, fantastic.

Closing her eyes to wipe the tears away she heard the door open behind her. In the reflection of the mirror, in her mother's favourite dress, the man from the alleyway smiled.

DEEPER THAN DARK WATER

Gary Power

Rupert pushed a finger into the hole that had been crudely
drilled into his forehead and gave the frontal lobe of his brain a
prod. It felt good. He smiled a simple sort of smile and
prodded again; this time it made him feel naughty and that put
a goofy grin on his ashen face. He ambled down the corridor
studying the numbers on the closed doors. When he reached
his own room he pulled his finger out, sniffed it, tasted it, and
then flicked the squidgy brain matter onto the carpet before
entering.

Rupert had been a junior doctor with a promising career
ahead of him. That was until he received the invite to spend a
sabbatical period at the 'Carl Rosenberg Neurological
Institute'.

Leaving the institute was never going to be an option.

His door was slightly ajar. Through the gap he saw the
silhouette of Stephanie standing by his window. Stephanie had
been his girlfriend. She used to stay over from time to time
when he started at the institute. It wasn't long before she too
became one of Carl Rosenberg's guinea pigs.

She was naked and dreadfully emaciated, like a barely
fleshed skeleton. Her face was gaunt and there was an
abandoned look in her sunken eyes (aftercare at the institute
wasn't exactly high on the agenda). Stephanie had been the
subject of a radical lobotomy experiment. To monitor the
pressure building up inside her head, a bolt had been inserted
into her skull during the operation, but it had long since ceased
being of any clinical use. Now her brain was starting to expand
through the bone flap in her skull. Bacterial meningitis hadn't
set in yet, but it would soon. She looked grotesque. Rupert
didn't mind though because he loved her, and love is blind.
They were an odd couple, him so tall and gangly and she just a
slip of a woman. Ever since her operation she'd become

91

increasingly promiscuous and Rupert liked that. He didn't bother to close the door when he went in; Stephanie preferred it if the others could see.

Static interference on the telephone extension in Dr Felix Carter's accommodation was building to a crescendo of white noise. He rapped the mouthpiece of the phone against his bedside table and managed to clear the line for a few precious moments.

His girlfriend, Rebecca, seemed amused by his mounting frustration.

"Felix … I finished work early today so I'm going to sort a few things here and come over later tonight … unless, of course, you've got another woman there?"

"Yeah, right," he chuckled, "I'm dying of boredom, Becks – the place is like a morgue. Christ knows how I'm going to benefit from my time here. To be honest, I'm wondering about knocking it on the head already. The digs are basic to say the least. I've only got a single bed; it's like being a student again. And you'll need directions to get here – the place is impossible to find."

Rebecca giggled saucily.

"I want to see your room before you decide to pack it in – it'll be fun playing at naughty students. And don't worry about me finding the place; I'll use my sat-nav."

"I tried that. The Institute seems to be off the map. Getting a mobile signal is too hit and miss to rely on. Best come to the village and I'll meet you there; there's only one pub, the Maypole I think it's called. How soon can you get here?"

There was some muttering and then he heard a heavy sigh.

"Father needs to talk to me about something important that's cropped up. You know how *everything* is important with him. I'll leave as soon as I can."

Felix picked up a picture of Rebecca propped against a heavy and curiously erotic brass figurine on his dresser. She'd written, '*Love you forever, X,*' boldly in crimson lipstick across the bottom of the photograph.

"Must keep *father* happy," he muttered softly enough for her not to hear.

"Did you say something, Fee?"

The line started to fade again, this time accompanied by several sharp cracks. Rebecca carried on talking but a penetrating hiss drowned out most of what she had to say. She sounded excited but Felix only caught truncated snippets of her enthusiastic banter.

"What's the place like?" she asked in a moment of blissful clarity. "Have you met the great man yet?"

"No. The mysterious Mr Rosenberg is yet to make an appearance. And as far as this place is concerned, think *The Shining* meets *One Flew Over the Cuckoo's Nest* – sort of bleak and surreal with a few gormless patients wandering around like extras from a zombie movie. The grounds are certainly impressive though and the building is pure Gothic, all buttresses and big windows. You'll see what I mean when you get here. I think there must be other people in the building; I've heard them but not seen anyone. Oh, and there's something else; there's something moving about in the loft. If it's a rat then it must be a bloody huge one."

Rebecca laughed at that. Felix loved hearing her laugh.

"Sounds creepy. Don't you go investigating till I get there. You know how accident-prone you are. You'll probably fall through the ceiling."

There was a momentary pause – a sort of thoughtful interlude without words.

Rebecca broke the silence first:

"I can't wait to see you, Felix. Keep the bed warm for me – you won't be sorry."

He closed his eyes and imagined her there.

"That's a promise, Becks."

He wanted to say, 'I love you', but what sounded like light footsteps above distracted him and robbed him of the moment.

Maybe one day he'd tell her.

Definitely one day.

He looked at the photo again.

"Just hurry up and get your cute arse here," he demanded.

"Well, I'm not so sure my arse is cute, but I will get …"

And that was all he heard.

The lights flickered and the line went dead. But before he was cut off there was a moment when Felix thought he heard the sound of laboured breathing, as though someone else was listening in. He struck the phone sharply against the cabinet again, partly out of frustration, this time to no avail.

A hefty thump from above startled him. It was followed by a slow, dragging sound on the ceiling. His eyes followed the noise from one side of the room to the other. Further investigation was an option, but he'd have to move the bed and pull the dresser underneath if he was going to reach the loft hatch – and the way he was feeling that was far too much effort. Since having his supper an overwhelming sense of lethargy had set in. A subservient man who he assumed to be a convalescing patient had brought a tray of bland-looking food to his door. The man avoided eye contact and kept communication to a minimum. The meal had been surprisingly pleasant and was accompanied by a carafe of unusual but very palatable red wine that eventually sent Felix, still clothed and watching an antiquated television set, into a deep and restful sleep.

A whimpering cry emanating from the attic just a few hours later woke him from his peaceful slumber. Turning onto his back, he saw that the loft hatch was open. That stirred him a little more. Illumination from the blank screen of the TV set filled the room with eerie, monotone light. The hiss from the television was annoying, but not aggravating enough to rouse him completely from his semi-comatose state. With a heavy sigh he rolled over and found a young girl, maybe twelve or thirteen years old, standing at his bedside. A mop of unkempt hair was draped about her bare shoulders like a grubby cape. At first he thought she was staring at him. But then he saw the vacant, black pits where her eyes should be. One half of her head had been crudely shaved and there was a livid scar on her exposed scalp.

"I want your eyes," she said in a voice that was too deep and husky for such a frail little thing. She was holding a large screwdriver the end of which had been sharpened to a point, and her arm was raised as though about to stab at his head. Felix wondered if he was still dreaming, until she lunged with the screwdriver and slashed the side of his face. He kicked at the quilt that was covering him, threw it over her head and then pinned her to the ground. Several times the screwdriver pierced the cloth narrowly missing him. The eyeless girl struggled with a strength that belied her small frame so he pushed harder until she stopped moving.

When finally he released his grip she remained motionless.

"Are you finished attacking me?" he asked.

A small arm slumped lifelessly from beneath the quilt.

He stared in disbelief.

Palpating her wrist, he found that she had no pulse.

"Oh God, no ..." he gasped.

He'd only meant to restrain her.

He backed off to the window still trying to make sense of what had just happened. That was when he became aware of movement in the shadows at the far end of the room. Not a child this time but a gathering of adults. One of them turned on the lights. They were mindless, wretched things. In the stark light he saw that some were naked while others were wearing soiled hospital gowns. Brutal surgery had disfigured them all in some way. An obese woman covered in weeping sores staggered towards him. Her movements were erratic and uncoordinated and her breathing painfully laboured. She reached out for him and tried to speak but her words came out as incoherent grunts.

Some of those behind her began to weep mournfully while others cried quite hysterically. They were harrowing outbursts filled with torment and suffering. A skeletal man with white cataracts covering his eyes lurched forwards. There was seething anger in his expression. With his bony fingers clenched into a fist, the man ground his teeth and growled like a rabid dog. He glared at Felix as though possessed by the devil. Felix backed away. The others closed in as pack instinct took over and he realised that they probably saw him as the cause of their barbaric disfigurement.

He looked from the window and thought about jumping. Twenty or so feet onto a concrete patio didn't seem a good idea, especially as the grounds were now teaming with similarly maniacal patients.

With ironic timing Tubular Bells began to play from his pocket. His Exorcist ringtone seemed morbidly appropriate considering the circumstances, but answering it was not an option ... unless, of course, it was Rebecca.

If it was, he'd have to warn her to stay away.

Glancing briefly, he saw that it was.

Her text read: *'I'm on my way. U got that bed warm yet? Becks xxx'*.

When he looked up he saw that the fat woman had found the photograph of Rebecca propped against the figurine. She held it up for Felix to see and then furiously ripped it into obsessively small pieces.

"Oh shit ..." he said. He definitely had to stop her coming. He hit reply and to his relief and surprise heard Rebecca's voice.

"Felix, are you okay?"

"Becky. Don't speak; just listen. Don't come here. You hear me? Go to the village ... wait at the pub ... The Maypole ... I'll come to you there."

"Felix ... is that you? I was a bit longer with father than I meant to be, but on my way now ... it won't take me long."

"No Becks ... Stay away!" he shouted.

"I can't hear a word you're saying, babe. If you can hear me, I'll see you soon ..."

"Rebecca ... don't ... come."

96

She hadn't heard a word, and time was not on his side. He'd just have to stop her before she reached the institute – and he had to make his own escape before that.

Felix had the advantage of strength and speed. Looking at the patients, agility didn't appear to be on their side. He guessed that he could break through despite their numbers. He'd run and he'd keep running until he was well away from the godforsaken place. Rushing them was probably his best chance.

The unclothed, gaunt woman suddenly let out a gut-wrenching cry. She'd stumbled upon the young girl that Felix had smothered. With tears streaming down her face, she directed her impassioned rage at him. Clearly, the lifeless child cradled in her arms was her daughter.

"No," gasped Felix.

The woman's distressed cries cut through him like a knife.

"She ... she attacked me. I didn't mean to ... I'd never kill a child ... never."

"Myyy ... bay ... bee ..." she uttered in a voice that was horribly distorted by cruel and savage surgery, "my ... poor ... babeeee."

She looked at Felix with hatred in her eyes and he realised that he had to make his move now.

He charged towards the door, striking out as he barged his way through the gathered throng. They crumpled beneath his blows. But there were far more than he'd anticipated and he was forced to scrabble over their feeble bodies, crushing their brittle bones as he fought his way into the corridor. They were too weak and uncoordinated to stop him, but he wasn't in the clear yet. Blocking the far end of the corridor was a tall man in front of who stood a sickly thin woman. Felix gathered his strength and prepared himself for a final charge, but it wasn't the man's size that brought him to a sudden halt.

"Rupert?" he said in complete disbelief, and then looking at the woman, "Stephanie!" He recognised them both; they had been close friends at a time during his studies when he needed support most. They stared back and he saw in their eyes some degree of recognition. Revulsion overwhelmed him when he caught sight of the festering scars inflicted upon them. Frantically he tried to make sense of the situation.

"You … you travelled. Everyone thought you'd both taken off. I tried to contact you but you never replied. How did you end up here?"

Stephanie spoke first. Or rather, she tried to. With huge effort she contorted her face and formed a word.

"Feeeeliiiix …" she said, and then she grinned with a Cheshire cat smile.

Felix looked once at Stephanie and then at the pus and brain oozing from the infected hole in Rupert's forehead. The tall man was distracted by the commotion that Felix had left behind. But there was something else. He saw a sudden look of concern in Rupert's eyes and so he turned. And as he did, he caught a glimpse of the gaunt woman bringing the brass figurine down on his skull with all the strength she could muster.

Upon regaining consciousness, Felix found himself lying on a cold, hard table. His body was covered with surgical drapes and his head immobilised in a skull clamp. An elderly and distinguished looking man wearing a surgeon's gown was drawing a large circle somewhere above his left brow.

He tried to move but his body didn't respond. He tried to speak but his tongue just lolled around in his mouth. He could move his eyes though and he could see that he was in an operating room.

The aged man moved into his view.

"We finally meet, Doctor Carver. Please let me introduce myself; I am Carl Rosenberg. I'm glad to see that no damage was inflicted on you by my patients; you have suffered superficial contusions and quite possibly a minor subdural haematoma, but nothing too serious. You see," and he briefly chuckled, "your brain is very precious to me."

Deeper Than Dark Water

He indicated for an assistant to turn a switch on the wall and several video monitors flickered to life, the largest being ceiling mounted and directly in Felix's line of vision. The camera was focused on his head and he could see in lurid and graphic detail that skin and muscle had been peeled back from a large, blood smeared patch of his skull. Several burr holes had been drilled into his cranium in preparation for surgery.

His blood ran cold. Suddenly the world was a distant place and the image on the screen impossible to take in.

"I have great plans for you, Felix. Assisting me today will be Justyna, a very talented young lady from Tarnow, Poland."

The petite, pretty nurse smiled and politely nodded as though to introduce herself. "Also assisting is a gifted theatre technician by the name of Anthony, or 'Ant' as he likes to be known. Ant, perhaps you'd like to put on some music to entertain us while we work. He has a very eclectic taste in music you know."

The pleasant banter was quite surreal considering the circumstances, but the menacing composure of the surgeon's manner was even more chilling.

Rosenberg crossed his arms, leaned forwards and gazed unnervingly into Felix's eyes.

"That's quite enough of introductions. Now as to the operation, first I will remove a flap of bone from the left frontotemporal region of your cranium. I don't want you to miss any of this; I've linked up a high-definition camera so that you'll be able to see just how I work. I imagine you'll find some of my techniques quite fascinating. Human consciousness is like a vast and unfathomable sea. As you go deeper so the water becomes darker, colder … and quite disorientating; that oceanic world soon becomes a mysterious and implausible place. I want to venture deeper than the dark water, Felix. I want to explore beyond the human condition."

Rosenberg picked up what looked like some kind of drill and briefly powered it up. The motor screamed and Felix cringed, or rather, he tried to. His body wouldn't respond, much to Rosenberg's amusement.

"This is a surgical saw or craniotome as it is better known. I'll use it to cut out a portion of bone in your skull. For reasons that will become apparent, you'll find that you are unable to move. I've induced complete paralysis for the purposes of this operation. The slightest movement would spoil my delicate surgery. I'm going to make a few alterations to the areas that affect mood and consciousness, working eventually towards your limbic system. After that, your behaviour will be closely monitored for several weeks. I'm afraid I've had to dispense with consent forms for obvious reasons but I can tell you that you will have a complete loss of inhibition and most likely some major personality changes. Memory will be all but wiped out and you will also experience what may well be on occasion quite disturbing hallucinations. I appreciate that my approach is extreme but my studies in the perception of human consciousness are, to be perfectly honest, beyond compare. I am a genius, Felix. My methods and research know no boundaries. And just in case you're wondering, the institute is government funded; it's just a little bit 'off the radar'. Research like this isn't exactly palatable with the whingeing public."

He gazed deeply into Felix's eyes and grimaced.

"*Cogito, ergo sum*: I think, therefore I am."

Rosenberg looked distantly into space for a moment.

"I so wish I'd said that first," he mused.

He chuckled to himself as he slipped on a surgical mask and it was then that Felix realised he was at the mercy of a completely insane maniac … and that death would be a preferable outcome.

Rosenberg powered up the craniotome again and pushed it into one of the burr holes above his left eye. The blade snagged a loose flap of flesh and a spurt of blood shot across the surgeon's face. He pressed harder and the whine became deeper as the saw began to cut through bone.

And then the craniotome suddenly, much to the surgeon's

intense frustration, stopped working.

The doors to the operating room had been flung open and from the corner of his vision, Felix saw Rebecca. She'd wrenched the plug from its socket and now she was staring in disbelief at Rosenberg.

Felix let out a loud sigh of relief.

"What the fuck's happening here?" she screamed. She snatched the saw from the clearly shocked surgeon and for a moment looked as though she was going to strike him with it.

Leaning over Felix and with tears in her eyes she scrutinised the bloody mess that had been made of his head before glaring furiously again at Rosenberg.

"What have you done to my Felix?" she cried.

Rosenberg just stared into space. The jolt of Rebecca's unexpected entrance had left him and his two assistants quite bewildered.

Felix became concerned when she disappeared from view and tried desperately to call for her. The surgeon appeared momentarily stunned, but the man was deranged and Felix doubted that Rebecca fully understood the danger she was in.

"B ... Beck ... eee ..." he grunted. Speech was slowly returning, and he knew that was a good sign. There was even a tingling sensation in his arms and legs. The indications were that he was going to be okay. They were in a sterile operating room. The skin flap could be sutured back into place quite easily, and, most importantly, his brain was still intact. The situation was certainly salvageable.

When Rebecca returned she was gowned and donning latex gloves. She picked up the craniotome, gave it a quick burst, and looked at Rosenberg who had now taken on the humbled stance of a scolded child.

"I just don't understand you sometimes, father," she snapped, and then stabbing a finger at Felix added, "I brought this one in. I've been grooming him for months; that makes him mine to operate on. I thought we understood that."

MARSHWALL

Paul Finch

Like so many innocent objects, it took on a different aspect in the dark. When a glimmer of moonlight caught its teeth or the shiny globules of its eyes. When a whisper of breeze filled its ragged old shroud, and set it rustling around the rigid form and dusty limbs. When the deep gloom clung to its hair and its leather and its ancient, worm-eaten hide, an amorphous mantle of shadow only hinting at the strange miscreation beneath.

For countless years it occupied its forgotten corner. Alone. Hidden by clutter. Out of sight, out of mind. Waiting.

*

Marissa's mother hadn't even wanted her to go home to Halvergate for the occasion of her father's funeral, so three years later, when Marissa and Duncan received a letter from old Mrs Gray, requesting that they let bygones be bygones, it was quite unexpected.

My Dearest Daughter,

I am not a well woman. Age and infirmity are fast catching up with me. I don't wish to give the impression that I sense an impending doom – but the lonely years I've spent in the absence of your beloved father have led me to re-evaluate.

The hurt that existed between us was once intolerable. Indeed, at the time I'm sure we both felt there was no way back. But in a world as indiscriminately cruel as our own, where the only ones you can safely rely on in times of crisis are family, I think we should finally put our differences aside. Time heals all, even the greatest of sadnesses. But time also runs out, usually when one is least expecting it to.

With this in mind, I extend my warmest invitation to you and your young man to come down here and visit with us at Marshwall. You would both be most welcome.

Your loving mother,
Leticia

"Marshwall?" Duncan said over his tea and toast. "Sounds great, doesn't it?"

Marissa was thoughtful as she sat at the other side of the breakfast table. Autumn rain streamed down the window. Below it, noisy vehicles flooded in both directions along the Mancunian Way, their outlines blurred by spray.

"It's quite a pretty place actually," she said. "Fifteenth century cottage. Well kept. Course, I haven't been there for a few years."

Duncan read the letter himself. "Doesn't sound like an old cow ... isn't that what you said she was?"

"Well ... she *could* be an old cow, yeah. But that's the point, isn't it? She'll now be a *very* old cow. Seventy-five, at least."

"Seventy-five and she's not a well woman. That doesn't sound good."

Marissa shrugged as if it was unimportant, which perhaps it was. She hadn't spoken with her mother for a long time, something ridiculous like nineteen years. "Wouldn't surprise me if she was exaggerating. Mother was always quite manipulative."

Duncan munched on another piece of toast. "Thought you said the old fella was the main problem?"

"He was the dictator. But she was his creature. Backed him to the hilt every time. 'Listen to your father, he knows best'. Jesus, the number of times I heard that crap."

"Parents, eh? Nightmare. Especially if you're inclined to be a rebel and they're set in their ways."

Marissa looked the letter over one more time, then folded it and shoved it into her dressing gown pocket, before leaving the table. Duncan poured himself another cuppa. He didn't care much for secrets, but he'd always known that the problem between Marissa and her parents had cut both parties deeply, and even though it was far in the past, neither side had shown any inclination to forgive and forget. However, it was interesting to learn that Marissa's seventy-five-year-old mum owned a fifteenth century cottage. He'd known she lived somewhere called Halvergate, which he thought was out in the wilds of Norfolk – Marissa's slight rural accent still betrayed these origins – but though the house's name, Marshwall, didn't sound too prepossessing, its great age made it an interesting proposition. Assuming it was in good nick.

When he went to the bedroom and stopped in the doorway, Marissa was in front of her dresser. A willowy, green-eyed blonde, still only thirty-eight, she'd always looked good in the tight blue skirt, white short sleeved blouse and blue high heels that she wore as part of her daytime uniform – even if it did only qualify her to sit behind the counter at a small street-corner estate agency. His own suit hung in the wardrobe; as a self-employed financial advisor, there wasn't the same onus on him to be in the office for nine (or much before lunch, these days).

"Anything else you haven't told me about your past?" he asked casually.

"Like what?" she said, brushing her hair.

"Well … do you have any brothers or sisters?"

"You mean, when mum's estate is divvied up, will we have to share it with anyone?"

He slouched in and sat on the bed. "Alright, you've got me … but look, you haven't shown any sign that you like the old woman all the time I've known you. I didn't think it would cause offence to enquire."

"I'm an only child, Duncan, you've always known that."

"I've not known it, I *assumed* it … because there've never been any phone calls or Christmas cards."

She stood up, straightened her skirt and fixed the nametag on the lapel of her blouse.

"You can't blame me for asking," he said. "Anything that'll get us out of this poky little flat."

She checked her make-up, and pulled on her blue jacket.

"Fifteenth century cottage," he persisted. "I bet that's worth a tidy sum."

"It belongs to my mother."

"Yeah, but like you said … she's seventy-five, and I'm sorry, but I think you should go and make friends with her again."

She pecked him on the lips. "So do I."

Duncan was surprised. He followed her to the apartment door, where she put on her raincoat and mittens. "You do?"

"Yes … but not for the reasons you're thinking. It's gone on too long, this nonsense."

She trotted down the stairs into the communal hall, which smelt of damp and, as usual, was heaped with junk mail and crammed with bicycles belonging to other residents, most of whom were students.

"Is this place nice?" he called down after her. "Marshwall, I mean?"

"It could be amazing," she said as she opened the front door. "But if we do end up taking possession, we'll sell it the very first chance we get."

"Why?"

"Don't even ask."

*

Duncan Mackintyre and Marissa Gray had lived together for four years now, having first met through mutual friends. Duncan, who was six-foot-three, had been slimmer back then, dark-haired, handsome and experienced – not to say a little worldly (he had a string of relationships behind him, though he'd never married), and had made an immediate impression on her. His carefully cultivated image of urbane playboy had helped, as had his job, which had allowed him to set his own undemanding hours and still turn over an average eighty grand a year. Of course, all that had been before the financial crash.

Since then, his earnings had dwindled alarmingly, in some months to virtually nothing. He consoled himself with the knowledge that Marissa had never seen him in his absolute pomp, so she didn't really know how far he'd fallen, though she was aware that he'd once had a house in Wilmslow, which he'd had to sell, and that the gym and sports club memberships, which had kept him in good shape for so long, had been allowed to lapse. About the only thing he had left from those halcyon days was his soft-top MG convertible, which he swore he would never be separated from, though occasionally it had the potential to cost him an arm and a leg, spare parts being so expensive. If nothing else, he supposed, it would enable them to ride down to Norfolk in style.

"Can't hurt to let your mum think you're shacked up with a winner," he'd said.

Marissa hadn't responded, not for the first time implying indignation that she wasn't.

It was the third Friday in November when they set off, hitting the M6 south around mid-morning, diverting east onto the A14 in early afternoon, and then taking the A11. It was never going to be an easy journey on a Friday, endless heavy traffic extending it for hours. And when they finally did reach the quieter roads of the Norfolk backcountry, they had to stop continually in lay-bys to consult a map, their sat-nav having given up the ghost fifty miles back. At least the weather was on their side. November had commenced with its customary howling gales, swirling leaves and driving rain. But today was still and quiet, and several degrees above freezing, so they didn't have ice to contend with either. A thin wash of milk-grey cloud obscured the weak sun, though this broke apart later on to cast a mellow haze on the flat bare fields and russet woods of East Anglia. Until the sun went down of course, at which point the twisting rural lanes turned tar-black.

"No worries," Duncan said airily. "We'll be there for six o'clock."

But they were still on the road at seven. By this time, even Duncan felt tired and irritable, though strangely, Marissa, who'd been vexed earlier on that the journey had taken so long, was sitting stiff and upright as though apprehensive. Whenever he spoke to her now, she merely nodded or replied in monosyllables. It was only as they covered the final few miles, a straight stretch of lane hemmed on either side by utter darkness, that he realised the truth: she was nervous.

"Can I help?" he asked.

"What do you mean?"

"Obviously something's bugging you."

"Coming back here after all this time, I suppose."

"Wish I knew what you meant by 'here'. Can't see a damn thing."

"These are the Halvergate Marshes. We're following the line of an old Roman road. Used to connect Norwich to Yarmouth. Kind of a causeway really."

"You mean it's all bogs out there?" Duncan had been wondering why not so much as a tree or signpost, let alone an actual building, had flickered through his headlights recently.

"Pretty much."

"And does this causeway ever get flooded?"

"Never has to my knowledge. But we're only nine miles from the sea, so I suppose it could happen. Worried it'll devalue your inheritance?"

He groaned. "I wish you'd stop talking like that. Inheriting Marshwall is a consideration – of course it is. Assuming your mum leaves it to you in her will. But it's not the be-all and end-all. If you want to turn around now and go back, fine. I'll never mention it again."

"Perhaps we *should* go back."

"It's your choice ..."

She glanced sidelong at him, intrigued by his determined

unwillingness to pry. "Have you never wondered, Duncan, what the actual fall-out with my parents involved?"

"Course I have, but it's none of my business."

"Someone died."

"Okay …?" The road curved and, fleetingly, some distance ahead – perhaps a couple of miles as the crow flew – he spotted a twinkle of lights. It was the sort of thing you saw on the coast when a house was perched on a headland. The road curved again, and the lights vanished. *Marshwall*, he told himself, though he was too distracted by what Marissa had just said to ponder this for long.

"I said someone died."

"I heard you."

"I wasn't always an only child." She stared sightlessly through the windshield. "But you'd never have seen it coming. Mother was nearly fifty when she had Albie."

"Christ … that must've been difficult for her."

"It was. And it didn't end with the birth. She hadn't expected to have another kid, even though she'd wanted one, so she doted on him. Said that now we were a 'real family'. But he was hard work, I'll tell you. Wilful, bossy. Mother thought that was marvellous; said he was his father's son. Anyway, it got worse as he got older … because she spoiled him rotten. By the time I went to university, he was six and a holy terror. Father wasn't much use around the house, so mother had to do most of it herself. Whenever I came home, she took it as an opportunity to rest."

"Great way to spend your holidays."

"That wasn't the whole story … I got some free time. But I did the babysitting thing quite a bit. One night in particular it was a real issue. It was my first summer back, and mother and father had gone off to a rotary club dinner, so I was in charge again. Trouble was I'd been supposed to be going out that night too. A few of my school friends were having a reunion in Lowestoft. I was furious to be missing it. And of course, when Albie started getting up to his usual tricks of being difficult and disobedient … well, put it this way, I stopped paying attention. I was feeling angry, resentful. Treated myself to a glass of wine or two …"

She hesitated to continue. Ahead, Duncan again saw lights in the darkness. They were now much closer, shimmering through masses of leafless branches. "I take it something happened to Albie?"

"Yes." She was glassy-eyed as she peered into the past. "He insisted on doing something that he knew he shouldn't. Something I should have prevented, but … well … suffice to say I was too distracted."

A gateway swung into view on the left. There was no actual gate, but two tall stone posts framed an entrance in a wall of matted rhododendrons. They were thick with moss. The one on the left bore a rusted iron plaque:

MARSHWALL

From such an entrance, Duncan half expected one of those crumbling, gothic monstrosities that routinely featured in horror films, but actually, once inside the grounds, everything looked rather neat. The foliage, though thick, was cut back, and the drive covered with limestone pebbles, which reflected brightly in the MG's headlamps. They emerged from the outer ring of vegetation, and saw to their left, open lawns only partially strewn with leaves, suggesting that most had been raked away. On the right, warm light shafted out through the diamond-paned windows of the main house, which was built from yellowing brick; as they followed the drive around it, they passed numerous wings and gables. Ivy clad some parts, while in others heavy black beams were exposed. Its eaves were low, and the immense slope of its roof tilted steeply up into the autumn gloom. When they reached the main door, two lights designed to resemble Victorian gas lamps sprang to life, revealing a parking area and a large, silver-grey Freelander 2.

"A seventy-five-year-old lady with a four-wheel drive?"

Duncan said, applying the handbrake.

"Mother doesn't drive," Marissa replied, focused intently on the doorway. "That car probably belongs to Vicki Anderson, her friend and part-time housekeeper."

Duncan followed her gaze: the door was another impressive 'olde-worlde' feature; a massive oak affair studded with iron. Marissa's eyes never left it. She didn't so much look nervous or apprehensive now, as openly scared

"Hey … we knew this wasn't going to be easy," he said, taking her right hand and squeezing it. "But your mum was the one who instigated this meeting … and accidents happen. Maybe she's finally realised that."

Marissa made a brave attempt at a smile.

They climbed from the car, but before they'd removed their baggage, the front door opened and more warm light flooded out. The woman standing there was in her mid-sixties, but tall and robust looking. She had a strong, angular frame, only half concealed beneath a black poncho. Her hair was white, but long and lustrous. When she came forward, she was handsome rather than pretty, but maintained a cool, imperious air.

"Young Marissa, is it?" she asked.

"Hello, Aunt Vicki."

"My dear, what a fine young woman you've become."

"It's been a long time."

"Far too long. And your mother thinks the same." The woman called Vicki hadn't yet smiled, but not, Duncan suspected, because she was unhappy – more likely because she rarely smiled. She took Marissa's hands in her own. "I only ask that you treat her gently … and indulge her eccentricities. She's rather frail these days."

"She didn't specify what's wrong with her."

The woman sighed. "The truth is … there's nothing wrong with her. High blood pressure, a touch of arthritis perhaps. But she's obsessed with this idea that time is running out, and she genuinely wants to put things right between you … though I suspect that won't be easy."

Duncan stood to one side, listening unobtrusively. It wasn't exactly music to his ears that old Mrs Gray was not ill. But seventy-five was seventy-five, so it was just a matter of being patient, and of course polite. And convivial. And useful. Above all, useful. All the things the average well-heeled mother would want in a prospective son-in-law.

"The main thing is mother's okay?" Marissa asked.

"In herself, she's fine."

"And how's ... everything else?"

Duncan thought he detected meaning in that last question. He glanced from one woman to the other, wondering if something was being kept from him.

Aunt Vicki pondered this, before replying: "Let's cross one bridge at a time, eh?"

*

He'd been expecting a wisp of a woman, someone extremely feeble for seventy-five. But in actual fact Mrs Gray didn't even look that old. Her hair was tinted a delicate red-pink and neatly styled; she wore a fitted red dress and high heeled shoes. She was somewhat wizened, but subtle dabs of make-up brought out her green eyes in startling fashion.

Marissa had her mother's eyes, Duncan realised.

She also had her height, because Mrs Gray wasn't far short of six feet. However, she was thin, and as she advanced across the lounge to meet them, she did so stiffly, leaning on a cane. Arthritis, he recalled. So she wasn't one hundred percent.

As the old woman slowly approached, he glanced around the room. The oil painting over the grand fireplace just had to be a depiction of the late Henry Gray. Duncan had no specific idea what Marissa's father had done for a living; she'd always referred to him simply as 'a merchant'. But in this image he was a broad shouldered fellow wearing a brown tweed suit and waistcoat, with a large, square head tufted around the edges with white curls. He was rosy cheeked and ample jowled, and he smiled with beneficence. He didn't much resemble the tyrant that Marissa recollected, but he was hardly likely to have commissioned a painting showing an unpleasant side to his character.

Below the portrait there was a heavy stone mantel, and at one end of it a photograph of a little boy with a mop of sunny hair, wearing a manic grin. It was a charming picture, somehow enhanced by the subject's missing front teeth. Duncan glanced to the other end of the mantelpiece, half expecting to see a picture of the Grays' other child acting as a counterbalance. But the space there was empty.

Mother and daughter now embraced, but considering they hadn't seen each other in two decades, there was something cool and formal about it. There were no tears, there was no 'how've you been?' Perhaps more to the point, there was no 'I'm so, so sorry'. Feeling more than a little awkward, Duncan glanced behind him, hoping that Aunt Vicki had come in as well. But she hadn't. He heard a dull creak from somewhere upstairs.

"We only have a cold spread for dinner," Mrs Gray said in a vaguely apologetic tone – not regarding her long-lost child with even half the emotion that Aunt Vicki had (and she'd been aloof enough). "We didn't know what time to expect you."

"It's always difficult these days," Marissa replied. "The traffic from north to south is horrendous at weekends. Mother, this is Duncan Mackintyre. We've been going out together for four years now."

Mrs Gray took Duncan's hand in her own, which was twisty and liver-spotted. "You seem like a sturdy young man, Mr Mackintyre. I hope you've been looking after my Marissa?"

Duncan thought it best not to tell her that at present it was the other way around.

"What are you … about forty?"

"Erm …" Duncan was taken aback by the directness of the question. "That's right."

"And what is your area of expertise?" Mrs Gray had a strange way of interacting; there was distance in her eyes, as though she was actually peering through him and seeing someone else a long way behind.

"Mother," Marissa interrupted. "I think we're going a bit fast, don't you?"

"Fast, my dear?"

"Duncan's been good enough to drive me down here, and it's a long way. I don't think it's really fair to subject him to an immediate cross-examination. Don't *you and I* have things to talk about?"

Mrs Gray gave this some thought. "Yes ... we do. But perhaps you'd rather eat first?"

Once they'd taken their bags upstairs – rather to Duncan's surprise, they'd been allocated one bedroom between them, with a double bed – they came back down and reconvened in the dining room. The house was deceptive. Not as spacious on the inside as he'd expected, but it was cosy and nicely appointed. With all its original fittings – low beams, oak wainscoting, huge brick hearths complete with soot-blackened ironmongery – it would still fetch a nice price. He had to conceal how giddy this thought made him; was it unrealistic to predict eight or nine hundred thousand?

Mrs Gray might have apologised beforehand about the cold collation, but it was a damn sight more appetising than the soggy hamburgers and chips they'd forced down at a service station around lunchtime, consisting of sliced ham, chicken and turkey, boiled eggs, salad, cheese and cold sausages.

"So, Mr Mackintyre," their hostess said, "as I'm prohibited from asking any questions about you, maybe you have some for me?"

"Oh ..." Again Duncan was caught on the hop. "How are you?"

She tittered in response. "That's a safe enough starter, I suppose. I'd like to tell you that I'm very well, thank you, but alas that isn't so."

"I hope it's nothing too serious."

"Of course you do."

There was nothing obviously scathing in her tone, but that had seemed a curious comment. Duncan remembered what Marissa had said about her mother being an old cow. They ate for a while in silence, Mrs Gray picking at her food like a bird.

"I expect that a lonely outpost like Marshwall will seem fairly quiet to you, Mr Mackintyre," she eventually remarked. "After your life in the big city."

"It's nice to take a break from all the noise," he replied.

Mrs Gray turned to her daughter. "And how about you, my dear? Won't Marshwall seem a little ... unexciting these days?"

"Excitement isn't everything, mother. This is my home. And I love it dearly."

Mrs Gray pondered this. "Marshwall isn't the sort of place, Mr Mackintyre, where one can easily find distraction. Though that wasn't always true, was it, Marissa?"

Marissa didn't glance up from her plate, but when she spoke, she did so quietly. "We need to talk, mother. But I warn you, I've not come all this way just to be reprimanded again."

"Hmm ..." Mrs Gray considered. "Here's hoping you don't have a handsome young gardener in your employ up in Manchester, Mr Mackintyre."

"Mother!" Marissa looked daggers at her parent.

"Else, Marissa here might feel it appropriate to put on her skimpiest bikini – quite the skimpiest bikini you'll ever have seen! – and go out and flaunt herself."

"Sunbathing!" Marissa hissed. "It was hardly a criminal offence."

"Agreed," Mrs Gray said solemnly. "There were no criminal offences committed that day. However ... that *evening* it was a different matter."

"You know how difficult Albie could be ..."

"Regardless of that, my dear, you were supposed to be watching him."

There was a shuddering creak from above their heads. The two women took no notice.

"I *was* watching him," Marissa said. "I just wasn't prepared to chase him all over the house."

Mrs Gray turned back to Duncan. "You don't have French windows, I trust, Mr Mackintyre? If you do, pray it will never be a simple thing for Marissa to open them and beckon whoever happens to be hanging around on your lawn."

"Fifteen minutes!" Marissa had reddened in the cheek; her emerald eyes flashed anger. "That's how long I was … *occupied*. I didn't think even Albie could get into trouble in that time. In any case, we've had this conversation before. Why do we need to have it again?"

"Because the last time Mr Mackintyre wasn't privy to it."

"Mr Mackintyre!" Marissa said, startled. "Mr Mackintyre isn't …"

She faltered, and for an alarming second Duncan thought she'd been about to say 'important'. He'd hoped that after four years he was more to her than a simple bed-warmer. But who knew? Marissa had always been her own woman.

"Mr Mackintyre …" Marissa continued, "is an understanding man who recognises that accidents happen. He is also a polite man who at this moment must feel very embarrassed."

Mrs Gray turned to Duncan. "*Do* you find these family issues embarrassing, Mr Mackintyre?" This was no apology; it was more like a challenge.

"I can think of family issues that are more embarrassing," he said.

Suddenly he was tired of being the observer, the anonymous extra. He had ambitions to be part of this clique, so it was time to assert himself.

"My father was a coal miner, Mrs Gray," he confessed. "He was officially disabled by the time he was thirty-six because of all the coal dust he'd inhaled. It never stopped him inhaling alcohol mind you. At least, that's the way it seemed, he drank so much. A quantity matched only by the amount of prescription meds my mother took on a weekly basis. Then there was my older sister, whose habits were strictly non-prescription. When *they* fought ... well, that was what you'd call embarrassing. Skin and hair flew. Literally."

Mrs Gray gazed at him with fascination. For the first time she seemed to be visualising him clearly. "Well, Mr Mackintyre ... I can see you're quite the catch."

"That's my family, Mrs Gray, not me." He knew this was a gamble but could only hope that his candour would pay off. "But if it helps, they paid for their sins."

"Indeed. How so?"

"They're dead."

Mrs Gray contemplated this as she turned back to her daughter. "What we have here, Marissa, is a very honest young man. It seems that he, at least, has faced his demons."

"Yes, well, as we know, mother ... there are demons and demons." Without another word, Marissa rose and took their dishes through to the kitchen.

A few minutes later, after attempting to entertain his hostess with casual but ultimately inane conversation, Duncan also beat a retreat to the kitchen, where he offered to assist Marissa with the washing-up.

"Still trying to impress?" she said, referencing the fact that he rarely did this at home.

He ignored that and stood alongside her at the sink, drying while she washed.

"I know what you mean ..." There was another long creak from somewhere overhead. He glanced upward, briefly distracted. "I mean ... about how difficult she can be."

"Smart move though, opening up to her like that."

"Do you think so, or are you being sarcastic again? I know it was a risk. I was trying to show solidarity ... like I know life can be tough as well." She handed him a large cooking pot. "And trying to divert some of the flak away from you."

"That was sweet. But it wasn't necessary." She handed him

116

another pot.

"Just out of interest … if Aunt Vicki's your mother's housekeeper, why are *we* doing the dishes?"

"Aunt Vicki isn't here."

"I've heard her upstairs."

"You heard nothing."

"Marissa …"

"You heard nothing, Duncan." She avoided his puzzled frown. "She was going home, earlier. She doesn't stay here at night. No one does if they've any sense."

*

At first, as Duncan listened to the dull *creak-groan*, he wondered if it was someone walking around on the floor above, though it sounded a bit too regular to be normal footfalls; it made a curious repeating pattern – *creak-groan, creak-groan*.

Then he remembered that there was no floor above.

But it was Marissa who sat bolt upright in the darkness. Overhead, the noise continued – *creak-groan, creak-groan*. "What the hell is that crazy bitch doing?" she whispered.

"What is it?" he asked, still fuddled with sleep.

"I can't believe she's kept it." She jumped out of the bed and fumbled around for her dressing gown. "Turn the lamp on, will you?"

When he finally found the bedside switch, Marissa had already put her gown and slippers on and was heading for the bedroom door.

Duncan was only in shorts, so he pulled a T-shirt on and followed. Outside, the landing was so dark that the light shining from their bedroom had next to no impact.

"Fuck!" Marissa swore, blundering into the small banister at the top of the stairs. "I once knew this wretched place like the back of my hand."

Duncan glanced over his shoulder, thinking he'd just heard a sigh. All the unused bedrooms were closed, but the door to Mrs Gray's room stood half-open. Blackness skulked beyond it. "What about your mother?" he said, pointing.

"She's not in *there*, you idiot." Marissa stumbled to the far end of the landing, where another narrow stair apparently led up to the attic. "She's up *here*."

Duncan glanced again towards Mrs Gray's room, hearing another sigh. It sounded like Mrs Gray herself. She was clearly asleep in there. "Mariss ..."

But Marissa had already vanished from view. He hurried after her up the spiral stair. In the narrow, twisting space, the repeating *creak-groan* from overhead was much louder, as though a machine was operating. But it ceased abruptly when they were about half way up. Duncan didn't immediately notice because he was too busy tripping and stubbing his bare toes on the uncarpeted woodwork.

"Blast!" he said. "Isn't there another light?"

"Here," she replied, reaching the top and hitting two switches one after the other.

The first brought a dull, unshaded bulb to life directly over their heads. It created only sufficient radiance to illume the shroud of cobwebs hanging over it, and the naked plaster walls on either side. The second light came on in the attic itself, which lay just beyond an open doorway on the left. This was a little brighter, though not impressively so. Marissa went straight in, Duncan close behind.

The attic, which was triangular shaped and seemed to fill the entire roof space of the house, contained an enormous amount of clutter, no doubt the usual boxes, packing cases and discarded furniture, though it wasn't easy to tell as all had been covered with grimy dustsheets. However, nothing and no one moved in there.

Marissa peered from one end to the other; Duncan noticed how the anger had drained out of her. "I was sure ..." she said. "I was absolutely sure it was ..."

"A squirrel?" he suggested. "On the roof? They can make a

hell of a racket."

"Squirrels don't ride back and forth on wooden rockers."

"What?"

She strode forward, yanking sheets away, kicking up miniature choking fogs. A coat hanger appeared, followed by an old bureau, its upper shelves crammed with ancient paperwork. Next came a wingback armchair, badly sprung. Then a filing cabinet so old it could easily date from the Second World War.

"Perhaps if you'd tell me what we're looking for?" he said, following her.

But she'd come to a halt. They were now at the farthest end of the chamber. No household object was easy to identify when a sheet was thrown over it, though this was less so than most – it was no shape that Duncan could recognise, though he knew why it had caught her attention. The other sheets' folds were so heavy with dust they were almost black; this one was dingy, but much cleaner than the rest.

He thought again about the sounds they'd heard. Had someone been moving this object? If so, they'd surely have met that person on the stair, wouldn't they?

He glanced uneasily over his shoulder. There were many niches, many concealed places. "You know, someone could be hiding in here," he said.

"No one's hiding." She tore the sheet away.

Despite everything, he was disquieted by what lay beneath. In the midst of the general drabness up here, its bared teeth, which were pearly white, its glinting amber eyes, the bright green leather of its harness, reins and saddle, its flowing scarlet mane and its sky-blue body covered with large pink polka dots made for a garish combination.

Duncan had always found rocking horses vaguely unsettling.

He wasn't sure why. It was the same with dolls and puppets, as if a few blobs of bright paint and some silver bells were insufficient to hide the unfeeling coldness underneath.

This particular rocking horse didn't have any bells attached

– not any more, though apart from that it was in reasonable condition. It was a large specimen, a good four feet at the withers, and though made from wood, there were only a few signs of decay. Its limbs were intact, its four hooves mounted on two heavy oaken rockers.

The thought struck him like a dash of iced water.

"Jesus … that noise?" He stared at Marissa, but her face was twisted with anger.

"That stupid old cow," she said with venom. "That stupid, ridiculous old cow! She's kept it all these years!"

"How could I throw it away?" The wavering voice came from behind them.

They twirled around.

Mrs Gray's face was pale and smudged with make-up, her hair in disarray, her overlong nightie trailing on the floor as she approached from the attic door. "How could I? It's the only link I have to him?"

"Mother, are you mad?" Marissa demanded. "This revolting thing is a memento of disaster. You should have thrown it away decades ago."

"How dare you suggest …?"

"It's a piece of trash. It has no purpose here."

"You would say that, wouldn't you?" The old woman's face became peevish. "The only job you had to do all night was prevent your brother riding it unsupervised. But of course you were too busy doing something else …"

"If it was so dangerous, you should have thrown it away as soon as father brought it back from that jumble sale."

"But Albie wanted it. He loved it."

"And you couldn't deny him anything, could you?" Marissa pushed the horse's nose; it tilted forward and began to rock – quite violently. The noise it made was exactly the same as they'd heard from the bedroom. She turned to Duncan. "As you can see, this thing is an accident waiting to happen. But oh no, Albie had to be allowed to have it, because mother could never say 'no' to him."

Mrs Gray looked genuinely astonished. "Are you having the nerve to blame me?"

Marissa rounded on her. "I know about my negligence, mother, and how much I let the family down. But it's time you learned about your own. Duncan, why don't you do us all a favour …? Take this disgusting thing outside and break it into firewood."

"No!" Mrs Gray squawked. "Please, we must keep it …"

"Mother, he's gone."

"You know that isn't so."

"What's she talking about?" Duncan said.

Tearfully, Mrs Gray gripped his arm. "You heard it rocking again, Mr Mackintyre. I know you did. That's why you came up here."

"Weren't *you* rocking it?" he asked. He glanced from one woman to the other, but neither immediately answered. "Hey … what the heck's going on here?"

The old lady wiped at her tears, attempting to regain her haughty dignity. "No doubt my lovely daughter has told you that we parted ways some nineteen years ago because of this same tragedy. But it isn't true." She glared icily at Marissa. "You lasted quite a few months after that, didn't you, darling?"

Marissa gazed boldly back. "I had to make arrangements to leave. That was all."

"She made these arrangements, Mr Mackintyre, after a few too many sleepless nights."

Again, Duncan glanced from one to the other. "Are you … are you saying this thing rocks on its own?"

"Of course not," Marissa retorted. "It's a hunk of lifeless wood." But from her taut expression he could tell that she wasn't being entirely truthful. "I advise you, Duncan, if you want to be part of this family, you throw that thing away right now."

"No, I beg you," Mrs Gray said. "Please …"

Marissa folded her arms and waited; a stance that brooked no argument. Duncan took the rocking horse by the reins and tried to drag it. It was heavier than he'd expected, but it slowly began to slither across the planks.

"No!" Mrs Gray said again, this time with a bird-like screech. "For the love of God!"

Duncan looked at Marissa, but she remained firm. "It's been in this house too long, Duncan … and it's caused far too much trouble."

He continued lugging the weighty item, gradually crossing the attic, stopping here and there to kick smaller items out of his way. Mrs Gray wailed, fluttering around him in her voluminous nightgown like a demented butterfly.

Again, Duncan glanced at Marissa. "Listen, if it means this much to her …"

She pointed at the attic door.

"Marissa, I'll never forgive you," Mrs Gray wept. "I swear, I'll never forgive you for this, I … I, *oh my God* …" She came to a tottering standstill, her breathing fast and ragged. She rammed a clenched fist between her withered old breasts. "Oh … oh my God … Marissa!" She groped out towards her daughter, who caught her arm. "I … I can't … I can't breathe …"

"Of course you can breathe."

Mrs Gray shook her head, eyes bulging like baubles. "No … I can't."

"Just try to relax."

"I can't breathe!" The woman's voice had become painfully shrill.

At a nod from Marissa, Duncan abandoned the horse and grabbed their hostess's other arm. Together, as gently as they could, they assisted her down the stairs into the cottage's lounge, where they sat her on the sofa and laid a quilt over her shoulders. It was a couple of minutes before she was able to recover a little of her composure, but she was still shaking. Her fingers had knotted together as she sat there; she'd gone white as paper, beads of sweat glittering on her brow.

"How are you feeling now?" Duncan asked.

"I'm ..." Mrs Gray looked confused, as if she didn't quite know where she was. "I'm alright ... I think."

Marissa led him to one side. "A quick visit to hospital's in order. I don't like this."

He nodded. "I'll get dressed."

"No ... just me. You stay here."

"Why?"

She lowered her voice. "Because while we're out you can get rid of that damn rocking horse. You've only been here one evening, and you've already seen the anguish it causes."

Duncan glanced at Mrs Gray, who seemed oblivious to their conversation. "You sure? She seems pretty attached to it."

"Duncan ..." Marissa's voice fell to a harsh whisper. "She's just a batty old woman. Once it's gone, she won't even notice." She turned around. "I know it's late, mother, but I'm taking you to hospital."

Mrs Gray nodded vaguely. Marissa got quickly dressed, then put a pair of slippers on her mother's feet, and swathed the quilt around her. They stood her up and walked her towards the front door and out onto the drive. Only now did the old lady seem to realise what was happening. She glanced over her shoulder, as Marissa part assisted, part pushed her into the MG's front passenger seat. "Mr Mackintyre ... don't do it, I beg you!"

"Mother, come on," Marissa said impatiently.

"Mr Mackintyre, please ... don't take away all I have left."

Duncan could only watch from the entrance, as the car's tail lights receded through swirls of exhaust and vanished among the rhododendrons. All she had left, he thought, turning and looking at the rambling Elizabethan house. Batty old woman indeed.

He made his way back upstairs, his bare feet padding on the wooden treads of the spiral stair. The light was still on in the attic. He entered, yawning, glancing at his watch. Half-past three. Hell of a time to be hauling lumber.

The rocking horse was waiting for him, brilliantly coloured

beneath the room's central light. Again, that word 'garish' came to mind. Not to mention 'ugly'.

He circled the object. The black pupils in its amber eyes seemed to follow him – that was a famous optical illusion of course. The same was said to happen with portrait paintings. He stood with hands on hips. Marissa wanted it out, but where to take it then? Was there a compost heap around the back, or some dense undergrowth where he could stash it until morning? He certainly wasn't going to go rooting in the outbuildings for an axe and saw. Not at this ungodly hour.

He was still working on the basis that old Mrs Gray had rocked the horse herself, as she possibly did every night in her grief, and had hidden when they'd first come up here. But now he remembered that he'd heard her breathing in her sleep. He wondered if the horse could have rocked itself as part of some natural phenomenon. Had it been located on a section of canted floor maybe? Was its weight unevenly distributed? Had a draught set it in motion? None of these things seemed likely … and then, suddenly, a rather neat idea occurred to him. Mrs Gray desired to keep the tawdry object, and he obviously didn't want to upset her too much. Meanwhile, the problem her daughter had was that it rocked too much.

Why get rid of the whole horse, when he could more easily dispose of its rockers?

It was so obvious a solution that, as he headed downstairs, Duncan wondered why no one had thought of it before. A small utilities room was accessible from the kitchen, and after rummaging through a few drawers in there, he found what he needed: a screwdriver.

Be useful, he told himself, as he trekked back up. That was always the way to win over prospective mothers-in-law. Make yourself useful.

But when he arrived back in the attic, he wondered what had changed.

The rocking horse was exactly where he'd left it, but now there was a stillness in the room, which he hadn't noticed before. That was an odd thing to tell himself. Why shouldn't the room be still – there was nobody else here? Yet this was slightly different: it was an unnatural stillness, the sort of stillness you got in a game of hide-and-seek, when you fancied someone was concealed nearby.

Putting such irrational thoughts down to fatigue, he strode to the horse, squatted and examined its hooves. A single screw had been driven through the middle of each one, in opposing directions from front to back. The extreme age of these fixtures and the dense rust in which they were caked would cause a problem. But Duncan was on the verge of making *both* the women in his life extremely happy, and he wasn't going to let anything get in the way of that. So he worked hard for the next ten minutes, droplets of sweat squeezing from his furrowed brow as he twisted the screwdriver back and forth. Only with much grunting and straining did he manage to break the ancient seals and, in each case, eventually, extract several inches of gleaming silver screw. A couple of times, he thought he sensed movement behind him. He glanced over his shoulder, wondering if he'd spot a dustsheet fluttering in an unexpected breeze, or, who knew?, a scampering rat … anything that might have been the cause of so much discord in this house (that would *really* win him kudos). But on no occasion did he see anything untoward. Again, he put it down to his imagination.

When the job was done, he lifted the horse off its rockers with relative ease, though it was still heavy. The rockers were heavy too; they were at least six feet in length, made of oak, and rimmed along their undersides with aged steel. It wasn't surprising the entire house had been shaken. He carried them downstairs anyway, feeling pleased with himself. Now everyone would be happy. Mrs Gray could keep her memento of better days, and Marissa could sleep at night. And so could he.

But it was only a short time later, about quarter of an hour after he'd got his head down on the pillow and switched his lamp off, when Duncan was woken again …

*

He wasn't quite sure what had disturbed him – a dull *thud* of some sort. There were always sounds like that in the flat. Idiot students messing around till the wee small hours; the landlord doing occasional much needed repairs.

But then he remembered that he wasn't in the flat, and that there weren't any students upstairs. Nor any workmen.

His eyes snapped open in the darkness.

Prolonged silence.

He definitely must have dreamed it this time. He'd removed the rockers, so it couldn't make that sound again, no matter how hard it tried.

Another hollow *thud*.

Duncan sat up, the quilt falling off him. A few seconds ago he'd been fast asleep; now he was wider awake than he'd ever been.

Another *thud*.

There had to be a natural explanation.

Thud.

There was.

He'd removed its rockers. Dear God in heaven! – the realisation trickled through him like iced water. *What in Christ's name had possessed him to do that?*

The next *thud* drew his eyes upward. The bedroom ceiling was invisible in the dark, but he knew that the sound he'd just heard was in a different position from the one that had gone before it. As was the next one that followed, and the one that followed that, and the one that followed that – all of them lumpish, clumsy, yet growing steadier, surer – and each one closer to the place where the attic door must stand.

Duncan leapt from the bed, his flesh tingling.

The next *thud* sounded different: more muffled, but of course it would do – the spiral stair descended through a stone

126

shaft.

Thud – this one was further down the stair.

Thud – this one was further down still.

Duncan giggled, before slapping a hand to his mouth.

Thud – this one louder, closer.

He dashed across the bedroom in the direction where he thought the door was – and rebounded from the wardrobe, nose stinging, hot blood gushing over his lips.

More *thudding*. Much louder now. On the landing in fact; and something else – a slow, repetitive creaking. The twist and groan of flexing timber. Duncan fought his way through the dark, finally locating the door. He groped down its jamb until he found the bolt – thank God for 'olde-worlde' fittings! – and rammed it home.

Thud … virtually outside.

And then silence again.

Duncan retreated until he reached the bed. He toppled backward onto it and corkscrewed over to the other side, where he flung himself down into the open space next to the window. Sweat stippling his brow, he peered through the blackness, which, as blackness always eventually did, had now diminished a little. He could just distinguish the rectangular outline of the door.

Something scraped on the landing carpet, and creaked, and the door shuddered.

Pressure was building on it from the other side. The next creak was torturous: the agony of straining wood. He could picture it bowing laboriously inward from its frame, could hear the deep groan of its iron hinges as they distorted, as their nuts and bolts were slowly wrenched from their moorings.

The bedroom window was the only option.

Most folk always imagined this was how they'd escape a burning building. Yet when they looked down from this lofty perch, they nearly always balked. It was perhaps a measure of Duncan's terror that he never hesitated. When he found the latch too stiff to manipulate, he put his shoulder to the sheet of diamond panes, which collapsed outward in a clattering cascade. He literally vaulted out, even though jagged shards sliced his flesh, even though he then fell twelve feet, tearing handfuls of ivy en route – the only thing that slowed him down sufficiently to prevent serious injury when he alighted on the paved footpath below.

It was bitterly cold for a half-naked man. But adrenaline was pumping through Duncan's body, and fleetingly he felt nothing as he crouched there.

He wasn't sure which side of the house he was on. They'd arrived in the pitch-dark, so he'd gained no impression of its layout. Directly in front lay a strip of lawn, and beyond that another belt of rhododendrons. Instead of chancing such an impenetrable tangle, he went sideways, circling the building, running as fast as he could over grass and gravel, unmindful of the sharp stones and spiky twigs, rounding corner after corner, passing a succession of darkened ground-floor windows, and suddenly finding himself on pebbles.

Ahead of him, the drive veered off through its tunnel of foliage. As he sprinted down it, he sensed Marshwall falling away to his rear, a receding black outline on the star-speckled night. There were new moments of horror as, briefly, he was enclosed by shambling masses of vegetation, but he'd soon passed between the gateposts and was out onto the main road with its solid tarmac surface and its broken white line.

It didn't matter which way he ran from here, so long as he ran – which he did, legs working like pistons. The sweat sprayed off him and no doubt he left bloody footprints, but he pounded along hard. The vast emptiness on all sides, which the first time here had been vaguely oppressive, now provided relief. The cold wind cut across him; he could smell the salt marshes. The real world again – where he was not an intruder, not an interloper. From somewhere behind came a colossal splintering of wood.

Duncan shot a panicked glance over his shoulder. The road dwindled into blackness. Marshwall was already so far behind that he couldn't see it. He lengthened his stride all the same, even though the breath rasped in his chest and saliva boiled from his mouth.

But whimpers struggled from his lips when he heard that awful sound again.

It was different this time. Of course it was. Firstly because of the tarmac, a *clacking* rather than a *thudding*. And secondly, because of the open road, no clumsy, awkward clumping this time, more the fast drum-roll of an approaching gallop.

Duncan swerved off the blacktop. The ground tilted steeply downward. But he didn't care. He blundered pell-mell into the darkness, ploughing through soft muck, scrambling amid leafless, clawing brush. He never saw the dry-stone wall, even as he ran headlong into it. It struck him at waist height and flipped him over it neatly.

He landed on the other side on his back – but in a chill, semi liquid mass, which quickly began to suck him down. In almost no time the bulk of his body was beneath the glutinous surface, which though it gripped him like heavy clay was also soft and silky – and provided no purchase whatever. When Duncan finally thought to reach behind him, his fingertips brushed the wall's footings, but by then it was too late. With a gentle *plop*, the slime closed over his face.

*

"Any particular reason why you waited three days to report this?" the elderly police officer asked.

"I haven't been here since last Friday evening," Vicki Anderson said. "Apparently there was some kind of scene, though – Mrs Gray thought he'd stormed off."

The policeman zipped up his anorak. It was almost December, and squalling rain and wind was blowing across the Halvergate Marshes. "He wouldn't have wandered off the road, would he? In the dark?"

"I'm afraid I can't say. I only met him once … for a couple

of minutes."

"And how's young Marissa holding up?"

"She has her mother to comfort her."

"Yes ..." The officer didn't look too encouraged by that. "Well, obviously we'll be in touch if we learn anything ... but Mr Mackintyre is not what we'd class as a vulnerable person. I'm afraid it can't be a priority for long."

"I understand."

He climbed into his patrol car and waved from its window as he drove away along the pebbled drive. Vicki went back inside, ensuring to close the new front door behind her. She paused before entering the lounge, where Marissa, wearing a dressing gown and slippers, was sitting on the sofa, pensively sipping coffee. Her mother, who was standing by the fireplace, saw the housekeeper in the doorway and came over to join her.

"A sad business," Vicki muttered.

"He obviously wasn't right for her," Leticia replied dismissively. "Young men of that sort. He won't be the first to have run from commitment."

Vicki looked sceptical, but merely asked: "How is she?"

"She'll be fine ... she has her family. What more could she need?"

Henry Gray smiled benignly down from over the mantel. A few yards to his right stood the rocking horse. Also in a place of honour: dusted, polished, retouched with paint. And permanently fixed in its brand new concrete base.

EXPLODING RAPHAELESQUE HEADS

Ian Hunter

It was in Scotland of all places that I saw the painting; those few months when I was rattling around Europe, cramming in as much culture as I could as if it was about to be rationed to us Americans, or the world was coming to an end and this would all be rubble, while we were dust. It was in the Scottish National Gallery in Edinburgh, a big grey, temple-like building with imposing pillars, which sat at the bottom of a small hill they called the Mound, below the old houses that stretched up and down the Royal Mile from the castle to the palace down at the other end.

I came round the corner, eyes drifting between the brochure in my hand and the paintings on the wall, when suddenly there it was, a section devoted to Salvador Dali. Although they didn't have much in the way of exhibits and things started with various black and white photographs of the man himself taken at different times during his life, but all seemed to show him with wide eyes and eyebrows raised, either in a questioning or condescending pose. In many his moustache was tapered to two deadly points. One photograph showed those points skewering two flowers, in another they were curled upwards, climbing over his cheeks, ready to impale his eyes. In some photographs, he was standing beside famous people. I recognised Harpo Marx, Alfred Hitchcock, Sonny Bono, John Lennon, even Raquel Welch, and Alice Cooper.

It was obviously a bit of a thing to have your picture taken with Dali, but I have to confess that I didn't recognise Coco Chanel, although the little card below the photograph told me her name anyway. Sadly, the rhino Dali was almost kissing in one photo seemed to go unnamed, like the headless manikin he carried in another shot, as if the jointed dummy was his dead, robot bride from a bad 50s B movie.

My kind of stuff.

Walking on, the blizzard of photographs ended and the small exhibition started with his painting *Oiseau* or *Bird* to you and me. What was it about? It looked like the skeletal remains of a dead bird, almost prehistoric, decaying on a beach, with part of the body missing to reveal the corpse of a young bird inside. Then there were a couple of sketches of things that looked like skeletons adorned with various pieces of meat. Entrails and sausages, steaks and cuts. Next came a storyboard for a proposed film on surrealism and a proper painting called *Le Signal de l'angoisee – The Signal of Anguish* – depicting a woman who was naked, except for a pair of stockings, standing in a strange landscape being watched by someone you couldn't really see through the square window of the building behind her. It was disconcerting, it was creepy, it made you stop and look back at the painting to see if the watcher had stepped forward, revealing themselves, but, no, they always stayed in the shadows.

And that was good, that was something out of left field, which couldn't be topped, or so I thought, but I was wrong. They had kept the best for last. Kept it for me, because it changed my life forever.

Tête Raphaëlesque éclatée.

Exploding Raphaelesque Head.

If you don't know it, Dali's painting was inspired by the bombing of Hiroshima and uses a classic Madonna-like pose typical of the Renaissance artist, Raphael, but has the head fragmenting. Some of these fragments looked like pieces of twisted silver. Flesh turned to metal, possibly transformed by the alchemy of nuclear forces, while the splitting parts around her neck are darker, almost stone-like, but in strange, sharp, conical, wriggling shapes that resemble shapes seen in some of Dali's other work. This may be a painting depicting the instant after the explosion, still head-like before it shatters in a thousand different directions, as the woman looks down, demurely, almost in prayer.

Exploding Raphaelesque Heads

I couldn't take my eyes off it. I stood staring, oblivious to the other people who flowed behind me, tried to get in front of me for a better look, but I denied them with my closeness to the canvas. Eventually, after several minutes had passed and my eyes had finished taking in every square centimetre of the canvas, I snapped out of my reverie and spoke to a member of the gallery staff. I made some vague, rambling enquiries about buying the painting, which were instantly laughed off, until I insisted that I had the money to buy it if they named their price. That received a more hesitant, less certain laugh, which attracted the attention of some security staff who stood in the corners, hands behind their backs, watching my every move until I went to the shop in the Gallery. There I bought all the books I could find with Dali's work in them. They even had a few tacky products inspired by the very painting that dominated my thoughts. A jigsaw, a tea towel, various notebooks, a shopping bag. I've added a few tacky products of my own over the years, all with a production run of one. Some I've commissioned from other artists, some I've made myself. If you ever come to my house, which is admittedly highly unlikely, you will see two walls covered in a reproduction of that exploding head. It also adorns my bedroom ceiling. I try to make it the last thing I see at night and the first thing I see in the morning keeping my eyes firmly closed until I am in position to gaze up at it.

But all of these things, they are never enough.

After I had made my mind up, after I had foolishly thought I was ready, my first subject was male, in his thirties, found sleeping rough beneath the pier – what was I thinking about? I almost died. He spat at me as soon as I took the tape off his mouth, struggling violently in the chair I had tied him to, trying to rock from side to side before he fell over. I've seen enough movies to know if that happened he would break the chair and be on me. I thought I could get the grenade into his mouth when he was shouting. It wouldn't fit, and I had already pulled the pin. We both had about five seconds. I dropped the grenade under his chair and dived behind one of the blast walls I had constructed in my special studio. There wasn't much left of him, and what was left, wasn't pretty, and was, well, everywhere. Wrong, wrong, wrong and I thought my ear drums had burst with the noise.

My second subject was a homeless man and this time things went slightly better. I drugged him and took out all his teeth with the help of a hammer and some pliers, and managed to squeeze the grenade into his ruined mouth in plenty of time, especially with the pin protruding outwards. Still, what a mess. Grenades were clearly not the answer, but at least the money I splashed on state of the art earplugs, connected to a digital processor, was money well spent.

My third subject was a male hitchhiker. I killed him first – how? Well, that doesn't matter, but it was better he was dead as I had started to experiment with different kinds of explosives and wanted to make things as simple as possible. This time I used ammonia gelatin, placed in the mouth. Again, messy, but not without potential.

The fourth subject was an old beggar, and an old boozer too. I used Semtex this time, obtained from shadowy contacts of a guerilla artist I know. This time I tried a different, more ambitious place to put the explosive, namely inside the skull. I should have been a surgeon, instead of the third waster son of a logging tycoon. I'm good at this. I shaved some of the old man's hair off, before peeling back the scalp, and sawing through the bone, and then again and again at different angles until I was able to pull out a rough circle of skull before removing part of the brain. Too much Semtex was an obvious, beginner's mistake and I also noted that I needed to remove more of the brain in future.

By now, I'd learned all I could from the men. I didn't need them anyway; they were just practice. Dali's painting is the fragmenting head of a woman. Killing these male subjects first had made things easier from a planning and preparation point of view, but from now on, it was going to be women only, and they would all be dead if possible. At peace, serene. Madonna-like.

The fifth subject was my first female, and my brilliant idea was to try and take the top of her skull out from inside her head, and make it easier to explode and come apart. It took hours to achieve anything like the desired effect, leaving me exhausted with another mess on my bloody, gloved hands. What was there before the explosion didn't even resemble a head very much, so you can imagine what was left afterwards.

From now on, the skull would have to stay.

My sixth subject was a drug addict, and I went back to basics with the hole in the top of her head and a slightly lower amount of plastic explosive. Not enough for the desired effect, but getting there.

A woman possibly in her early thirties was my seventh subject. It was hard to tell her age. She'd clearly had it tough by the state of her, so in a way I was doing her a favour. I picked her up by the old bus station. Sadly, I over compensated with the explosive charge, and her head sort of imploded, collapsed in on itself, totally the wrong result, possibly due to where I placed it within her skull, I would need to do much better next time.

Now it was time to go up a gear, time to find a different sort of woman. Three at most, I hoped. Two to practise on and the third would be the charm. Sad, but true, and I'm not being insincere, not really, but none of my female test subjects so far could be classified as 'lookers', not after the drugs and the booze and the abuse have worn them down. Two out of three have had broken noses and all have cheeks riddled with broken blood vessels.

Victim number eight was a high school beauty and a real test of my mettle.

Her youth and good looks gave her some of the qualities of the subject in the Dali Painting, which strangely off-putting. What a set of lungs she had as well, constantly screaming the place down. Even though my place is out in the country and my studio well hidden within the depths of the estate I still kept her drugged at the end. Glued her eyes shut, and puffed up her lips slightly with collagen filler. She was almost perfect, almost.

Ninth victim was me being really stupid and acting on impulse after finding a woman at the side of the road, trying to get her car to start. Anyone could have come along and seen me. Seen us. Anyone. What an idiot I can be at times, although I did take care to push her car down one of the old forest tracks and saw it tumbling between the trees towards the old lake where it should be rusting at the bottom. I was also pleased to note the similarities to the Dali painting when I slowed down the film I have been taking of all my explosions, slowed it down to almost frame by frame, the incandescent Hiroshima moment.

For my tenth victim I scoured a lot of online model agencies until I found the ideal woman to hire, being very careful to cover my tracks for when she was inevitably reported as missing. That face. That nose. Those lips, they hardly needed filler at all.

As for the curve of her eyebrows? Well it was divine. The hair wasn't, of course, but still you can't have everything. Crucially, her hair was longer than I needed it to be, but I still had to be very careful when I cut it, very careful when I styled it. I wasn't even really sure if she needed to be alive when I did all that. Not being sure, I thought it better to drug her then wash and cut her hair. Shame I had to cut into her scalp to plant my little charges.

Now it is perfect. She is perfect. Head and neck severed from her body and carefully mounted. Drained of blood. Lips perfectly full. Eyes closed, head angled downwards, Hole cut out of the top of the head with an angled light source shining down from above. I know the angle isn't going to mirror Dali's exactly, but I don't want anyone to see the Semtex placed inside her. Now there are six cameras pointing at the head.

136

Exploding Raphaelesque Heads

One from each side. One from above. One slightly below, looking up as she looks down.

Dali would be proud of me.

THE BEST CHRISTMAS EVER

John Llewellyn Probert

"Your brother is useless!"

Dr David Mainwaring paused at the bottom of the staircase and turned to see his wife beckoning to him from the drawing room. Whatever it was she wanted to discuss, it was obviously intended to be out of earshot of the children, who were still unwrapping their Christmas presents in the lounge. He took off the overcoat he had only just put on and hung it on the polished pine newel post as calmly as he could manage.

"What's the matter now?" he said, following her beckoning form into the silence of the oak-panelled room. Once inside and with the door safely closed, Mainwaring turned to smile at his wife. Even when she was angry Madeleine was very attractive, and the glare in her flinty blue eyes this morning offset the silver tinsel that she had arranged meticulously in her hair to perfection.

"Look at this!" she hissed, thrusting a brightly coloured box at him.

It was much heavier than Mainwaring was expecting, and he found himself having to support the brightly coloured cardboard oblong with two hands. He looked down to see a cartoon of a smiling young man in overalls wielding a spanner. Above the picture the words 'Junior Tool Set' had been arranged haphazardly in garish multi-coloured lettering, presumably to increase the appeal of the product to its target age group.

"Isn't it ridiculous?" Madeleine snapped, tapping with a manicured index finger at the writing on the side of the box.

"'Daddy will be soooo jealous!'" David read the words, in yet more colourful lettering, before moving onto print that was far more formal, tiny and almost illegible that it had to be important. "'A bumper pack of fifty-five real but child-sized metal tools in a sturdy wooden box, suitable for ages eight and over. Use only with adult supervision.'" He looked up at his wife. "Well, Stephen's nine, so what's the problem?"

Madeleine rolled her eyes and tapped the picture on the front of the box again. "They're real tools, David," she said. "Look – there's a real saw and a real hammer. Those are real chisels." She pointed to an admittedly dangerous looking pair of metal pincers. "And God knows what those are for."

"They're pliers," David said, still nonplussed at his wife's reaction, and actually rather surprised that Roger had managed to come up with something age-appropriate for at least one of his children this year. Last time, he had given Stephen a colouring book suitable for a three-year-old, and Tabitha, who had just turned seven three days ago, had received a book on fashion design.

"They're dangerous," his wife seethed. "Didn't we always agree that we wouldn't allow the children toys they could hurt themselves with? Nothing that could encourage them to think of violence as play? No guns, no swords, nothing that exploded or made loud noises, no violent video games, and most definitely nothing that they could cut themselves with."

David nodded wearily as Madeleine went through the list. Of course he agreed with her on principle, but it had made getting presents for the kids occasionally difficult, and frequently very dull.

"It does say 'Use only with adult supervision'," he said. "And I don't mind being the one who does the supervising. He's going to need to learn about these things sooner or later and I'd rather help him now than learn that the first thing he's done at university is cut his own finger off with a chisel."

Madeleine sighed. "Stephen shouldn't need to learn any of that," she said. "Hopefully the school we are paying a considerable amount of money for him to go to will ensure that he leaves with sufficient qualifications to be able to pay people to do those kinds of jobs."

The 'we' was not lost on David. Madeleine's involvement with the family finances always tended to be the opposite of contributory, her taste for a new pair of shoes every week and the absence of any gainful employment being the two main subtractive factors in the Mainwaring family's financial equation.

"Has it occurred to you that he might want to do it as a hobby?" he said, as calmly as he could. "Boys like doing things with their hands, you know. I wouldn't have dreamed of trying to become a surgeon if I didn't know I had some degree of manual dexterity beforehand."

Madeleine took the box from him, laid it on the ground, and grasped his right hand in both of her own. "There's a world of difference between transplanting a kidney and putting up some shelves," she said.

"True," David replied. "But you have to start somewhere. I honestly don't have a problem with this, Madeleine." He looked at his watch. "And now I'd better get going or I'll be late."

"Are there really that many patients on the ward on Christmas Day?" she asked.

Her husband shook his head. "But if there's even only one I need to go and see how they're doing. After all, no one really wants to be in hospital over Christmas." He kissed her cheek. "Hopefully I'll be home by lunchtime."

"You'd better be," Madeleine replied. "Fortnum and Mason's didn't drop off that turkey yesterday for nothing, and Mary wasn't up all last night preparing it so you could let it go cold."

Mary was their housekeeper. Childless and alone, at sixty-eight she had been happy to spend her Christmas Eve preparing the Mainwaring family's Yuletide feast before being given the today off.

"Did you remember to give Mary her Christmas bonus before she left?" David asked.

Madeleine looked aghast as she remembered the envelope sitting on the mantelpiece. "Oh my God, I completely forgot," she said. "That's probably why she stomped off in a huff an

140

hour ago."

"Yes, it probably is," said David, relieved he was going into work and would be spared his wife's indifference to everything but herself for a couple of hours. "I suppose we can give it to her at New Year."

"Then she'll have something to spend in the sales." Madeleine beamed as if the whole thing was some kind of thoughtful act dreamed up entirely by her.

"I suppose she will." If she comes back to work at all, David thought.

"Well if she's unhappy we can always get a new one." To Madeleine other people's lives existed merely to make hers more comfortable. "We could ask the Pendleton's where they got theirs."

"And when would we do that?"

His wife's face assumed the indignant expression of a spoilt child who has been told that their favourite hamster has just died. "Oh, for God's sake, David! Surely you remember that we're having dinner there tonight! It took me ages to sort out a babysitter while you were swanning around in your hospital being important."

Which meant the first call she had made had been successful, otherwise he would have had to deal with it. "Who's coming round?" he asked.

"That fat girl from the village. You know the one – a bit slow but she seems to be good with the children."

David didn't bother to tell his wife off for being rude because there was no point. "You mean Sophie," he said. Sophie was nineteen and worked behind the bar at the Coach and Horses, which was probably as far as she was going to get in life before marrying and discharging several similarly simple children into the world.

"Sophie, Sukie, something like that," said Madeleine. "Anyway, she'll be here at seven and we need to be ready to go by then."

Which means you'll be ready about an hour later, David

thought, opening the drawing room door and grabbing his coat. Madeleine followed him out as he went into the lounge to say goodbye to the children.

They both looked up as he entered. Dark-haired Stephen was putting together the Mousetrap game his grandmother had given him, while little blonde Tabitha was sitting cross-legged beside the tree, colouring in a picture of a fairy princess using her new box of crayons. Even though he was late, David couldn't help but marvel at how quickly his son had managed to put together the intricate plastic pieces.

"You've done a fantastic job there," he said, crouching down by the boy.

Stephen looked at him, all smiles and sunshine next to the baubles and decorations of the tree. "Will you play with me, daddy?"

David felt his heartstrings being tugged as he replied. "Not right now. But I promise I will when I get back from the hospital, okay?"

"Okay." David tried not to take the boy's despondent reply to heart too much.

"Daddy! Daddy!" that was Tabitha. "Come and look at what I've done."

David leaned over to inspect his little girl's handiwork. As he did, his daughter coughed and wrinkled her nose.

"What's that smell, daddy?"

He grinned at that and looked up at Madeleine. "That's the aftershave your mummy bought me for Christmas," he said. "I'm glad I'm not the only one who thinks it's a bit overpowering."

"What does overpowering mean?" Stephen asked, putting down a tiny green plastic hammer.

David made the children giggle by pretending to be knocked out before kissing them both goodbye. At the front door Madeleine stopped him and once again she didn't look happy.

"All right," she said, glowering. "I know you didn't like my present, but there's no need to joke about it in front of the children!"

"Oh for goodness' sake, Maddy." Now he was getting exasperated. "It was just a bit of fun with the kids. It's nice aftershave really."

"No it isn't," she said. "I can tell you hate it. Well, don't worry, I'll take it back to the shop on Monday and get something I can appreciate instead."

If there was an appropriate way to handle her outburst, David was way past the point of caring, and he closed the front door behind him with a slam.

*

The doorbell rang just as Madeleine was about to throw David's aftershave into the kitchen bin. It was Mr Pople, their next-door neighbour. Mr Pople was a retired clergyman who insisted on 'popping round' at the least excuse. He was a widower and lived on his own and it was for this reason that the one tiny piece of Madeleine's heart that was not made of selfish stone relented and let him in.

"Well, well, well, and what's going on here then?" said the little, bespectacled man as he beheld the children and their scattering of presents.

"It's Christmas," said Tabitha, presumably just in case the poor man was unaware of the date.

"Indeed it is," said Mr Pople, focusing his attention on the little girl. Behind her, Stephen concentrated even harder on the instructions for the model kit he had been given, hoping it would make him more invisible. "And what is special about Christmas Day?"

"We get presents," Tabitha replied, all wide-eyed and innocent.

"And?" Mr Pople had to wait a little while for the answer he wanted, and only eventually got to hear it because Stephen whispered it in Tabitha's ear.

"Baby Jesus?" Tabitha said, looking around to see where

this new distraction Stephen had told her about might be.

"That's right." Mr Pople was smiling now. All was right with the world because a seven-year-old had remembered one of the guiding principles of his doctrine. Satisfied with her for the moment, he turned his attention to Stephen.

"So how are things going in school, Stephen?" he asked.

"Very well, thank you." Stephen was only nine, but he was already aware that honesty was not necessarily the best policy in such situations. Tabitha was yet to learn this essential fact of life.

"I don't like school," she piped up, with a shake of her little blonde head.

Mr Pople looked taken aback, as if such a thing was impossible. "Well, why ever not?" he asked.

"Just don't," she replied with the degree of elaboration one tends to expect from a seven-year-old.

That wasn't good enough for Mr Pople. "Well you must learn to like it," said the vicar. "School is where you learn about things, where you make friends, where you make something of yourself."

"Archie Parsons smells," said the little girl, quite inexplicably before throwing down her crayons and going in search of her mother.

She didn't have to go far. Madeleine Mainwaring was just coming back in from the kitchen.

"Something smells delicious, Mrs Mainwaring," said the vicar.

"Thank you," said Madeleine, before realising what he might be angling for, "we've got relatives coming for lunch and I'm already worried there might not be enough to go round." Whatever her failings, David Mainwaring's wife had always been very good at thinking on her feet.

"You know," said Mr Pople, swiftly changing the subject to avoid the embarrassment that would be worse than death for a man of his background and upbringing, "I could have sworn when I came in you were carrying a bottle of aftershave in there."

"Oh, it was a Christmas present for David," she replied, looking sheepish. "But we both decided it was a bit overpowering so I've left it by the sink to remind me in case Uncle Roger would like it when he comes round."

"Uncle Roger! Uncle Roger!" Tabitha started bouncing up and down in a display of enthusiasm that even she herself would have been embarrassed by were she any older.

Madeleine just smiled and nodded. She would get out of that particular lie to the children once the vicar had gone.

Mr Pople, however, had turned his attention back to Stephen, who was busy taking the Mousetrap game to pieces to see if he could rebuild it differently.

"You know," said the old man, pointing at the brightly coloured pieces of plastic, "that's what your daddy does."

That caused Stephen to pause and look at the vicar as if the man had truly lost his marbles. "No he doesn't," he said.

"Oh, not with pieces of plastic that clip together of course," Mr Pople continued, "your Daddy does it with real people."

This merely served to confuse Stephen even further, and he gave the vicar a blank look, so Mr Pople tried a different approach.

"Your Daddy takes people apart and then puts them together again, so that they are better than they were before. Of course he has to use a lot of special tools to help him, but he's the clever one." He ruffled the boy's hair to Stephen's immediate irritation. "Maybe you'll be like your dad one day, eh? And then everyone in the town will be as proud of you as they are of him. You'd like that, wouldn't you?"

"Of course he would, Mr Pople," said Madeleine, using her taking control of the situation voice. "But first, little children have to wash their hands, don't they? If they're going to be nice and tidy and ready to eat Christmas lunch by the time Daddy gets back?"

The two children scampered off to the bathroom. Having been unsuccessful in getting Mr Pople to leave by that method,

Madeleine decided to employ less subtle means.

"You'd better get going, Mr Pople, or you'll be late for your lunch."

"Oh, I'm not having anything special," said the vicar, not moving even a single encouraging inch towards the front door.

Madeleine grabbed him by the shoulders and forcibly turned him round. "Well, we have a lot to do so we'll have to continue this lovely chat another time," she said, almost having to manhandle him out of the room. The vicar paused by the front door. Almost as if he were desperate to find any excuse not to leave, he spotted the brightly coloured cardboard box that David had put by the door on his way out.

"My, what a wonderful tool set!" Mr Pople said, deliberately loud enough that the children should hear. "I think there's a very lucky boy in this house who's going to make a lot of very fine things with this."

"Actually we think it's too dangerous," said Madeleine, opening the front door and willing the little man through it. "See you soon, Mr Pople." It was an admission of inevitability rather than an invitation, not that the vicar probably saw it that way as he bade her good day and set off into the chilly December morning.

*

David was back by one, by which time Madeleine had managed to arrange the food that the shop had produced, and Mary had prepared, to the extent that she felt able to claim responsibility for it all. With the family fed and the washing up left for the housekeeper, it was only a couple of hours before Madeleine began bleating about getting ready to go out.

As David had predicted, Sophie arrived at dead on seven, while Madeleine was still in the shower.

"Hello, Dr Mainwaring." The babysitter greeted him with a bovine smile, as he opened the door wide to admit her ungainly bulk. The girl waddled into the lounge and demonstrated her ability to hug both children to the extent that they almost seemed to disappear within the substance of her being. Slightly breathless after their release from the confines of Sophie's folds, Tabitha went back to her new junior sewing set while Stephen returned to his attempts to create something surreal out of his Mousetrap game.

"What are you doing there, son?" David asked, doing his best to ignore Sophie's rasping breathing coming from the sofa behind him.

The little boy shook his head. "Don't know yet," he replied. "I want to make something special."

"Well you're doing a very good job of it," said David, putting a hand on his shoulder. "You know, you're a clever lad. I bet you can make something really special with just what's in this room."

His son's eyes brightened. "Do you really think so, Daddy?"

"Oh yes," said David, encouraged by his son's response. "I hope to see something very impressive indeed when we come back."

Stephen glanced around the room, his eye caught something for a second, and then he was looking at his father again. "You will, Daddy," he said. "I promise."

"And remember," David got to his feet. "That toolset that Uncle Roger got you is only to be used when?"

Stephen looked down at the carpet, even if he was quick with the answer. "When an adult is watching," he said, as if he had been denied the keys to that particular kingdom.

"Good boy," said David as he heard his wife managing to clump down the stairs and complain about her earrings at the same time. "We'll be back around eleven," he said to Sophie, who gave as much of a nod of acknowledgment as was possible considering the amount of fat that occupied the space between her chin and her chest.

The couple said goodbye to the children and left. As the front door was closing, Stephen looked up at Sophie.

"Are you an adult?" he asked.

*

David and Madeleine were back later than they had promised, but it was Christmas, and the Pendletons had been so generous with the alcohol that it would have been rude if they had left just as the second bottle of Campari was being brought out. David paid the taxi driver with notes of an indiscriminate and blurred denomination that made the man smile broadly enough to suggest that a terrible and unrectifiable mistake had been made, but he would worry about that in the morning.

The lights were off in the hallway, the lounge door was closed, and it was very quiet.

"I wonder why Sophie's not watching TV," said David as he struggled with the door chain.

"She's probably asleep," said Madeleine, loud enough to wake even the most comatose of hippopotami. "She's probably polished off all the leftovers from lunch. I'm so pissed I'm going to bed." She began to make her way upstairs. "Good luck dragging that girl out of your armchair," she said.

"Don't forget to say goodnight to the children," David called, trying to keep his voice down. They would probably be asleep, but if not, he knew they would want Mummy and Daddy to say goodnight to them.

Numerous glasses of wine, port and Campari had rendered David's eye-hand coordination non-existent, and Madeleine was out of view by the time he managed to secure the lock.

He was just about to open the lounge door when Madeleine came thundering back down the stairs, tripping on the last but one and falling into David's arms.

"Steady on," he said.

"The children," Madeleine mumbled, her breath strong enough to render him twice as intoxicated as he was already. "The children, they're not there!"

"Nonsense," David mumbled. "You probably went into the wrong room, that's all."

"I'm not that drunk," said Madeleine, swaying to indicate that oh yes, she was. "I'm telling you they're not there!"

David was about to check for himself when the silence was interrupted by what sounded like the grating buzz of an electric drill coming into contact with something hard.

It was coming from the lounge.

David's eyes widened in horror, and they widened still further once he had managed to get the lounge door open. By then of course, Madeleine had already fainted.

Sophie was where they had left her, but now heavy-duty nails had been hammered through her wrists to keep them in place on the arms of the chair. Despite the fact that her eyes were open, the eyelids stitched back to her face to prevent them from closing, there was nothing to suggest that she was still alive.

She was not the only dead thing in the room.

David's horrified gaze swept from the pinioned, dead fat girl to the space beside the Christmas tree. It had been cleared of all toys, and a sheet, that until very recently had been white, lain upon the carpet. The red stains and splotches, along with the clumps of blonde hair scattered across it were upsetting enough, but were nowhere near as horrifying as the gruesome centrepiece.

Parts of it were Tabitha, parts of it were Stephen's Mousetrap game, and parts of it were the leftover turkey carcass from lunchtime. The pieces had been assembled seemingly randomly but in an approximate pyramid shape. On the very top of the bloody pile was the fairy off the top of the Christmas tree.

A bloodstained Stephen put down the power drill. His eyes lit up as he saw his Daddy enter the room.

"Hello, Daddy," he said, before instantly registering that his father was less than happy with what he had done. "I'm sorry I made a bit of a mess," he said, doing his best to look apologetic. "But please don't worry about Tabitha. I just wanted to see if I could make something of her, just like the vicar said. And I did use anaesthetic, like they do at the hospital."

Down by Stephen's feet he saw the empty bottle of the aftershave he had described as 'overpowering', and next to it, lying on its side with the cap missing, a bottle of bleach. "I used most of the aftershave on Sophie but it didn't work very well so I used bleach, on some cotton wool and stuffed into her nose and throat like on the telly. Tabitha wouldn't keep still so I had to hit her on the head with the hammer, but after that she behaved herself and she was all right about everything."

Stephen picked up the plastic blue bleach bottle with fingers encrusted with gore and held it out for David to see. "It says it kills all known germs dead, but Tabitha isn't a germ, so I knew it would only stun her."

The only sound David could make was a croak as he took a step forward.

"I'm sorry, Daddy," said Stephen, realising his father was less impressed than the little boy had hoped for. "I'll go to bed if you want me to, but I did promise Tabitha I'd put her all back together again when I was finished, just like you do when you make people better." When that did little to alter his father's expression the little boy added, "And you did say an adult had to be watching so that's what Sophie's doing for us. Hello, Sophie!" he waved at the girl's blank sagging face. "Sophie's been very quiet for most of the evening as well. Mummy said the aftershave would overpower her but the chisel in her neck worked much better at stopping her making all those noises. I promise I'll tidy it all up tomorrow, but could I just have five more minutes, please? I don't want today to stop." He wiped clotted blood from his face, picked up the saw, and smiled angelically. "Thank you, Daddy," he said. "This has been the Best Christmas Ever!"

Dedicated to Sir Charles Birkin

THE PYGMALION CONJURATION

Mike Chinn

His breathing slows and vision blurs. He gazes up one last time at the magnificent creature rearing over him. She is everything he'd ever wanted in a woman; she is all women. His women. It's so unfair, he thinks …

*

Sex magick!

From the moment Dennis Crawleigh heard that phrase, he couldn't get it out of his head. It reverberated in his subconscious like an echo of promise. *Sex magick.* What was it? How did it work? Was it some hocus-pocus to get young and attractive women into bed? Just to get young and attractive young women to notice he had a pulse would be something …

Sex magick …

To be fair, Dennis wasn't a bad-looking man. But on the wrong side of thirty, with his fine blond hair becoming a memory, he could just reach the lofty heights of five feet on tiptoe and he'd been wearing the same glasses for twenty-five years. He owned a house – left to him by an aunt – but remained determinedly unemployed. Dennis had little confidence in himself, and even less belief that any woman would consider him more than a distant friend. Any kind of short cut was welcome.

And sex magick …

It took just over a week for him to be bitterly disappointed. A search of the Internet on the local library's computers soon disabused him of all his eager fantasies. It seemed that sex magick was, in reality, just an excuse for people to strip off and get busy – all the while pretending to be part of some powerful ritual. Dennis wasn't surprised to discover that Aleister Crowley – of whom he'd heard – had been a strong

151

supporter of the idea. Crowley had been, Dennis was certain, just a dirty old man with a persuasive tongue. He quite envied him.

However, it left Dennis feeling quite deflated. No magick was ever going to get him a girlfriend; never mind sex. There was Rohypnol, of course, but he didn't think he'd ever be that desperate …

The matter would have rested there, if it hadn't been for the dream Dennis had one Friday night after he'd gone to bed with a bellyful of budget lager sitting on top of two rounds of cheese on toast. He found himself in a dark, misty place, surrounded by vague, flowing shapes on which he could never quite focus. He wandered for an aimless period, sure that he should be scared, but instead feeling curiously excited. Eventually the mists parted and revealed an imposing figure sitting on what looked like a giant red and purple mushroom. It was a man with a penetrating stare, a vaguely supercilious smile, and what looked like an embroidered seat cushion jammed on his large, bald head. The smile broadened into a leering grin at Dennis's approach, and the man lowered his head slightly. His eyes seemed to glow.

"You were right, you know," he said. His voice sounded flat and muffled – as though coming from the bottom of a large, padded box.

"I was?" Dennis blinked. "What about?"

"The sex magick." The man winked slowly. "Just like you thought …"

"Eh …?"

The distant, muffled voice sighed patiently in Dennis's ear. The bald man was standing next to him, a friendly arm thrown across Dennis's shoulders. "There are … rituals which, when performed correctly, bring about – how can I put this …?"

"Me having sex?" Dennis suggested.

The man sighed wearily. "Quite. But it will take patience, diligence and hard work …"

Dennis shuffled. Sensing his reluctance, the man patted his

shoulder and hugged him closer. "Oh, nothing you can't handle, old chap. I'm sure the apple hasn't fallen *that* far from the tree."

"Apple?" Dennis was losing the thread.

The man sighed again and began thumbing through a huge, brassbound leather tome that hadn't been there a moment earlier. "Crawleigh ... Crowley – do you think a letter here or there makes a difference? Do pay attention, old man!" He stabbed a finger at a dense paragraph of illuminated script that looked like no language Dennis had ever seen. "Page six hundred and sixty-six—" He sniggered.

Dennis felt himself pushed closer to the massive page; he could smell its incredible age. From somewhere above him he just made out the muffled words: "Read, mark, learn and inwardly digest – that's what my old form master always said. Pathetic old queen. Still, he had a point." The hand on Dennis's shoulder slipped down his back – briefly cupping his backside. "Do what thou wilt shall be the whole of the law—"

Dennis awoke with an aching bladder and the thick smell of rot in his nostrils.

*

The dream stubbornly refused to fade as the day trudged on. If anything, it grew more real – becoming a genuine memory. Dennis could not only still smell that decaying old book, he could visualise it perfectly. The heavy black leather cover; the grotesquely ornate brass fittings; the heavy pages – too stiff and thick for paper – with their chewed corners and cracking edges ... Even its title: *Incantamenta Et Ad Voluptatem Et Lucrum.* Not that he had a blue clue what that meant, but it sounded ... promising ...

Dennis headed for the local library. He was pretty well known there: Miss Grant – the Chief Librarian – had shown him how to use the Internet when he'd first started researching magick. As he walked in, she glanced up from her computer and smiled at him. She always had a smile for Dennis; it was one reason he felt relaxed in her company – that and the fact she was probably old enough to be his mother.

"Mr Crawleigh." She peered over glasses that were even more old-fashioned than Dennis's. "Can I help?"

"I'm trying to find something out about an old book." He fished a slip of paper out of his pocket and placed it on the counter in front of her. He'd printed the Latin title as neatly as he could from memory, not at all confident of the pronunciation. Miss Grant picked up the paper, pushed up her glasses and read the words; her brow puckered slightly.

"A little different from your normal reading, Mr Crawleigh," she commented, handing him back the slip.

He shrugged self-consciously, cramming the paper away. "I was just wondering if you could tell me anything about it … I don't imagine the library has a copy."

She smiled again. "I don't imagine so, either, Mr Crawleigh." But she tapped at her keyboard, staring with more brow-creased intensity at her screen. After a few seconds she exclaimed softly.

"That's a very rare volume, Mr Crawleigh. Unique, even. The only copy in Britain is at the British Library in London."

Dennis's hopes drained. Of course it was; and he had no intention of wasting money traipsing all the way down to London just because of some dream. It was so unfair—

He became aware that Miss Grant was looking at him again. "Crowley," she said.

"Beg pardon?"

"Aleister Crowley. The Wickedest Man in England, they called him …"

"Yes …" There was a very cold draught suddenly blowing down Dennis's back. "What about him …?"

"The copy in the British Library once belonged to him – or so it says here. It was given to the Library in 1950 – three years after his death – along with other volumes and a variety of papers." Behind the glass lenses, Miss Grant's eyes twinkled. "Have you taken a sudden interest in the Great Beast, Mr Crawleigh?" She tapped a finger against the side of her nose and smiled. "Don't worry – your secret's safe with me …"

Dennis tried not to huff – this was getting him nowhere. "I can't get to London—!" he began.

Miss Grant pointed over his shoulder at a cluster of computers filling a space that had once contained bookshelves. "The Internet, Mr Crawleigh …"

Of course! He laughed softly. "Never thought of that …"

She returned to her own work and Dennis sat himself back down at a console. Entering *Incantamenta Et Ad Voluptatem Et Lucrum* into the search engine produced dozens of hits. He selected the first, and there it was: an image of the book from his dream. Every creased page, scratched brass hinge and scuffed leather cover. He'd found it!

He started to read the on-screen notes.

The first thing he learned was that the authenticity of the *Incantamenta Et Ad Voluptatem Et Lucrum* was in some doubt: not a few experts considered it a hoax perpetrated by Crowley (him again, thought Dennis) a century or so back. Most of the book was given over to a variety of spells or rituals, the majority of which – Dennis wasn't surprised to discover with the help of a handy Latin-English translator – were to conjure wealth. Or create gold from base metals; or create jewels from simple stones; or how to find wealth; or how to summon a demon who would tell you where to find wealth, or how to create gold or jewels … Naturally in every case, the participants of the ritual had to perform it naked, and round it all off with a good old fashioned orgy. In all, pretty repetitive and unimaginative. If it was one of the Great Beast's jokes, it wasn't much of one; or perhaps back in the early twentieth century, sensibilities were more easily offended. Dennis began to think everything – the dream, book – was just a coincidence after all. Wish fulfilment, in a way.

Then he remembered the dream-Crowley mentioning a page

number ... what had it been ...? Something about it had amused the old man ...

"The number of the Beast!" Dennis laughed – much louder than he'd intended – earning him a *"Shh!"* off Miss Grant. Dennis mouthed an apology and went back to flipping pages on screen. Six hundred and sixty-six: 666. Dennis imagined that would have given Crowley a good belly laugh.

There was quite a dense block of text on page six hundred and sixty-six, followed by two more pages of what looked just like bullet points. Dennis highlighted the lot and ran it through the translator. It was another ritual – but not for the acquisition of gold or money, or any kind of riches. Entitled *The Pygmalion Conjuration*, it was to satisfy much older, baser lusts than wealth.

Dennis skimmed through the opening chunk of text: a very circuitous, verbose description of what the ritual was meant to achieve. But Dennis read between the over-written lines: any man or woman who could master the spell would be able to have whoever they wanted, whenever they wanted. *Real* sex magick. Dennis flopped back in his seat, staring at the screen. This was it! Exactly what he'd been looking for!

Dennis printed off all three pages, folded the sheets into his coat and closed down the Internet. He gave Miss Grant a cheery thumbs-up when she asked if he'd found what he was looking for – and headed home.

*

Dennis couldn't believe he was actually going to go through with the ritual. On the one hand, he was mortified that someone might find out; whilst on the other, curiosity had a hold of him: what if it worked? And if it didn't – well, he'd be the only one to know, and apart from feeling a bit of a prat, he'd be no worse off than he was now.

The ritual called for several items – he supposed they were talismanic – a sword, incense, candles, a knife, a wand, a small

156

pentacle and a vase. After thinking carefully for a while, he eventually came up with a toy light sabre he'd had since a kid (batteries dead), a packet of joss sticks left over from his teenage years, some shrivelled candles kept in the back of a kitchen cupboard for emergencies, a carving knife, a length of bamboo cane, and a pentacle carefully drawn on a sheet of paper. The vase, it turned out, was just for flowers. Carefully, he laid everything out neatly on the dining table.

The text was very particular about cleanliness, so the next morning he showered thoroughly. All day he drank nothing but glasses of water, and didn't eat a bite. As night drew in, feeling clean, fasted (and a little light-headed), Dennis was ready.

As per the instructions, he put on a clean bathrobe, lit the joss sticks and candles, placed the sheets of paper with the ritual on the dining table within easy reach, and picked up the bamboo wand. He wasn't sure whether he had to or not – the text was unclear – but it felt right. Taking a deep breath he began intoning the words in a suitably solemn voice, trying not to laugh. The syllables seemed to echo briefly, before fading away in an odd manner – but he may have imagined it. As he chanted he tried to visualise exactly what he expected out of the ritual; luckily, years of living alone had honed Dennis's imagination, and he found he could visualise it pretty well.

He saw women – beautiful, sexy women – arrayed before him, in varying degrees of undress. Woman from the TV, from movies, from newspapers and magazines – many of whom he couldn't put a name to, but he knew their faces intimately. And they were all looking at him with unrequited desire: he was the only thing in the whole world that they wanted. They smiled at him, eyes half-lidded; reached out their hands. He could almost hear their wanton pleas, smell their perfume, feel their touch …

When it was over, he dumped himself awkwardly on the carpet – almost collapsing – tired, his body sheened in sweat even though he was cold. Above everything else, he wanted a beer – but he was afraid that might sully the purity of the ritual.

He would wait. Tomorrow he'd see if the Pygmalion Conjuration had worked – see how many women he could … *will* into his bed. That was the word. *'Do what thou wilt shall be the whole of the law'* – he understood Crowley's famous maxim now.

*

The next day he could barely eat breakfast. His stomach was a writhing sack of butterflies, and all seemed to be wearing boots. Even though he was starving, all he could force down were half a round of toast and a mug of tea. Like a kid with a new toy, he had to get out and see if the ritual had worked. Discover if the Pygmalion Conjuration had granted him mastery over the women of the world …!

He dressed quickly, barely noticing what he was throwing on. Outside it was unseasonably cold; Dennis pulled up the collar of his coat, rammed hands into pockets and made for the park. He sat on a bench facing the duck pond and waited. And waited. Apart from two swans and a moorhen on the pond, he seemed to have the park all to himself. There was a tattered copy of a red-top newspaper abandoned on the bench beside him; he read it front to back whilst he waited. Still nothing. He folded the newspaper into a coat pocket, stood and walked to a coffee-stall just outside the park: he had no intention of freezing to death while he waited. Cradling the huge cardboard cup of the cheapest coffee on sale, he returned to his vigil.

The coffee was all gone when the first women approached. Both were in their mid-thirties, Dennis guessed – both a foot taller than him, one black with long, highlighted hair, the other white and blonde. Both gorgeous. They were laughing at some joke, heads together, oblivious of everyone and everything. All the better. As they passed Dennis's bench he fixed his eyes on them, willing them to turn and join him. To first share his bench, then agree to come home with him and share his bed. He put into it every bit of mental effort he could muster; sweat trickled down the side of his face despite the chilly air.

They kept on walking – didn't even so much as glance in his direction.

Dennis flopped against the bench's rigid back. Damn!

A girl – probably not far out of her teens – passed the receding women, coming straight towards Dennis. She was a little shorter, with pale brown hair halfway to her waist – dancing side to side like she was in a shampoo advert. Dennis closed his eyes and tried reaching out with his mind – feeling for her thoughts. Nothing. By the time he opened his eyes again, she was fifty yards down the path.

Damn! Damn! Damn! Damn! FUCK!

The next couple of hours unravelled slowly. Women and girls passed by – in increasing numbers as lunchtime hit – but he couldn't reach out or influence a single one. Mostly they ignored him – though one or two glanced nervously at him out of the corners of their eyes, before speeding up and vanishing. Eventually, he gave it up as a bad job; plus he thought it was increasingly likely someone might call the police. He stumped home: embarrassed and angry with himself for believing such stupidity. Had he grown so desperate – reached the Rohypnol stage after all? Obviously he had.

That night he sat in his battered chair, nursing a cheap lager and flipping morosely through the battered red-top newspaper, which he'd forgotten all about. He gazed at the picture of a half-naked model on one page, lost in a hopeless, bitter longing; and a familiar ache in his groin. Wishing that once – just once – a girl like that (or to be honest, even a fraction as sexy) would just say hello to him. Just once. Was that so much to ask? It was so unfair—

"Hello."

The word was spoken so softly that Dennis didn't hear it at first.

"Hello!"

He glanced up, almost dropping the part-drained can of lager. He did let the newspaper go, though – partly so he could get a better look. Standing in front of him, stiletto heels digging into his thinning carpet, was the model from the newspaper. Dennis blinked, looked first at the lager can and then at the girl. She was still there. Sexy and voluptuous and pouty.

"Hello, Dennis." Her voice was warm and husky – just like he'd imagined it would be. She had huge, honey-coloured eyes; her smile was wide and promising. He tried to say hello back, but his voice broke on the second syllable and all he managed was a strangled: *"Hell—"*

She dropped smoothly into his lap, her browned arms encircling his neck. She smelled vaguely resinous – some modern scent, he thought. Her breath was warm and tickled his ear as she whispered to him. When her mouth closed on his, Dennis finally let the lager can go.

*

He awoke with a start, looking around his bedroom. He was alone. Obviously last night had been a dream – another dream! But so detailed and memorable …! He pulled himself out of bed – a little surprised to find he was naked. He pulled on his bathrobe, jammed feet into slippers, and shuffled downstairs.

The old newspaper was scattered across half of the floor. Next to his chair the lager can was lying on its side, a wet patch leaked out across the carpet. Dennis sighed, vaguely disgusted at himself, and scooped up the sheets of newsprint. He was just about to screw it up when it occurred to him something was wrong. He leafed through the pages, finally reaching the one where the model's picture had been. There was a huge blank space – just the banner and a small square of inane text. The half-naked model herself was missing – or to be exact: her picture was missing.

Dennis dropped the paper back on the carpet. He dashed back up to his bedroom, seeing for the first time just how dishevelled his bed sheets were. He bent down; sniffed. Yes:

apart from the familiar odour of his own sweat there was the faintest, resinous scent. It hadn't been a dream. Dennis really had spent the night with a ... with a—

He sat heavily on his wrecked bed, head spinning.

"Fuck me," he whispered eventually. "It worked ...!"

*

Dennis had quite a collection of photographs and glossy mags. He picked out one magazine at random and flipped through the pages, finally settling on a full-page snap of a famous film beauty, taken five years earlier at Cannes. Dennis stared at her picture, wishing she was alive, wondering how she'd feel (he knew what her voice was like), how she'd smell. At some point – he couldn't pinpoint when – he was aware that her picture wasn't on the page any longer. But she was standing in his bedroom, smiling – warm and friendly.

"Hello ..." he just about managed.

"Hello, Dennis," she purred, and slithered to his side.

*

Dennis figured out the Pygmalion connection eventually: the mythical sculptor who brought a statue to life. Thanks to the ritual, he was doing it with photographs. All he needed was to want it enough, and he could summon a succession of gorgeous, willing, warm and full-blooded women. They didn't care about Dennis's lack of experience, his enthusiasm over patience. They were there for him, no matter what.

He found it didn't need to be a full-length picture, either: somehow, he – or the spell – created the entire woman. Even a black and white photo transmuted into natural flesh tones. The only downer was the original picture was gone forever and so – during his post-coital sleep – would be each woman. Dennis assumed they ceased to exist once he lost consciousness, but he didn't worry unduly about it. He had plenty of pictures. If

161

he woke up in the middle of the night in the mood for a little more fun, he could just shuffle out another photo and call up a new bed-partner.

Horror movie actresses preserved in their youthful prime in old books; singers as they'd been at the start of their careers, trapped on CD covers; newsreaders; weathergirls; celebs from lists A to Z who were simply famous for being famous (and wearing very little). If Dennis had a picture of them, there was no limit. (Though he quickly learned that attempting to enjoy the exaggerated voluptuousness of cartoon characters was a step too far). How many men – he reasoned after the first three or four days – wouldn't want to live out their fantasies in living 3D?

One morning he uncovered a class portrait from his final year at school and found that – with just a little more effort – he could extract each and every girl from the print. The ones he'd fancied from afar to those he'd hated (often at the same time): all at his beck and call for a day. When he'd finally struggled out of bed hollow-eyed and pale, the old photograph – pockmarked with white gaps that had once been people – looked desolate and forlorn. Dennis ripped up the ruined snap and binned it.

It was inevitable the day would come when his source material ran dry; his stack of literature and cuttings reduced to a collection of blank pages and empty photographs. He was down to a cheap, dog-eared celebrity magazine someone had left on the bus.

He gazed at his gaunt expression in the mirror; acutely aware that he'd not stepped outside his house in … he had no idea how long. His thinning hair looked practically gone altogether, his bathrobe was … well, disgusting, frankly. He looked – Dennis had to admit to himself – like a junkie denied his fix for too long; although that irony wasn't lost on him.

"Get a grip!" he mumbled at the reflection.

He took a shower – wondering just how long it was since his last one – dressed in clean clothes and checked the fridge for anything edible. The milk had soured and he didn't have any eggs or juice. Green and blue colonies of mould smeared the two remaining slices of bread. All that the kitchen cupboard held were one can of ratatouille and two of carrots.

He dragged on his coat. Locking the front door behind him he stepped out into a cold, bright day. Immediately a headache started up behind his eyes.

"Mr Crawleigh?"

Dennis blinked, trying to focus on the figure swimming in front of his pulsing eyes. After a moment, it sharpened into Miss Grant from the library. She was staring at Dennis, her expression … He wasn't sure what her expression was, but he thought concern was in there somewhere.

"Miss Grant …"

She stepped closer; it was all Dennis could do not to back away. "You look – well, you don't look at all well, Mr Crawleigh. Have you been ill?"

"I've …" He shivered – the cold, obviously. "No – I've not been too good, Miss Grant. Flu, I think. But I'm getting better. Just off to get something to eat, in fact." He forced a smile. "First proper food for a while."

"Well …" She seemed to be examining him closely. There was something different about her that Dennis couldn't quite figure out. "You see that you do eat, Mr Crawleigh. You look like you could do with a good square meal …"

He gave her a jerky nod. "I will, don't worry. I'll be up and about in no time." He turned away. "I'll see you …"

She replied something that Dennis didn't catch, but he wasn't going to pause and ask her to repeat it. He was cold, he wanted to get to the shops and back as quickly as he could and – embarrassingly – he had just grown an extremely pained and urgent erection. It wasn't just the cold making him hunch.

*

He returned from the shops and emptied out the blue plastic

bag they'd supplied. For a moment he was confused: where was the food? Had he left it in the shop! He must have had a second bag that ...

But as he gazed on the selection of tabloid newspapers and celebrity mags it occurred to him there was no second bag. There was no food. He didn't need it.

He opened a newspaper, riffled through it to the society page. The daughter of some tycoon stared out at him, awaiting his command. He looked at the picture, stared through it, and took her hand – pulled her to him.

His erection was back – a delightful agony. He didn't waste time taking her to his bedroom. He just took her.

*

His head was ringing. Dennis turned over in bed, groaning: he felt sick and weak; all his joints ached. The mother of all hangovers – without him actually having drunk anything. The ringing persisted. It wasn't his head – it was the front doorbell. Someone was pushing it with an annoying rhythm. He wished they'd stop.

After what felt like hours it became obvious that whoever was downstairs had no intention of stopping. Dennis rolled from his bed, wincing at the tiniest movement, staggered to his feet and pulled on his crusted bathrobe. He weaved down the stairs, clinging desperately onto the bannister with fingers that were vague and insubstantial. Making it to the front door he tried to fling it open angrily. Instead, he almost overbalanced.

"What?" he croaked.

"Mr Crawleigh!"

He blinked, forcing the silhouette on his step into some sort of focus. It was Miss Grant – although he guessed more from her voice than recognising her against the stabbing daylight.

"What?" he repeated, clinging onto the front door. He thought he might throw up.

"I thought you said you were getting better!"

He felt arms encircling him, supporting his sagging frame. The world pitched and yawed around him; he barely registered he was being half-carried back upstairs. Miss Grant lowered him onto his bed where his swimming head gradually stilled. His eyes got back a little focus. Miss Grant was looking down at him, her face angular with concern – but there was still something about her ... Something different ...

"Your glasses ..." he muttered, but she didn't seem to hear him. Instead, she was gazing around his bedroom: at the scatter of half-blank glossy magazines and torn-up newspaper.

"You have been a busy boy," she said. Her voice was so neutral, so calm. He started to speak, but she silenced him with fingers against his mouth. "High time we did something," she said, and backed out of the room.

Dennis lay on the bed, his thoughts an incoherent mess. All he could wonder was how he'd come to this state: he was disgusted at himself. But even in that moment of self-loathing his thoughts drifted to Miss Grant: how she'd changed, how she somehow looked younger, sexier.

If only he had a picture of her ...

She re-entered the bedroom, carrying a tray. Dennis guessed she was going to try and feed him – though even the thought of food made him gag. She placed the tray in a corner and stood back from it, facing Dennis.

"Now, Mr Crawleigh – we need to sort you out!"

He tried to smile, to nod in agreement. His attempt at a 'Yes' came out a meaningless hiss.

Miss Grant was unbuttoning her heavy coat. She threw it carelessly onto the bed; beneath she had on nothing but underclothes. Dennis stared, gape-mouthed, as she pulled off her slip, bra and briefs. Despite his weakness, he felt arousal drift through his emaciated body like a warm infusion. Her body was a young woman's – not the middle-aged librarian he'd imagined.

She bent and picked something off the tray. It took him a moment, but Dennis recognised the carving knife he'd used in

165

the Pygmalion Conjuration back … when was it …? He craned his stiff neck, trying to see what else was on the tray: it contained every item he'd put together for the ritual – except for the instructions. What …?

Miss Grant closed in on him, knife raised. Dennis tried to flinch away, but he could barely move. With a series of quick slashes, she cut the filthy robe away from his body, leaving him cold, exposed – his erection all too obvious. She glanced at it and smiled; it wasn't a pleasant smile.

"We'll have none of that, Mr Crawleigh." She reached down with the knife, touching the frigid blade against his hot flesh. His erection shrank away.

"Better." She stooped over the tray again, lighting joss sticks and candles. Then she stood over him, carving knife and light sabre crossed over her breasts. She sucked in a deep breath, closing her eyes. When she re-opened them, Dennis finally recognised the huge, honey-coloured eyes of the model he'd had that first night. And her breasts: so like the pert breasts of a Hammer actress he'd lusted after for so long, and eventually enjoyed. Her arms … her legs; she was still Miss Grant and yet …

She was smiling at him again: it was sharper and more deadly than the knife she was clutching. "Where do you think they all went – after you were finished with them?" She was gloating. "The Conjuration is much deeper and more subtle than you realise, Dennis – may I call you Dennis? I feel like I know you so well." She leaned closer, caressing his face with the tip of the knife. "Did you think it was just for your benefit?" Her teeth nipped the air, millimetres away from his nose.

She straightened. Holding the light sabre above her head, with her other hand she traced a thin line down Dennis's body – throat to scrotum. He tried to shrink away from the point, but failed.

Miss Grant laughed. "Don't worry, Dennis – I'm not going to cut you up. Or damage you in any way. For one thing, he needs you intact." She carefully placed knife and light sabre on the bed. "And for another, I won't need to."

She reached down, delicately pinching his nose shut between the fingers of one hand; placing the palm of her second hand over his mouth.

*

Whatever Dennis was sitting on, it felt pretty uncomfortable – like a hard, uneven mound. He wriggled, but he couldn't settle: his backside managed to be both numb and sore at the same time. He tried looking down, but mists obscured just about everything. He was alone in a grey, silent world. He couldn't get down, either – it was as though he was chained to the mound.

"Buck up, old man." The voice came from nowhere, and everywhere: dampened and flat. "It could be worse."

Dennis looked around, and wasn't surprised to find Aleister Crowley standing next to him – although what he was standing on eluded Dennis's gaze.

"Could it?"

Crowley turned to him, a wide grin splitting his face. His eyes sparkled with malice. "No, on reflection, I don't suppose it could. Tough luck, old man."

"Your Conjuration didn't work! You promised—!"

"Actually I never *promised* anything, Dennis. And I can assure you the Conjuration worked perfectly. You – as you so elegantly phrased it – had sex, didn't you …?"

"Yes, but …"

"Well, then." Crowley stepped away from Dennis's perch. "That Miss Grant was quite a find, don't you think?" He paused and turned around. "Did you know her first name is actually Thelema?" He stared hard at Dennis, obviously looking for a recognition Dennis couldn't give him. "No? Oh, well."

"She killed me!" His situation suddenly occurred to Dennis.

"That bitch—!"

Crowley touched Dennis's mouth with a finger, silencing him. "Now, now. I'll have no name-calling." Crowley was growing fainter: his body dissolving in the ever-present mists. "She administered a *coup de grâce*, if anything; and your part was already over. Well done, by the way – I couldn't have succeeded without your … sterling efforts." Despite the mists, Dennis was certain he could still see Crowley's supercilious grin. "You remember: *sex magick* …"

Dennis tried to speak, but he remained mute.

"Sexual congress yields a tremendous degree of elemental power – that's why many rites conclude with what some so crudely describe as *an orgy*. The climax, if you like." He was all but invisible now – just a voice and cruel laugh. "The adept focusses that power – bends it to his will. Imagine how much power *you've* been generating over the past few weeks …"

Crowley's voice faded along with his body. The cold grey mists closed in around Dennis, vague shapes moving within them. He could no longer see any more than he could speak. Somewhere in his head, Dennis began to scream.

*

Miss Grant stood at the bedside, watching and waiting. She'd replaced the knife and fake sword (she'd felt such a fool waving that ridiculous child's toy!) on the tray and placed it on the bed by Dennis's feet. Then – still naked as Crowley had instructed her – waited for the resurrection.

She spared a moment to glance down at her own rejuvenated body. Even presented with the evidence of her new eyes, she could barely accept it. The years had fallen away – just as the Master had promised; piecemeal, her body had been renewed – replaced – by each and every one of Dennis Crawleigh's sordid couplings. Even though, as she'd looked in the mirror, she still saw Thelema Grant – it was an improved version. So much more alive, so fresh; seductive, sexier. The next time the

Area Manager called in to the Library, she had no doubt she could persuade him to find her a better job. She sniggered – she'd almost thought *better position* ...

Dennis's corpse sighed; his eyes opened. With a groan, he carefully sat upright, swung his legs off the bed, and stood. Miss Grant helped him – the Master was still unsteady on his new feet. "Did it work?" she asked. The other's eyes fastened on hers, glowing with an inner light. He smiled with a confidence and arrogance she'd never seen on Dennis's face.

"Yes. Oh, yes!" He threw his arms around her, kissing her cheeks. "My dear Miss Grant – Thelema! My own Galatea!" He released her and went to admire himself in the bedroom mirror – studiously tiptoeing around the litter of paper on the floor. He stared for almost a minute, fingers absently caressing his head and face.

"Pity about the hair," he said, eventually.

Miss Grant busied herself snatching up the papers. She tried not to see all the empty spaces; tried not to think what it meant. "Better burn all this. Lord knows what would happen if someone saw." She straightened. "Pity about Dennis. Although I understand the need for sacrifice."

The Master had turned away from the mirror. "What do you think best: Dennis Crowley or Aleister Crawleigh? Or something entirely new?"

"Might I suggest something entirely new ...?"

"Of course." His teeth flashed. "No connections or loose ends."

Miss Grant piled the papers untidily on the bed. As she did so, she realised the carving knife was no longer on the tray where she'd replaced it. The Master stepped in close to her; his heat, his power, engulfed her.

"You realise, of course, that Dennis wasn't the sacrifice ..." She felt the point of the knife – hard and chill – against her spine. His last words to her were, "Sometimes I hate myself ..."

169

THE BOY

David Williamson

No sooner had he walked through the front door after another long hard day at work, than his wife was on at him.

"*He's* been a little swine again!" she screamed, pointing at their eleven-year-old son who was busy cowering in a corner of the living room. All afternoon, he'd been listening to those dreaded words; 'Wait till your father gets home! He'll give you what-for, my lad!'

And the sad thing was, the boy *knew* he would get 'what-for' as he seemed to get it at least three or four times a week, but he just couldn't help himself. He was simply a normal, naughty, pain-in-the-arse boy, no better or worse than any other boy his age. Okay, maybe *slightly* worse; certainly no angel by any stretch of the imagination, but then no demon either.

His father had barely had time to take his coat off, and his wife continued her verbal assault on him, bombarding him with every tiny misdemeanour, every minor infraction of the rules carried out by his son during the day.

"*And* he called me an old cow, too! I told him you'd give him what-for when you got home … I *warned* him!"

The boy's father was in his early fifties, and truth be told, he was not a well man. These days, he would have been diagnosed as still suffering from the effects of post-traumatic stress disorder following the nightmarish scenes he had witnessed during his time serving in the army in the Second World War. Sights that he never spoke about, not to anyone. Sights that had left him a nervous wreck of a man, only able to function on any level at all because of the cocktail of drugs supplied by his understanding GP.

The father's nervous tic grew more pronounced the more his wife continued to berate him about their son's behaviour, and when at last his short fuse ignited, he dragged the boy roughly from his hiding place, somehow managing to remove the thick leather belt from his trousers at the same time, and thrashed the squirming child as his mother looked on, a smug, self-satisfied smile on her hard face.

When it was over, for today at least, the boy ran sobbing to the bedroom he shared with his younger brother and flung himself onto his bed. Although his father administered the beatings on a regular basis, the boy somehow knew that he didn't *want* to carry them out, that he didn't *enjoy* doing what he did. It was just his way of shutting his wife up, of stopping her constant nagging, of getting a bit of peace and quiet after a hard day.

The boy also remembered that it hadn't always been this way.

He recalled the day it had all started, when he had been taken to a neighbour's house and left there for what seemed like months, but in reality was probably no longer than a few weeks. One minute, the then three-year-old was happily playing with his Dinky cars on the lino in the kitchen, the next, he had his coat thrust onto his back and was marched six houses up the street and deposited with some strange woman and her daughter. People he didn't recall having ever met before. Then his father was gone, saying he'd be back when he could, as the young boy cried himself into a bewildered sleep on the stranger's settee.

He knew it had been around Christmas time; he remembered that, because the strange woman had taken him to visit Santa's Grotto at the big department store, and he had sat on a fat man's lap who had given him a small plastic toy boat filled with toffees.

During those days, weeks … months? he only saw his father three times, and then only when he called round to give the neighbour some money, presumably for looking after the boy. His father would promise to be back and see him soon, but the days seemed to drag on endlessly and each time the boy saw his father during those fleeting visits, it only served to stir up more feelings of abandonment and seemed to highlight the fact that he was no longer wanted, no longer loved by his daddy.

There was no sign at all of his mother, his one-time loving, caring mother. She seemed to have vanished from the face of the earth.

Then, finally, it was over.

His father came to collect him, wearing his big old tweedy overcoat. He held the boy's hand and they walked the six houses back to their home. The small boy looking up at his daddy, smiling with joy, elated that they were back together again, thrilled to be holding his daddy's hand.

They entered the lounge, and there, silhouetted in the bay window, backlit by watery January sunlight, sat his mother on a hard-backed kitchen chair. She was holding something carefully in her arms; something wrapped in a small blue blanket and she was smiling, not at her son, but at the bundle she held so gently.

"This is your new brother!" she said proudly, without preamble. The father held the three-year-old firmly by the shoulder, maybe in an effort to comfort the boy from the shock news that he now had a baby brother.

The small boy was led slowly across to where his mother and new brother sat, almost as though he was in the presence of royalty and had been granted a special audience.

Mother pulled the blue blanket away from the baby's face so that the boy could get a better look at his new sibling.

"There," she cooed. "Here's your brother. What shall we call him, eh?" she asked in a sugary-sweet voice, her eyes still fixed adoringly on the infant.

The boy was in shock. He was too young to know anything about babies or understand where they came from. All he *did* know was that he had been dumped with strangers for weeks on end without setting eyes on his mother, and only the briefest of glimpses of his father. And now *this*? This *stranger* who'd come from nowhere and was apparently his brother? The brother sitting on *his* mother's lap, in *his* place? And she was smiling at it!

"Rover!" said the boy, suddenly.

"What?" asked his mother, still too engrossed with the newborn to listen to her elder son.

"Rover ... call him Rover!" repeated the boy.

His mother laughed, giving subliminal permission for his father to do the same.

"We can't call him *Rover* ... he's not a dog ... he's your *brother*!"

The boy thought for a moment while his parents laughed at him.

"Chum then ... let's call him Chum," suggested the boy, in honour of a pet who'd died back when he was still crawling.

His parents laughed again, his mother with a strange look in her eye. She was smiling, but there was something behind the smile, something the boy had never seen before. It was something *nasty*, as though she didn't like him anymore.

"No, we've already decided to call him Clive ... Clive's a *nice* name ... not a dog's name."

"Clive's a *stupid* name!" said the boy, and he felt his father's grip tighten on his shoulder.

So, Clive aka Rover, came into the boy's life and stayed there.

As it turned out, Clive was a very sickly child. If anything was going around, any sort of childhood malady, he was sure to pick it up and he'd be screaming the place down day and night, which made their father, whose nerves were shattered at the best of times, even more nervous and uptight than usual.

Then after a while, another strange thing happened.

The boy's father just vanished one day. He'd come home from the local infant school, and dad was gone! It was even more strange, because dad always picked the boy up after school in his little van, but on this occasion, there was no one there waiting for him and after hanging about long after all the other kids had left and gone home, he decided that his dad wasn't coming and had walked home on his own.

"Where's daddy?" asked the boy of his mother, who was

busy trying to comfort the eternally sick Clive.

"He's gone away for a while," she snapped, without elaboration.

The boy was confused and scared. It reminded him of that other time.

"Has he gone to get another baby?" the boy asked, earnestly.

His mother shook her head and snorted with derisive laughter.

"No he hasn't!" she spat. "Now get that uniform off and wash your hands ready for tea."

"But where's my *daddy*?" whined the boy.

A firm slap to the left side of his face silenced his whining. "I said, he's gone away for a while. Now get changed, you little sod!" This and the glare that his mother gave him made it clear that the subject was closed.

He didn't see his father for many weeks after that, and despite asking where he was on a regular basis and receiving another slap for 'being defiant', he was never given an answer.

All he did know was that he was forbidden to go into the back bedroom and that the doctor would pay regular weekly visits to the house and whisper with his mother. Then the boy would be locked in the front room and he'd hear the doctor climbing the stairs and a bedroom door closing.

Then the visits stopped. His mother became ever more hostile towards the boy while Clive became ever more wonderful in his mother's eyes.

After what seemed like an eternity, his mother; Clive in his pushchair (although he was now big enough and old enough to walk on his own), and the boy, went for a walk together. A rare event, and the boy had to ask his mother where they were going.

"We're going to meet daddy from the station," she replied, rather nervously, adding, "and you'd better bloody well behave yourself!"

His father had lost a lot of weight. His old tweedy coat was hanging from his once broad shoulders as though it belonged to someone else and stranger still, he no longer had any teeth, just a gaping mouth full of red raw gums!

But the boy was thrilled to see him again, teeth or not, and he threw his arms around his father's waist and burst into tears.

The walk back home was very quiet, neither of his parents speaking to one another, as Clive grizzled in his pushchair demanding the attention of his doting mother.

Over the coming weeks, the boy heard the words 'convalescent home' and 'nervous breakdown' a lot as his mother chatted to neighbours over the garden gate. None of it made any sense to him of course, but his dad was back and that was all that mattered. He was a lot twitchier than he remembered, the tic in his eye had been joined by a non-stop flexing of the fingers in his right hand, which would get a lot worse in direct proportion to how much his wife nagged him.

Suddenly, the boy could do nothing right. Every action or gesture was pounced upon by his mother as a sign of 'defiance', every word was deemed to be 'argumentative' or 'rude' so much so, that it was almost impossible to do or say anything without her uttering those fatal words:

'Just you wait until your father gets home!'

And when he wasn't receiving a belting from his harangued father, he would feel whatever came into his mother's hands around the back of his legs, or worse, the back of his head. One time, she'd actually hit him alongside the head with a frying pan snatched from the hotplate, and then he got another beating from his father because the frying pan had been full of fat and his mother had had to clean the kitchen!

There was no escape. He had been promised his own bedroom at one time, but his mother and father now had a room each for some reason, so he was forced to share with Clive. His father, never a very good handyman, had cobbled together a set of bunk beds from two narrow ex-army beds held together with some angle iron. To make matters worse, Clive had been given the top bunk and he delighted in wetting the bed at night, which rained down on his brother beneath.

The Boy

His mother and Clive found this very amusing, even though she had to clean the mess up every morning and change all Clive's bedding, though not the boy's, no matter how damp and smelly it became, it would have to last a fortnight. And the more she doted on Clive, the more he would go out of his way to torment his older brother, which in turn appeared to make their mother happier.

The boy was now eleven and his brother eight when he decided that enough was enough; he would kill Clive and things would go back to the way they used to be. Just him, mum and dad … all happy again with no more beatings and no more Clive around to ruin everything.

But how do you kill someone? It looked so easy on the telly; you shot someone or stabbed them with a sword … easy-peasy. That was on TV however. How would *he* get rid of his brother and yet not get into trouble again? After all, despite his apparent 'defiance' and 'rudeness', the boy was no fool and he knew he would be in very serious bother if anyone knew he had done it.

He prayed every night that one of Clive's endless illnesses would kill him, and there was briefly a moment of real hope when his brother was taken to hospital suffering from some mystery virus, but he returned within a week to continue his tormenting ways.

Time passed, and the boy kept the notion of dispensing with his brother on the back burner, as the six-week school holidays had arrived. His last such break before 'the big school'. Freedom!

The boy was out every day with his friends, making camps in the park, playing football, climbing trees and having fun from dawn until dusk in the bright summer sunshine. He'd more often than not return home late for tea, covered in mud and dirt and get a slap for his tardiness and being mucky, but it was all worth it to get out of that depressing house, and more importantly, away from Clive and his snivelling.

Then his mother got a part-time job in a baker's shop and

the boy was told that *he* would have to look after his younger brother until their mother returned from work.

Not only did the boy have to suffer the ignominy of having his friends taking the piss because he had his baby brother tagging along everywhere he went, but Clive would tell their mother everything his elder brother got up to, which would inevitably lead to more punishment.

Fortunately, their mother didn't entertain the idea of grounding the boys, as she knew full well that the house would be wrecked in her absence, so they were allowed to continue roaming free, so long as the boy agreed to look after his brother and keep him safe. Great for Clive, dire for his brother.

Every day that passed, the boy hated Clive a little more and the feeling seemed to be entirely mutual, as Clive would relish any and every opportunity to cause grief for his brother when they returned home each evening.

The worst occasion being when the gang of boys had seen a drunken flasher one day in the park, and, after failing to persuade Clive to go and touch the man's cock, they had stripped ferns, uprooted the stems and then used them to chase the drunk and whip his genitals until he had screamed for mercy and ran. Comically, he had tried to pull up his pants and trousers whilst running, but had fallen over a molehill. The boys had seized their chance then, thrashing him mercilessly until he crawled off bleeding and sobbing into the bracken.

The boy received the worst beating of his life for that little episode. Not because he and his friends had punished a paedophile, but because he had endangered the precious Clive with his antics. Clive and his mother sat side by side on the settee, an identical smug smile on each of their faces as the boy came back into the room after his thrashing and tried to sit in a chair, his buttocks ablaze with pain.

"That'll teach him to look after me properly, won't it mummy?" whined Clive.

"Yes it will, my darling!" confirmed their mother.

*

The Boy

The old sewage works had always been a great place to play and hang out. Despite, or rather *because* of, all the DANGER – KEEP OUT! signs, the gang always felt compelled to go there and rummage about in the various tunnels and shafts, and the long abandoned pump house, which still stank of shit even after all the years of disuse.

Rats scurried in dark corners, bats lived in what remaining roof hadn't been vandalised, stolen or simply collapsed from old age and lack of repair.

It was a magical place, full of mystery and adventure, a veritable treasure trove of excitement to anyone with half an imagination.

Clive had no imagination. He would whine constantly that the place stank, that it was too dirty, too scary, too far away from home, though in reality, it was less than a mile.

The boy used his newly learnt words on his brother. "Fuck off, Clive, you little shit!" and the rest of the gang laughed long and hard. There wasn't a single one of them that didn't feel the same way about Clive.

Clive stuck out his bottom lip and began to whimper. "I'm telling my mummy you said that!" he whined and would have run off back home there and then except for the fact that he didn't know the way … and was far too frightened to move about the old sewage works on his own.

"Let's play hide and seek!" called one of the boys, to unanimous agreement from the others. All bar one that was; Clive, naturally.

"NO! I DON'T WANNA PLAY THAT!" he screamed, his words echoing eerily around the high walls of the pump house.

The boy walked over to where his brother stood, his fist clenching and unclenching, resisting the almost overwhelming urge to punch Clive straight in the mouth.

"Okay, you sissy-boy … *we'll* play and you can find us, if you're too chicken to hide!"

"NO!" screamed Clive.

"TOUGH!" his brother retorted. "You can play, or you can

178

fuck off back home on your own … and I don't care what dad does to me!"

Clive's lips puckered and tears rolled down his grubby cheeks as the rest of the gang looked on, smirking at the standoff. It had been a long time coming and they were enjoying every second of it.

"It's up to you, Clive. We can leave you here with the rats and the bats, or you can try and find us and then we can all go home."

Clive slowly realised that he was in a no-win situation for once, wiped his snotty nose on the sleeve of his jumper, and nodded, accepting defeat.

"Wahoo, let's go! Close your eyes and count to twenty!" And with that, the rest of the boys scattered around the huge old pump house, fighting amongst themselves for the best hiding place.

The boy had already decided in advance where his hiding place would be, and he headed across to the far wall, scrambling over a large pile of rubble towards his goal.

He had been to the pump house many times before being lumbered with having to take Clive everywhere with him, and he knew that there was an old covered cistern with a heavy, cast iron lid on the inspection hatch. He also knew, that although the pump house had long been redundant, the access hatch and all the machinery in that part of the plant was still maintained, as there was a sluice gate separating the cistern from the canal which ran outside the works, and this was on very rare occasions used when the canal threatened to flood after heavy rainfall.

It was easy, therefore, to lift the well-oiled inspection lid and clamber down the vertical ladder that went into the old Victorian, brick-lined cistern. It hadn't rained in an age, so he knew he would be safe from risk of flooding. The lid was heavy, but he hefted it a few times to make sure he'd be able to open it again from inside, then closed it silently behind him and descended the metal ladder.

The Boy

It was pitch-black now that the lid was closed, but that didn't worry the boy one bit, as he knew that no one would find him down there. And Clive *certainly* wouldn't have the balls to look in such a place.   And if he did manage to overcome his terror of dark places and scramble down the metal ladder and discover his hiding place, the boy would make certain that he would never leave alive. He suppressed a snigger, and sat down to wait on the dry rubble-strewn floor of the cistern.

"Nineteen, twenty … coming, ready or not!" announced Clive, half-heartedly and he proceeded to make a great pretence of looking for the hidden gang of boys.

In reality, he hadn't closed his eyes while counting to twenty. In fact, he had made a point of watching where exactly his brother had been heading towards, and he made a beeline in that direction.

As soon as he saw the heavy lid covering the access chamber, he knew immediately where his brother would be hiding and grinned broadly to himself. That was just too easy!

Then he spotted the wheel that operated the sluice. Liberally coated in grease it would be as smooth to operate as the day it was installed way back in Victorian times.

Clive released the safety brake and began turning the wheel as fast as he could. He could hear the sluice gate opening in the cistern beneath his feet and the barely audible muffled cries from his brother as the cold, dirty grey canal water poured into the old tank with a roaring sound.

The shock of the water battering into his body made the boy go rigid with terror. The force of the deluge knocked him off his feet and swept him into the far corner in the inky black darkness of the cistern. He tried to stand, groping blindly to reach the safety of the vertical ladder, but every time he attempted to clamber to his feet, the sheer force of the water knocked him over again.

He screamed at the top of his lungs for help but was rewarded with a mouthful of foul tasting water which forced its way down his throat, up his nose and into his lungs, making him choke and retch. Turgid canal water mixed with one-hundred-and-twenty-year-old Victorian shit that had washed out from the crevices in the brickwork and from the cracks in the cistern floor, filling his lungs with the foul mixture, drowning him.

He tried desperately to flounder his way to the hatch in the ceiling of the cistern as the water steadily rose, but he had swallowed too much water and when his flailing hands touched the vertical ladder, a brief glimmer of hope flashed through his mind, before he sank slowly to the bottom of the tank. Dead.

It was all a dreadful accident, of course.

None of the boys should have been in the old sewage works in the first place, and surely, no one would ever have been crazy enough to enter the cistern when it had been full of water.

The coroner returned a verdict of accidental death. And as no one amongst the gang had witnessed what had really happened, what else could the verdict be? He issued a strong rebuke against the owners of the site, for their complete lack of any form of security, but that was that. Case closed.

Clive and his mother stood beside the open grave while the priest jabbered on with the funeral service. Father hadn't been able to make it; he'd had a bad relapse and was 'away' at a convalescent home for the foreseeable future.

As the service ended and Clive and his mother walked away from the graveside, they held hands, turned and smiled at one another.

"It's just us now, mummy," said Clive.

"Yes, just us, darling." said his mother, happily.

THE LAST WAGON IN THE TRAIN

Andrea Janes

At first glance it looked like any other wagon train.

It was stalled in the desert in traditional semi-circular formation, curled in on itself defensively, like an animal resting. The small openings in its canvas tops peered out like suspicious eyes. Each wagon was heavily packed; their wheels creaked and sighed as they rested in the earth, and in the breeze, small clatterings of wood and tin *tink-tinked* like distant cowbells.

Tackett saw it as he crossed over the ridge. He'd been walking slowly, shuffling over the hot sand for two days, one painful footfall at a time, resting at intervals. A measured pace. A desert pace. Go too fast and you'll kill yourself, stop and you'll die. He felt dizzy with the light and dust. But it was real, the wagon train. It was real. And he trembled slightly with relief.

He willed himself to stand up straight and shake off the dirt that clung to his trousers and coat. It wouldn't do to appear weak and hungry. He didn't know yet if these strangers were friend or foe.

A lone man stood near the train, holding his horses' reins with one hand as they nosed something in a bucket. He stood tall and upright, and looked thin but not starved. *They have food*, Tackett realised.

Tackett raised his hand and the man waved back. He stopped feeding the horses, who whinnied, then stilled until all motion ceased. The air settled.

"Trouble?"

"Horse broke her leg," said Tackett. "I been walking."

"You shoot her?"

"Yes."

"How far you going?"

"California."

The man whistled. "That's a long way."

"I know."

"Where'd you leave your horse?"

"A ways back."

He eyed Tackett. "Travelling light," he said.

"I have what I need. Mostly. Could use some water, though." It was an understatement.

"I got some." The man handed Tackett a canteen.

Tackett drank and it was like absolution. He meant it when he said, "Thank you."

"We've got plenty here in town."

Tackett squinted. Town?

The man gestured for Tackett to follow him.

They picked their way among the rocks to the wagon train. Each crunch of their footsteps echoed. The sun was merciless. The sky was violently blue.

Tackett hated this scrubby landscape. It reminded him too much of the illustrated Bible stories Aunt Mabel made him read as a child. He was afraid Moses would jump out from behind a rock and start screeching the Ten Commandments at him, or worse yet, his Aunt Mabel would.

"What's your line?" asked the man as they walked.

"Oh, general handy-work," Tackett said slowly. "Figured I might go out to San Francisco. But the way was longer than I thought."

"It was longer than any of us thought." The man paused. "I'm a wheelwright."

"Good trade."

The wheelwright nodded. "It is."

They stopped in front of one of the wagons.

"This is my town."

Tackett squinted at the wheelwright again, cocked his head to the side. He listened to the absolute quiet. Not a breath or whisper anywhere, no movement, no glint of life beneath the sun. No voices, no girls.

"You'll see what I mean," the wheelwright laughed.

He stepped up onto the creaking tongue of the wagon and hopped into its dark open mouth. He poked his head out. "Come on," he said, gesturing. Tackett heaved himself in. Inside the air was dark and hot.

In the dim light, a series of objects took shape. A painted sign; crates banked with sawdust and old newspapers; jars and barrels. Piles of canvas and folded pieces of cloth. Slats of rope-bound wood sat stacked atop each other. Beside the slats, a bundle of tarpaper shingles affixed to a canvas sheet was wrapped upon itself like a rolled-up horse blanket and tied with twine.

"Look here," the wheelwright said. He brought Tackett's gaze back to the stacks of wood. The flat bundles were about fifteen inches across and maybe twenty-five inches long. Each was numbered with slashes of red paint: 1/41. 2 /41.

"This is the general store." The wheelwright indicated a bundle marked 3/41.

Tackett looked around and saw that every single wooden bundle was numbered.

"We can put this together in three hours," the wheelwright said. "Including the roof. We got the counters, we got every last barrel."

We?

"Come on."

He led Tackett to the next wagon and opened the slit in the front of the canvas. It was hitched right to the back of the one in front of it, Tackett realised. They were all like this, hitched to each other. The interior looked very much the same as the first wagon: slats of wood, bolts of cloth. Thick grey dust covered the floor.

"The preacher's house," he said. "Right down to the curtains."

Bolts of pink calico languished under a coat of dust.

"And there are more." The wheelwright waved his arm around in a semi-circle. "Each one with a store or a house in it, even a church. We brought everything with us. Everything."

Tackett shook his head. "I don't understand."

"We're bringing the town with us. It's gonna have a circumference of nine miles around, spread out over an area of a thousand acres." The wheelwright touched the side of the wagon reverently. A fat black fly buzzed as it flew out of the way. "We'll surround it by a wooden wall twenty feet high. Houses, stables, stores, all laid out just like the streets we had back home. These first three wagons are Oak Street. It took every carpenter and woodcutter in town a year to build it and pack it."

Tackett was quiet. He thought about this for a minute. "So you all brought *everything* with you?" he asked carefully.

"Yes, we have everything we need. We have a hundred—"

"Including food and water?"

"Oh yes, forgive me. I've been jawing while you're dying of thirst." The wheelwright led him to a third wagon. Tackett counted them as they walked. There were ten wagons altogether. On the tenth wagon, he could see a single black cross painted slightly side-ways on the canvas beside the opening. The opening was drawn tightly shut.

The water wagon was filled with wooden barrels. The wheelwright lifted the lid of one of these, dropped a smooth wooden dipper into it, and ladled some water into a tin cup. "Here you go."

Tackett's hand shook as he lifted it to his mouth and the cup rattled against his teeth. He kept his eyes wide open as he drank, looking around him and thinking about the tenth wagon.

He handed the cup back and it was refilled twice before they agreed he ought to take it easy for a while.

"Of course, you can have as much as you'd like once your stomach's ready," the wheelwright said.

Tackett nodded. He could already feel the pain that had burned in his head for the past two days begin to lift. His mind buzzed like the fly as he tallied up the barrels and the wagons, and the sheer, unaccountable stock of it all. He was dizzy with greed. He could kill the wheelwright now. But he had to make sure.

"Your town is mighty impressive," he said. "You got ten wagons full of food and water?"

"Food, water and supplies," smiled the wheelwright.

"And in that last wagon?"

"You must be tired." The wheelwright smiled. "You oughta take a rest."

The wheelwright gave him a blanket and left him to lie down in the shade beside the water wagon. It'd been days since Tackett felt shade. His skin was so stiff with sunburn it cracked and purpled and peeled in places; getting out of the sun was a blessed relief. What's more, it'd give him time to think.

He had his gun with him, and the bowie knife he'd taken off Watt's dead body after the scuffle. That had been bad luck. Watt had tried to double-cross him, and the horses ran off during the fight. Somewhere on the plain were two quarter horses with saddlebags full of stolen gold, while Tackett'd been stuck out there alone with a corpse. Well, his luck was about to change.

Based on what he'd seen and heard, he had but one man to kill. What happened to the others he didn't know, but he could guess. You don't cross a desert without a little death.

He'd grab everything of value and take both of the horses. Load one up with water and supplies. Tackett hoped these fools had stashed some gold, or bonds, or cash in that tenth wagon. There had to be something in it, the way the wheelwright had changed the subject.

Tackett slept until the hot sun finally died, soothed by the sound of the wheelwright hammering away at something. Nothing made him sleep better than the sound of other men doing work while he was resting.

*

It was dark when he awoke. He found the wheelwright sitting on a rock in the centre of the wagon circle.

"Evening," they said to each other.

"Sit down," said the wheelwright.

Tackett sat. "No fire?" He began to rub his hands together instinctively until he realised he wasn't cold. Strange. He'd never known the desert to stay hot at night.

"We don't keep a fire lit. Fires attract the Indians. Come on and eat."

They sat around the pit where there was no fire. The wheelwright handed him a piece of jerky.

He apologised. "We used to have much more food, once."

Tackett ate five pieces and washed them down with water.

The wheelwright snaked his long fingers over his trouser knees and cracked his knucklebones. "I'm worn out." He stood up. "Coming with us in the morning?"

"I'd very much like to, if it's all right with all the townspeople." Tackett sneered in the darkness.

"It's nothing at all."

Tackett stayed sitting beside the fireless pit and watched him walk away.

The wheelwright slept under the stars. He set up a nest of blankets right next to the first wagon, the so-called general store, not two feet from the horses. He'd staked the horses with rope. Could he really be that stupid? Tenderfoot. No wonder he had but two horses. Toting enough wood for twenty arks but didn't think to bring a chain to stake the horses.

The horses seemed to stare at Tackett, snicking and switching their tails back and forth. He sucked his teeth and glared at them, and they flapped their loose mouths as they whinnied right back. Something bothered him about those horses. They were black and glossy, and well fed; and, though he'd been too tired and dizzy to notice before, extraordinarily large. He didn't like them and, though he knew it was impossible, he got the sense they didn't like him either.

He spat and stood up.

Tackett walked softly over to the water wagon and let

himself inside. How much should he take, he wondered. He couldn't carry a whole barrel, not on horseback, but he could fill up three, four big water skins at least. Tackett lifted the lid of a random barrel and found it empty. No problem, there were many others. He lifted another lid. Nothing. A third lid. Empty, dry as dust. A fourth lid revealed a barrel with about an inch of water, and a wooden dipper floating in it. It must've been the same one the wheelwright had drawn from before, since every other barrel was empty.

"*Shit!*" No water, nothing. He'd had enough of this. He was going to grab what he could from that last wagon and get the hell out of here. This place was a crock of shit.

Tackett jumped out of the bone-dry water wagon. He moved swiftly toward the tenth wagon. Its opening was still drawn tight. He looked closely at the crude cross painted on it. He rubbed his eyes.

It wasn't paint, he realised. He ran his finger over the canvas and rubbed his finger against his thumb. It wasn't paint at all. It looked like charcoal. It had been smudged with a paste made of water and ashes.

He dusted off his hand, drew the wagon open and looked inside.

A pile of bones was stacked from the wooden floor box to the curving ribcage of the canvas roof.

Thighbones were stacked criss-crossed atop each other like a log cabin, knees jutting out at the edges and corners. Smaller bones, arms and shoulder blades, rested over that, and then piles of hipbones, sitting like bowls on a counter. Within each bowl, a single head. Each gleaming appendage rested in its place in a mass pyramid.

The skulls were yellow-white and slightly luminous in the shafts of moonlight. Some had long patches of hair drily clinging to them. On others there were the shallow horizontal cuts above the eye sockets that were sure signs of scalping.

Vertebrae dangled from the wagon roof, interspersed with bones of feet and fingers. The hanging phalanges stirred and clattered softly like chimes in the night breeze.

A voice behind him said, "I see you found our graveyard."

Tackett turned around and sneered at the wheelwright. The man was crazier than Aunt Mabel, and didn't have a goddamn worth stealing. "I had enough of this." Tackett lunged at the wheelwright and plunged the knife upward below his ribcage and into his liver.

The wheelwright put his hand over the wound, which did not bleed, and looked steadily at Tackett. "Are you coming or not?"

The faint *tick-ticking* of the hanging bones grew into a noisy rattle. The wagon vibrated slightly, and outside, the horses whinnied and stirred. Tackett's knife trembled in his hand; it was clean and bloodless in the faint starlight. "Shit," said Tackett slowly. "This ain't right."

The wheelwright shook his head. "Are you coming or not?"

Tackett didn't wait to answer. He pushed past the wheelwright and leapt from the wagon, staggering when he hit the ground. He heard the horses whinny again as they stamped and reared and then he watched aghast as they shifted in the moonlight from glossy black to shining white, as the light shone through their long skulls and gleaming ribs. Tackett froze. But it was only a flash, a vision, it wasn't real – it couldn't be. The horses were black and glossy again, and huge. They were massive. Their whinnying was louder now, nearly screaming, and in the air another sound joined the noise, the now-familiar *tick-tick, tick-tick* emanating from the tenth wagon as the wheelwright tottered to the ground.

His clothes hung from his bones in tatters. He clattered over to the horses and each articulated finger bone grasped its way around the rotting leather reins. He led the horses to the tenth wagon, which he unhitched from the others. He hitched the huge black horses to the tenth wagon and dust stirred as the entire wagon train began to creak and shudder.

"There ain't no two horses anywhere that can pull a whole train," Tackett breathed. The wheelwright turned to him and grinned.

The bones inside clattered again and from the rear opening, one settler, then another, dismounted from the rear wagon and took up the grim march behind the train. Their hollow eye sockets seemed to stare at Tackett but whether they saw him or not, whether they cared or not, he couldn't tell. They were moving forward, the restless bones.

The animals moved and slowly the wagon train came with them, all hitched together one by one, with the settlers following. The wheelwright moved away from them and walked over to Tackett.

"Come along," he said, and gently grabbed the bowie knife from Tackett's fear-frozen grip. From the darkness, two other figures appeared. Skeletal settlers, clad in ragged cloth, fragments of dry black hair clinging to their skulls. They dragged something behind them, something Tackett couldn't make out in the dark, not at first. Slowly, he recognised it as a wheel. In one of their hands, he could see, a settler held a length of rope.

Tackett tried to scream. *Please* he tried to say. But his mouth was filled with dust.

*

When Tackett came to, he was naked and the sun was up.

They had tied the wheel to the back of the wagon train. It bumped along in the dirt through the night, with Tackett lashed to it. Now it lay in the centre of the wagon train, which was once more a circle. The sun beat down on his naked flesh.

The wheel was a rough cross of St. Andrew, with four spokes, one for each limb. Tackett's head rolled and lolled where it might. His temples pounded. His bones were broken. His skin was burning again, stiffening, hardening, cracking. He tried to lick his bloody, encrusted lips but his tongue was dry.

The wheelwright walked over to him, holding a bucket.

"Good morning," he said. "Don't mind me. Just feeding the

horses." He walked away whistling, leaving Tackett lashed to the unholy wheel.

The wheelwright had a good knife but he was pleased with the one he'd taken from Tackett. It was wonderfully sharp. It was in his own vest pocket now, its heft next to his heart. The wheelwright let his horses finish eating first. They snorted their way through the bucket of meat and chewed it all up. He patted their heads when they emptied the bucket, which he put away neatly under the wagon. He wiped his hands and headed over to Tackett.

He drew Tackett's sharp knife from his vest pocket and polished the blade on his sleeve. Excellent edge, strong and true. Lovely work. The wheelwright grabbed the soft skin near Tackett's shoulder blade. He would start from the back. He always butchered from the back.

"A good jerky ought to dry in the sun and wind," the wheelwright said absently. "Fire attracts the Indians."

Tackett's back flayed off nicely. One sheet. One solid sheet. The blood was nothing to fear. A man only had a finite amount of blood. You could shed a man's blood, you could take a man's scalp, you could murder his women and horses and burn his food to ash, but there was only so much blood a man could give. The rest was meat and bone. And soon the meat would begin to dry.

Tackett found his voice and began to scream.

"Shhh, don't," soothed the wheelwright. "You would've come with us anyway. There isn't another town around for three hundred miles. There's nowhere to go."

"Who are you?" Tackett managed to scream, but the wheelwright only smiled. Tackett's throat dried and he could scream no more.

The sun burned and the world began to waver.

Tackett lay there, exposed to the wind, as he would lie until the flayed strips of his burning flesh would flutter off his bones. As he would lie until he would be packed in a barrelful of salt in the general store in the city of the dead, and his skull would rest in a bed of bones in a wagon train that travelled by night in the endless dust.

DAD DANCING

Kate Farrell

Aren't parents embarrassing when they dance? Especially
dads. It's that sideways shuffle they do, with elbows at the
sides and feet slithering. Sometimes they click their fingers
too. It's not really dancing; with heads flung back, they move
to a private rhythm that has nothing to do with the music, the
sounds from their youth: The Beatles, (not bad); Boney M,
(don't go there); The Bee Gees, (unbefuckinlievable). The
slither thing is bad enough, but worse is the disco dance, which
is beyond gross. For that one they sort of twist on the balls of
the feet, one arm up, one down, or spin slowly pointing at
whoever gets into their eye line. Look at me; I am s-o-o-o-o-o
dangerous. There's really nothing dangerous about a middle-
aged man wearing new jeans with a crease ironed in, and a
fancy shirt revealing a gold chain nestling in damp, matted
chest hair. However otherwise jovial, generous or charming
the parent, it is something no child should ever have to
witness.

Twins Nic and Anton were cursed with such a parent. For the
first ten years of their lives it was less of an issue though even
from a relatively tender age, they felt there was something just
not *right* about such displays. They had been christened
respectively Nicholas and Anthony by their mother, and were
called Nicky and Tony by their father. The sobriquets Nic and
Anton were of their own choosing. Now well into their
seventeenth year, they were armed with the vocabulary to give
voice to their discomfort. Of an age when poise and style were
paramount, their millionaire father from Peckham let them
down in so many ways. It wasn't just the dancing; it wasn't just
the gold chains and the sovereign rings and the glittering
diamond in one ear. This last was a six-month anniversary
present from wife number two, Staci. It wasn't just the accent,

193

which marked him out as the son of a South London costermonger. No, also to be taken into consideration was his height. And his weight. Even his name: Ron. Not Ronald, not even Ronnie, but Ron. One syllable, three letters, no embellishment, nothing. Ron. But mainly it was the dancing.

The boys were not effete, not by a long stretch; they played rugby and cricket for their overpriced school in Berkshire, climbed and skied in Scotland, and with their fellows chased the pretty village maidens who they gamely referred to as 'tarts'. They were growing into perfect specimens of manhood. For the past two years, they had enjoyed the hospitality of their peers during Easter and summer vacs. While dad went to his whitewashed villa with wrap-around sun terraces on a golf course in Mar-bay-ah, the boys headed to the Highlands or the Vendee. There they would dress in faded shorts and old-fashioned rugby jerseys with the collars turned up, lingering in the company of fragrant virgins called India and Kitty, Flora and Hermione. When they returned from the first such excursion, nothing back at home was ever quite the same again. Their father, who had amassed his not inconsiderable pile through plumbing supplies, was frankly appalled when they told him how the hot water packed up at the Hon. Angus's parent's place, as it so often did. And then there were the high flush toilet cisterns, with bits of old rope attached to the pulling mechanism!

"Bit of a hoot, really," they said, echoing Angus.

"Nah. You should bring some of yer mates here, let them see some decent plumbing, proper karseys," he had offered.

He was justifiably proud of the five-bed-five-bath house, a symbol of his upward mobility from Peckham to the leafy acres of Wimbledon Common. Each en suite was a different colour: peach, champagne, sea mist, eau de nil, sun blush. All very tasteful, very classy, and chosen by Staci after consultation with the developer.

"Mmm," said Anton.

"Yah, right," said Nic.

Dad Dancing

Christmas was looming. Before the twins were able to go and frolic on the ski slopes with India, Angus, and the gang, there was the small matter of the festivities to be endured. The Christmas period itself was bad enough with relatives descending on them, but at least there was some perverse fun to be picked from the carnage, and Dad's legendary generosity also helped. The real problem was New Year, more specifically, New Year's Eve. A big party. Catering. Live music. Karaoke. And dancing. Lots and lots of it.

Anton said, "The thought of it, Nic ..."

"Simply chills the blood," finished his brother, the older by six minutes.

Some weeks previously, they had tried to negotiate a peaceful withdrawal from the end of year revelries.

"Thing is, Dad, some of the gang will be heading up to Aviemore after Christmas. Ruairidh's people have a place. They'd love us to join them."

The reality was that an invitation was yet to be forthcoming, but the twins would worry about that at a later date. The priority was to avoid another ghastly New Year's Eve with Ron.

"I daresay they would, Nicky. I don't doubt it. However, I want my boys here for New Year. We'll have everyone round, just like we've always done. They all talk about it for weeks afterwards, and it wouldn't be the same without my boys."

Here the proud paterfamilias stretched up and clapped an arm round each of them, the fruit of his loins. He slapped their backs with an enthusiasm which neither son felt the occasion merited.

"Tell yer what; get yer mates to come here, Roar-ree and Anus and all the rest of 'em."

His sons chose to ignore the charmless pun on their friend's name.

"Plenty of room for everyone. Whaddaya say?"

He beamed up at them, turning his head from one boy to the

195

other, his small brown eyes twinkling with the excitement of it all.

Nic paled. Some time ago he and Anton had made an unofficial pact that none of their friends could ever cross the threshold of the family home. Not one. Never. It would be a slow and painful social death.

"Don't think so, Dad," he said.

"No," added Anton. "They've made their plans. It's a …"

"Family tradition thing. They go straight up there …"

"Right after Christmas every year," finished the younger boy, honing the lie.

They hoped Dad would empathise with the notion of family + tradition as it was close to his heart. They were to be disappointed.

"Well, never mind, eh. You can go and join 'em after New Year's Day."

Nic made a last effort, a reckless bid for freedom.

"Yah, but we sort of told them we'd join them before Hogmanay …"

"Hogmanay schmogmanay, you stay here."

"But it'd be rude not to keep our word," said Anton.

Ron's currant sized eyes glittered and turned as black as coals. He removed his hands from the boys' backs and walked around them, rubbing a hand over his cropped bullet head.

"They're rather expecting us," continued Anton.

Their father rounded on them, faster than a bull turning into the matador's cape.

"Fuckin' 'ell," he said. "What have I spent on your education? What part of 'no' don't you get? N – O equals 'no'. No. Got that?"

A stubby forefinger waggled under each nose, as Ron spun from Anton to Nic, then back again.

Nic towered over his father by some six inches and opened his mouth for one final attempt.

"But we told them …"

He got no further. Ron drew back his hand with the beringed fingers and slapped the face of his first-born. A pistol crack, a stinging, then it was over. Nic stood his ground and did not even touch the smarting cheek nor staunch the trickle of blood. As his face reddened with the blow, his father's was wreathed in smiles once more.

"Right, now we got that sorted. Good boys, good boys. We'll have a laugh, few bevvies, bit of a dance. Just like we always do," he said, treating them to a twirl in the manner of an overweight middle-aged Greek gigolo. He clapped his hands together, rubbing them with unbridled joy.

"Yeah, just like we always do."

The incident was not referred to again, and Nic and Anton chose not to speak of it when alone together. There was no need. Ruairidh's people eventually issued an invitation, and so with Ron's benediction, the brothers made plans to join their friends in Scotland early in the New Year for some skiing once the public transport system was accessible again. Next year there was the promise of seventeenth birthdays and driving tests and cars, which assuaged the disappointment somewhat. But only somewhat.

Christmas Day came and with it some spinster aunts and Staci's aged parents, who bought a giant jigsaw puzzle for the boys. Nic and Anton managed to smile and permit furry kisses from the old girls and bore it all with a stoicism that is only found in teenagers who have been given very large cheques to spend at will.

December 30th saw the house a hive of activity as a small army of party planners took up occupation in preparation for the event the following evening. Staci didn't want to wear herself out as she said it might bring on 'one of my 'eads,' but anyway Ron was happy to hand over management to a team of well drilled and highly paid professionals.

His theme, according to the printed invitations, was 'Saturday Nite (sic) Feeva (sic)' and guests were expected to arrive suitably attired. He had opted for a white suit with waistcoat, and a black satin shirt. In anticipation of the night to come, his mood brightened while that of his sons' darkened. The vast array of cheques, Christmas socks and jigsaw puzzles gathered dust in their respective bedrooms, overlooked and ignored, as their loathing for the forthcoming event grew and grew. With every chair that was moved, every glass that was polished they flinched anew. The ceremonial installation of the glitter ball in the conservatory was the final straw.

"It's like being crucified," moaned Anton.

"Yah, like the nails going in," agreed Nic.

"It's horrible, too horrible …"

"To contemplate. He and Barbi are having a dress rehearsal."

That was their private name for Staci. Her similarity to the plastic toy with the pneumatic body and overly large blonde hair was not lost on them.

"Trying on their disco king and queen outfits? Oh God, no. I don't think …"

"I can stand much more."

"No, me neither."

"If only …" said Nic.

"Yes, if only …" said Anton.

They sighed in tandem.

Anton looked at Nic. Nic looked at Anton. They had inherited their mother's very pale blue eyes and dark brown hair, plus her slender build and height.

As each boy gazed deep into his twin's pair of icy orbs, words were no longer necessary for empathy was total. Their mother had died when they were eight and it was a capacity they discovered within themselves from that time onwards. Their father found their silent communication unnerving to say the least, that and the tendency to finish each other's sentences. Staci agreed with her husband, it was downright creepy. In fact, she privately thought they were a pair of insufferable little snots, with their posh airs and their rugby matches, smelly, cracked old Barbour jackets, and skiing trips, and friends who spelled their names all wrong. I mean, Rory was spelled R-O-R-Y for God's sake, not Ruairidh.

Anton went to his father's room, the room with the super-king-sized bed, where Staci would join him on occasion. Birthdays, anniversaries, good wins for Chelsea, that sort of thing. The arrangement between husband and wife worked well enough, though she preferred to wait for the bruises to heal between visits.

Ron was standing in front of a full-length mirror in his dressing room, posing in the white suit and black shirt. The jacket was hooked over one finger and slung carelessly over his shoulder. He seemed strangely unembarrassed at being discovered thus, and unless he had lost weight in the week since Christmas, the only other possible explanation was that he was wearing a corset.

His second born was almost lost for words.

"Wow," he managed.

"Waddya think? Yer old man still got it then? Eh?"

His father came at him, aimed a jocular punch at his son's upper torso in the way so beloved of men of a certain age. He exuded bonhomie from every pore.

"Goodness," said Anton. He smiled.

"What you two rascals up to then? Getting yerselves something fancy sorted for tomorrow night? Something to get the girls goin' then, eh?"

This was accompanied by a nifty bit of footwork and a swift one-two jab-jab at Anton's body.

If he touches me once more I might just break his back, thought the boy. He was capable.

"Well, yes, we're working on something. Something a bit special."

He only avoided the two playful taps his father was about to place on both his cheeks by sidestepping a little and pretending to arrange his fringe in the mirror.

"Brilliant! Bleedin' marvellous!"

Dad Dancing

"Pleased?"

"Course I am. My two boys! Who wouldn't be?"

Anton took the plunge.

"So, well, all that unpleasantness before, when we said we wanted to go to Scotland straight after Christmas …?"

He let the question hang. He knew his father would pounce on it.

"Nah. All forgotten. Me and my boys, that what counts."

Ron looked ready to split in two; he was beaming harder than seemed possible. And was that a glint of something moist in his eyes? His lovely boys were planning something special for New Year's Eve, and it was all for *him!* Blessed, that's what he was. Blessed.

Anton sighed, suddenly downcast despite this tender rapprochement.

"Thing is, Dad …"

"Woss up, son? Woss wrong?"

"Thing is, Nic's a bit, well, he's still a bit hurt by um, what happened then. The slap thing? I know we had a great Christmas and all that, but you know how he takes things to heart, and well …"

He trailed off, leaving his father to ponder a while.

Having given him time to consider, he then applied his masterstroke.

"Dad, could you, would you tell him you're sorry? You don't even need to say it to his face. You could write it. Just let him know you're sorry. Then we can all start afresh. New year, new start, all that?"

Ron looked up at his younger son, in some ways so much the wiser than his sibling.

"Nicky put you up to this, 'as he?"

"Oh Lord, no. He'd be really hacked off if he knew …"

Anton smiled, a picture of innocence, and tossed his fringe out of his eyes to gauge his father's response.

Ron went to his bureau, took a blank piece of paper, wrote just one word on it and signed it. He folded it over, handed it

200

to the boy and said,

"Garn, now get outta here."

As Anton left his father's room and walked the length of the upper landing towards his brother's, he heard the dreaded opening bars of 'Stayin' Alive' and his father joining in with the lyrics.

Some hours later, the house, decked in all its seasonal finery, was in darkness. Staci slept in her own room, as she didn't feel strong enough for a visit with her husband just yet. She couldn't leave it too long though. Due gratitude must be shown for the Lexus. Ron slumbered in the master suite while frost twinkled on the stone lions at the gateposts.

The house held its breath for the excitement that was to come.

A figure crept into Ron's room; a shadow stole across the carpet and leaned over the hillock in the bed that was his body. Somewhere a clock struck three and the only other sounds were his own measured breathing, and the slightly shorter breaths of the intruder.

A hand reached out, touched the sleeping man on the shoulder, then shook him. Struggling with the duvet, Ron fought his way to consciousness, angered at the invasion of his domain.

"Whatthefucksgoinon?"

Anton revealed himself.

"Shhh, Dad. It's only me."

"Tony?"

"Dad, you need to come downstairs. I think there's someone in the garage. I couldn't sleep and I thought I heard something. I went into Nic's room, and he's gone down already."

Ron shot out of bed, and for a big man could move with some speed when stirred. Without even bothering to get slippers or robe – no need as there was under-floor heating and the house was kept at a constant temperature throughout the night – he hurried past his son, out onto the landing and down the curved staircase. He didn't stop to consider how his younger boy might have heard noises travel all the way from the downstairs garage area to the bedrooms on the upper floor, but logic did not dictate his reactions. Concern for his Aston Martin and for Staci's Lexus did.

"Those fuckin' caterers, they've been sniffing round all day. I bet one of them's behind it. Cunts. Woss Nicky gone down there for? Fuckin' idiot. He could get his head stove in."

With Anton hard on his heels, he went through a connecting door from the hallway to the garage, which was in darkness. Ron slapped the switch, once, twice, nothing happened. Unbeknown to him, the overhead light bulbs had been loosened some moments before. He heard a movement and saw a figure beside his Aston Martin, bending over the windscreen.

"Oi you, just fucking stop right there. Tony, go and phone the rozzers." He couldn't help himself, he often spoke like a character from a second-rate television drama. Anton stayed put.

In the murkiness of the garage, the only faint light was from the buffed bodywork of a quarter of a million pounds worth of motorcars. As his eyes grew accustomed to the gloom, the figure propped against his prize car began to take on a more familiar aspect.

"Nicky? That you?"

"Yah. 'S me."

Ron stumbled over to him. "Where'd the fuckers go?"

He slept in brown silk pyjamas with his initials on the pocket and presented no immediate threat. How the 'burglars' would have laughed!

"Panic over, there was nobody here after all," said Nic, lounging on the car's bonnet. "Must have …"

"Imagined it," added Anton, joining him at the car.

Ron leaned over, his hands on his knees, as if he had been running and needed to catch his breath.

"Thank Christ for that. Fuck me. Coulda been nasty."

"Could have," agreed Nic.

"Very," said Anton.

"Still could," said Nic, for his brother's ears only.

"Mmmm," said Anton.

Their father rose to his full five feet and five inches.

"Right. Well then, get away from the car, and let's go back to bed."

Neither son moved.

"I said, get away …"

"From the car. Yah, heard you," said Nic.

Until the night's act of assumed, if thwarted, heroism, the boys had been banned from the garage for the past three years since one of them – he never knew which – had scratched that season's Ferrari with careless parking of a bike. Their bicycles from that day forth were left in a specially constructed shed.

Suddenly and swiftly, working as one and with no prompting, Nic and Anton, graceful as black cats, moved towards Ron. They pounced. His feet left the ground as he was lifted onto a footstool, barely thirty centimetres high. Anton wrapped him in an embrace that was designed purely to pinion his arms at his sides and confound his struggles.

"Whoa," he said.

"Shut up," Nic said.

Before he was able to make another comment, he found something slipped over his head and tightened round his neck; it felt coarse and constricted his breathing immediately. It was jerked sharply by Nic who had moved behind him and as he struggled, he looked up and saw that it was in fact a length of rope that had been coiled over a roof beam. His head was inside a noose. The rope dug deep into his neck, and his face began to swell, though due to lack of light it was not possible to appreciate fully the colour it was turning. In rapid succession it went from carmine to burgundy to the yellowish purple of an old bruise. Anton released his arms and he stood precariously on the stool, wobbling, thrashing and turning, fully awake at last. Speech was not possible, only wheezing, and a bubble of blood trickled down from his nose to be absorbed by the silk pyjama top. His chubby fingers went to the rope, though there was no slackening of it, no loosening, no give, as the strong young man behind him applied all his own weight to the job in hand. Turning once too often, Ron lost his footing and the stool slipped from beneath him. He was gurgling and choking, spitting and sighing, dying at the end of a piece of rope. Never a pretty man in life, in death he was an obscene caricature of the hanged man: deep plum face, bug eyes ready to pop from their sockets, and a bloated fat grey worm of a tongue protruding from liver coloured lips. His arms fell to his sides, fingers spasmed like sausages on a griddle; his legs kicked, while his feet continued to describe invisible steps in the air. A pool of urine formed just ten centimetres beneath his feet and steamed lightly on the cool floor.

Anton recorded the whole thing on his iPhone 7, newly purchased with a Christmas cheque.

"Oh look, Nic. Dad dancing!"

The older twin came round to inspect his handiwork and watched the instant replay on the phone.

"Bloody good show."

Content with their night's work, they tightened the light bulbs in the sockets, removed their latex surgical gloves, and retired to their respective bedrooms.

On the windscreen of the Aston Martin was a folded piece of paper. On it, written unmistakably in Ron's own hand were just two words: Sorry, Dad.

GUINEA PIG GIRL

Thana Niveau

She was beautiful. Quite the most beautiful woman Alex had ever seen. But it wasn't just her beauty. What he loved most about her was the way she suffered.

He had been horrified the first time. He'd felt the stirring in his loins and then the growing hardness in his trousers. A sidelong glance at his mate Josh, whose film it was, then some uncomfortable shifting.

"Holy shit," Josh said with a laugh as the freak in the lab coat cut off one of Yuki's fingers.

She screamed, her beautiful mouth stretched open, her slanted eyes as wide as they would go. She screamed. Josh laughed. Alex got hard.

"Yeah," he said, to say something. Then he squirmed as Yuki's torture continued and his erection grew.

Oh, how she suffered.

That night he'd wanked himself silly over the image of her terrified, pleading face. He didn't dare go as far as imagining himself pinning her down on the filthy mattress in the basement room, fisting a hand in her long black hair and telling her how he would take her to bits, piece by piece. No, he didn't dare. The image flickered in the background of his thoughts but he shied away from it. Pictured himself instead as the guy who came to tend her wounds, give her water and a bit of food, hold her and reassure her that he would help her escape if he could, honest, but they were watching him too ...

It was sick.

He felt ashamed and disgusted once the last throbs of pleasure had faded and he'd cleaned himself up and thrown the handful of tissues in the bin, wishing he could incinerate them. He felt as filthy as the room she'd been imprisoned in throughout the film. He'd let himself go this time but that was it. He didn't get off on stuff like that, no way. In junior school some bullies had once tried to make him join in with torturing old Mrs Webber's cat and he hadn't been able to do it. He'd suffered then, suffered their ridicule and taunting, them calling him a pussy. But he wasn't like them, couldn't bring himself to hurt something else, something helpless.

So why did Yuki make him feel like this?

Days later he still couldn't get some of the imagery out of his head. It was just some dodgy Japanese torture porn film he couldn't even remember the name of but he remembered every moment of every scene Yuki was in. She was tiny and fragile, the way so many Japanese girls were. Sexy and girlish, slutty and innocent all at the same time. An intoxicating package in any context but seeing her so helpless and vulnerable had done something to Alex. That wounded expression, her eyes streaming with tears, her hands clasped as she pleaded in words he couldn't understand ... It got under his skin.

He'd wanted to dive into the film and save her, protect her, and yet that wasn't where his fantasies steered him afterwards. On the way to work his hands had clenched on the steering wheel as he sat in traffic and he imagined them wrapped around Yuki's slender throat. If he closed his eyes he could hear her gasping for breath. He could smell her urine as she pissed herself in terror.

Sick.

And yet every night his hand slipped down between his legs and all it took was the thought of her wide eyes and high-pitched cries to make him unbearably hard. He couldn't banish the images. All he could do was let them wash over him as he came so intensely his ears rang. Again and again.

Yuki Hayashi. Actress. Born 13 April 1989 in Hokkaido, Japan. Filmography: *Victim Factory 1 & 2*, *Love Hotel of the Damned* and *Aesthetic Paranoia* (filming).

Alex clicked on each film and read the synopses. They were all low-budget rip-offs of the notorious 'guinea pig' films from the 80s. Girls got kidnapped and tortured and that was basically it. Sometimes they also got raped.

The fourth one in the filmography wasn't finished yet and *Love Hotel of the Damned* didn't seem to be available anywhere, not even on Josh's pirate site. But Alex ordered the others.

Like all rip-offs, *Victim Factory* aspired to take things a step further than its inspiration. The gore was over the top, even by Alex's standards, and it was made worse by the homemade feel of the production. They looked like snuff films shot on someone's home video camera.

Yuki's debut was as '2nd victim' in an unpleasant scene where she was grabbed off the street and taken to an abandoned asylum. There she was stripped naked and thrown into a room stained with the blood of previous victims. To wait. After listening in terror to the screams and cries of another girl, Yuki was dragged off to the torture chamber next door for her turn. The killer bound her wrists tightly with rope and looped them over a large hook. He turned a crank that noisily hoisted her off the ground while she screamed and wept and kicked her pretty legs. Even her slight weight looked as though it was dislocating her shoulders and Alex winced. How could you fake that?

Finally, in a bizarre moment of artistry, the killer carved a series of Japanese characters into Yuki's skin with the jagged edge of a broken samurai sword. The subtitles only translated the spoken dialogue so Alex had no idea what the words inscribed on her flesh meant.

It drove him mad.

The exotic swashes and flourishes streamed with blood that looked disturbingly real, a striking contrast to Yuki's pale skin. Alex could almost believe that the mutilation had actually happened but for the fact that in the second film, the one Josh had shown him, she was unmarked. Pristine and ready for more. Ready to have her fingers and toes snipped off one by one, her mouth forced open with a metal dentist's gag and her tongue cut out.

He searched the Net for more information but the films didn't appear to be widely known. There was the occasional mention on a message board but Alex couldn't find any translation for the characters in the carving scene. Nor was there much information about Yuki. He found one screen grab from the first film, which he immediately stored on his phone. Her eyes pleaded with him through the image and he felt obscurely guilty, as though he'd imprisoned her in a tiny digital cage. But he didn't delete the picture.

The films made him feel uncomfortable, almost sick at times. And truthfully, he didn't enjoy the violence. When he played the DVDs again he only watched the scenes with Yuki and even then he felt funny afterwards. But he couldn't get her out of his head. The very thought of her was enough to make him hard and even though he tried to picture her whole and undamaged, the images of torture would quickly take over. He tried to imagine her voice, cheerful and sweet as she chattered on her phone before being abducted in each film, but the musical sounds always devolved into screams of pain and madness.

Her anguish was so excruciatingly real. He couldn't tune it out, couldn't un-see it. And he couldn't help the effect it had on him.

She was there behind his eyes every night, pleading with him to stop, her tiny body struggling helplessly against ropes and rusty chains. And no matter how much he tried to transform the images in his head, he always saw himself wielding the blades, the needles, the bolt cutters. Her blood ran like wine over his hands and he was drunk on the taste of her.

"Hey, mate, you know that DVD you were after?"

Alex froze, staring at his phone with apprehension. Then he took a deep breath before forcing himself to ask calmly, "Which one?"

"*Love Hotel of the Damned*. I found it."

"Oh, cool," he replied, as nonchalantly as he could manage.

"Yeah, some guy up in Leeds has it and he said he'd burn me a copy for a tenner."

"Thanks, mate. I'll pay you back."

"No problem!" Josh sounded pleased, no doubt proud of himself for tracking down the obscure film. If he had any suspicions about Alex's obsession it wasn't obvious. "I'll drop it by your place next week."

Next week. Alex felt his insides churn hungrily at the thought of seeing Yuki again, seeing her suffer and die in new and terrible ways.

The synopsis of *Love Hotel* made it sound like the worst of the lot. Same 'guinea pig' concept but this time set in one of those weird Japanese hotels he'd read about online. The kind where you could fuck a manga character on a spaceship or grope a schoolgirl in a room designed like a train carriage. He'd found the trailer for the film on a J-horror fan site and it looked seriously reprehensible. Even some of the hardcore gorehounds said the level of sexual violence was too much for them.

Alex slid down in his chair as his cock began to stir.

The film was even worse than he'd anticipated. Murky and grainy, as though someone had simply held up a cheap camera and filmed it playing on a TV. The poor quality actually made the gore seem more real.

Yuki didn't appear until halfway through and Alex almost didn't recognise her. She was thinner and paler and she seemed even more fragile. But she was still beautiful. She wore an elaborate gothic Lolita dress with frilly petticoats and a lacy apron and mop cap. But not for long. Her 'customer' cut the flimsy costume away with a pair of shears. From the way Yuki yelped and twisted, it was clear he was cutting her too. Blood trickled down one arm and over her belly and she stared straight into the camera for one heart-stopping moment. Alex had the uncomfortable sense that he was watching a genuine victim this time and not an actress.

His thumb hovered over the STOP button for a few seconds before he reminded himself that there was a fourth film on the list. *Aesthetic Paranoia*, which she was apparently still shooting. If this was real, surely she wouldn't have made another such film. Surely she'd be shouting "Police!" or "Help!" He was sure he'd recognise that level of distress even in a language he couldn't speak. No, it was just that weird sense of authenticity you sometimes got with ultra-low-budget films.

Yuki cried and begged in plaintive Japanese while the man stripped the mattress off the bed and threw her onto the bare springs. He bound her, spread-eagled, with wire that Alex could see biting into her delicate wrists and ankles. Then he threw a bucket of water over her and she screamed again and again, writhing on the springs.

The man lifted the head of the bed and propped it against the wall so that it rested at an angle. The camera zoomed in and around Yuki's naked, shivering body, shooting from underneath the bed to show the mesh pressing painfully into her back, the wires cutting into her skin. In close-up, the springs looked rusty and Yuki was bleeding in several places. The detail was too subtle not to be real and Alex began to feel lightheaded again. But he couldn't tear his eyes away.

The man held up a series of huge fishhooks with what looked like electrodes attached and Yuki screamed herself hoarse as the hooks were threaded through her skin one by one in a scene that went on for nearly ten minutes. When he was done, the man connected the trailing wires to a machine at his feet. He pressed a button and there was a terrible buzzing sound, followed by another piercing scream. Yuki leapt and bucked against the springs for what felt like an eternity before the current stopped. Wisps of smoke began to rise from the contact points and Alex thought he could smell something burning. Blood ran from Yuki's eyes like tears as she gasped and panted, too breathless to scream. The camera zoomed in on her face and she stared directly out of the screen again, as though she were looking through a window right at Alex.

When the buzzing sound began again Yuki tensed and started to plead frantically, this time with whoever was behind the camera. Alex closed his eyes against her screams and the metallic rattle of the springs and the zap of electricity. He held his breath as it went on and on, wishing it would end.

At last there was silence. Silence and the smell of scorched meat. He shut the film off and ran for the bathroom. He almost made it.

It was several days before Yuki came back.

Alex had put the three DVDs in a carrier bag, knotted it and pushed it to the back of the bathroom cupboard. When Josh had asked how he liked the film he'd forced a laugh and said it was rubbish, with crappy effects. And if his voice had trembled when he'd said it, Josh didn't seem to notice. Yuki's picture was gone from his phone and the J-horror sites he'd bookmarked were erased from his browsing history.

As disturbing as it had been, he knew it was fake. That was part of the point of films like that – to trick the viewer into thinking it was real. Actual snuff films were an urban legend. None had ever been found and they certainly wouldn't be readily available online in any case. People had been fooled by special effects before. And while it was a compliment to the makers of Yuki's films, Alex had seen enough.

He was in bed, almost asleep, when he first heard the sound. A soft rustle, as though someone were reading a newspaper in the next room. He froze. He had the mad urge to call out "Who's there?" even though there was no one else in the flat. Unless someone had broken in. It was that kind of neighbourhood but the flat was too small for a burglar to hide in without Alex knowing. A rat, then? It would have to be an awfully big one.

His heart hammered in his chest, drowning out any sounds that might be coming from the other room. Seconds passed like hours as he sat staring towards the open doorway, feeling like a child who'd woken from a nightmare. He should get up and switch on all the lights but the thought of putting his feet on the floor, exposing them to the empty space under the bed, was too frightening.

"Get a grip," he mouthed, trying to spur himself into action. But still he didn't move.

There was another sound. A soft slap, like a bare foot on the hard floor. Then another. And another.

His blood turned to icewater as the footsteps came closer and closer. A thin shape was emerging from the darkness of the corridor. Then he heard the dripping. He could almost believe it was some girl he'd brought home from a club and forgotten about. She'd just got out of the shower without drying off and now—

Except it wasn't. It was Yuki.

When she reached the bedroom, Alex bit back a scream. She stood in the doorway, naked and dripping with blood. Her arms hung loose at her sides and Alex's stomach clenched as he saw the symbols carved into her body. The calligraphy was more extensive than he remembered from the scene in the film. The cuts ran from the base of her throat, across her small breasts and down her torso.

A strangled sound escaped his throat and Yuki's head turned towards him. It was a careful, deliberate movement, as though she had only located him by the sound and was trying to fix his exact position. She turned and took a step into the room. Alex stared at her in horror, desperate to run but unable to move.

It wasn't real. It couldn't be real. It was a dream or a hallucination, just like the images in his head he hadn't been able to get rid of. But worst of all, he felt himself responding as he always had. Hot desire pulsed in his groin even as bile rose in his throat.

Each step she took opened the cuts further. Blood flowed over her body like water, pooling on the floor. What was almost worse was the residual grace in her movements. She didn't shuffle or sway drunkenly. Rather, she moved with the

212

precision of a dancer, each movement full of purpose. Blood gleamed in the light from the window, shining on her mutilated skin like a wet carapace, and Alex shuddered as he felt himself growing hard.

"No," he managed to whisper. "No, please."

Yuki responded to his voice, reaching out for him. Her eyes were empty pools of black but her lips seemed to be forming a smile.

It took all his courage to shut his eyes and wish the sight away.

He counted to three before his eyes flew open again in fright. Yuki was gone.

It was some time before he was able to get up off the bed and even then his legs threatened to buckle with each step he took towards the doorway. There was no blood on the floor, no evidence that anything had ever been there.

It was the middle of the night but Alex got dressed and drove all the way to work to throw the DVDs away. He snapped the disks in half and scattered them, along with the packaging, into the three large industrial bins behind the office building. He wondered if he ought to say something, but what? A prayer? He wasn't religious so he didn't imagine it would do any good. But surely it couldn't do any harm.

"Goodbye, Yuki," he whispered, and her name felt like an obscenity on his lips. "Please don't come back."

But she did.

It was four nights later and Alex was asleep. He was deep inside a pleasant childhood dream when his eyes fluttered open with a start and there she was, standing over him.

He screamed and scrambled away until he was cowering on the floor against the wall. Yuki cocked her head as if in confusion, her eyes streaming with black, bloody tears, her temples scorched and pierced by fishhooks. She looked thinner, more wasted.

Yuki raised one pale arm and reached for him. He could see the gleam of bone through the cuts on her chest. The wounds

213

gaped like tiny mouths with each movement, as though trying to speak the words they represented. Alex shuddered with revulsion as Yuki drew her hand down over his torso. Her touch was gentle as she took hold of his cock. He stiffened in her grasp, unable to move, unable to resist as she stroked him like a lover. She pressed her blackened lips to his and he closed his eyes with a sickened moan as he came.

Then he crumpled to his knees on the floor, crying.

"Mate, you look like hell."

Alex had been tempted not to answer the door but Josh had kept pounding, shouting that he knew Alex was home.

"Yeah," he mumbled. "Got some bloody bug."

"I've been ringing you for days. The guys at work thought you'd died or something. You didn't even call in sick."

Alex managed a rueful smile. "Too sick to."

"Well, is there anything I can do for you? You need food? Booze? Drugs?"

"No, I'm fine."

But his assurances didn't get rid of Josh. His friend muttered about how stuffy it was in the flat before planting himself on the battered sofa where they'd watched so many DVDs together. He shrugged out of his leather jacket, revealing a black *Faces of Death* T-shirt. Alex stared at the grinning skull and spiky red lettering for several seconds before looking away. Josh didn't seem to notice his uneasiness.

An awkward silence stretched between them but Alex couldn't think of anything to say. He couldn't tell Josh he was seeing ghosts, much less the specifics of the encounters. But Yuki's presence hung in the air in spite of his silence. He could still smell her blood and burnt flesh, still feel the slick touch of her fingers on his skin.

He'd scrubbed himself raw in the shower after the first time but it hadn't changed anything. She'd returned the next night, and the next. She looked worse with each visit but each time Alex's own body had betrayed him, succumbing to her touch even as he choked back the sickness welling in his throat. He couldn't resist or escape and each violation only seemed to excite him more.

He was pretty sure he understood what the symbols were now. Hours of online searching had led him to a website about curses. He didn't need to read Japanese to know that one of the characters represented 'desire' and another 'obsession'. He hadn't dared to search further to see if 'love' was also among them.

Josh was talking, telling him about some new film he'd just seen, one his girlfriend hadn't been able to stomach.

Alex felt his own stomach churn queasily.

"Anyway," Josh continued, oblivious to his friend's discomfort, "pretty weird about that actress, huh?"

Alex blinked. "What are you talking about?"

"Didn't you get my email?"

"What email?"

"The one I sent you last week. About that Japanese girl. The one in the film you had me track down?"

Alex felt a crawling sensation in his guts. So his fixation on Yuki hadn't been lost on Josh after all. "What about her?"

"She's dead."

The words seemed to come from a long way away, like a transmission he'd already heard. He couldn't speak. The skull on Josh's shirt seemed to be laughing now.

"Alex? You okay?"

He nodded weakly. "Yeah, I think so." Some part of him had already known, of course.

Josh went on. "I figured you liked her since you wanted all her films and I was trying to find a copy of that last one for you – *Aesthetic Paranoia*. She died on the set. Some kind of freak accident."

"When?" Alex managed to ask.

"That's what's so weird, mate. It was only a few weeks ago, before I even showed you *Victim Factory 2*. She was dead the whole time we've been watching her films. Hey, are you sure

215

you're okay? You're white as a fucking sheet."

That night Alex lay in bed listening for the familiar sticky wet slap of her feet. There was no point in trying to resist. Yuki would come for him, would keep coming for him, until there was nothing left of either of them. He'd met her eyes through the screen and she had chosen him. He was special.

He hadn't liked the way Josh had said 'we'. *We've* been watching her films. He didn't like the thought of Josh seeing Yuki the way he did.

She was no longer able to stand upright but she could crawl. Her hair hung in matted clumps around her face as she pushed herself towards him on rotting hands and knees. Her skin was peeling away from the bone in places, hanging like strips of charred, wet paper.

"I'm here," Alex said softly, tapping the floor to guide her.

When she reached the source of the sound she stopped. A heavy obstacle was in the way. She reached out a tentative bony hand to touch it. Her fingers moved over the grinning skull and the red letters that were smeared with blood, then found the tear in the material. She prodded the gaping wound in Josh's chest, gingerly touching the bloody edge of the kitchen knife while Josh stared vacantly up at the ceiling.

Yuki frowned, looking lost for a moment before recoiling from the unfamiliar body. Hurt by the deception, she raised her head and a feeble sound emerged from what remained of her throat. Alex could see the glistening strings of muscle trying to work to form words. His heart twisted.

"I'm sorry," he said. "But I had to know I was the only one."

She responded to his voice, turning her head towards him and then making her way to the bed with painful care. Too weak to climb up, she raised her thin arms like a child. Alex ignored the crunch of disintegrating bone as he lifted her up and sat her in his lap, his cock already swelling hungrily. Her lips hung in bloody tatters and he smoothed them into the semblance of a pout as he kissed her.

"I love you too," he whispered. Then he slid his hand between her ruined legs.